Shadow Invasion

SHADOW
─ ⬥ ─
WITCH

T.P. BRYSON

Gotham Books

30 N Gould St.
Ste. 20820, Sheridan, WY 82801
https://gothambooksinc.com/

Phone: 1 (307) 464-7800

© 2024 *T.P. Bryson*. All rights reserved.

No part of this book may be reproduced, stored in a retrieval system, or transmitted by any means without the written permission of the author.

Published by Gotham Books (November 29, 2024)

ISBN: 979-8-3304-3952-2 (P)
ISBN: 979-8-3304-4162-4 (E)
ISBN: 979-8-3304-4163-1 (H)

Because of the dynamic nature of the Internet, any web addresses or links contained in this book may have changed since publication and may no longer be valid.

The views expressed in this work are solely those of the author and do not necessarily reflect the views of the publisher, and the publisher hereby disclaims any responsibility for them.

TABLE OF CONTENT

Part I 1
Prologue 2
Chapter 1 3
Chapter 2 5
Chapter 3 8
Chapter 4 16
Chapter 5 17
Chapter 6 23
Chapter 7 33
Chapter 8 34
Chapter 9 36
Chapter 10 41
Chapter 11 45
Chapter 12 48
Chapter 13 55
Chapter 14 62
Chapter 15 67
Chapter 16 69
Chapter 17 73
Chapter 18 76
Chapter 19 78
Chapter 20 84
Chapter 21 88
Chapter 22 90
Chapter 23 93

Chapter 24	96
Chapter 25	103
Chapter 26	105
Chapter 27	108
Chapter 29	111
Chapter 30	113
Chapter 31	116
Chapter 32	119
Chapter 33	122
Chapter 34	125
Chapter 35	131
Chapter 36	132
Chapter 37	142
Chapter 38	148
Part II	151
Chapter 39	152
Chapter 40	158
Chapter 41	163
Chapter 42	166
Chapter 43	168
Chapter 44	176
Chapter 45	178
Chapter 46	181
Epilogue	227
Authors Notes	228

To my wife, Alana, whose amazing love and patience has sustained me for fifty-three years; to my Lord Jesus Christ whose eternal love and patience has sustained me throughout my life.

Part I

Rumors of War

There will always be wars and rumors of war. They are the warning bells of time, but as I look back on those days of my youth, the world was completely unprepared for the horrors that were coming. Even those of us who knew about the hidden dangers of multiple universes and demon hoards that resided there did not fully appreciate the threat the demons were to their freedom and way of life.

George Washington, a great American patriot, once said, "To be prepared for war is one of the most effective means of preserving peace."

We were not prepared, so now peace seems forever lost.

From the writings of Robert James Williams (2067)

Prologue

Shadow Strong: Two Years Ago

High Overseer Shadow Strong earned her title and fame through years of supremacy in the battle arena. No witch could match her strength and cunningness. No male Shadow had ever defeated her. Not an ounce of weakness held her back. Fast, agile, and observant, she always controlled her fate. That is what kept her at the top of Tiarnas' food chain. Although fate had dealt her this unexpected blow, she considered her situation as an opportunity. She and the thirty-seven surviving Shadow witches, found themselves stuck in this strange world without an army or orders for how to proceed. Thus far, they had escaped detection. She vowed to keep it that way until she found a way back home.

Blending into this world population would be easy for a Shadow witch with powerful magic. Shadow Strong had used the *soul eater* spell many times before. It would serve her and her sisters well in this world. Tonight, for the first time, she stepped out of the early evening shadows of Balboa Park wearing her new five-foot-ten human female body. The original owner was Kylie Harrisford, the daughter of one of the wealthiest men in the world. She had given little protest when she died. Not that Shadow Strong had given her a chance to object. Now, the young woman's body, life, knowledge, and memories belong to the Overseer. Shadow Strong had picked this body because of the way it moved with confidence and entitlement. The fact that it came with so much of this world's wealth was a stroke of pure luck. This body pleased Shadow Strong, as did the soft fabric garment she picked to drape over it for tonight's event.

As she walked through the park toward the evening's event, she noted that others glanced and smiled in her direction. Such a reaction confirmed that she had chosen well. Shadow Strong disappeared into the crowd of humans gathering for a gala event at the elegant Botanical Gardens.

Chapter 1

The High Overseer's Plan

Kylie Harrisford, the daughter of the billionaire Roger Harrisford who recently met an untimely end, stood next to the guardrail on the roadside lookout point, admiring the lights of El Palmar. Dressed in a tight fitted black leather jumpsuit, Kylie's tall female figure silhouetted against the glow of the full moon over the ocean in the distance. The clear night gave her a broad view of the community that spread from the edge of the foothills to the ocean. The city lights fanned out about five to six miles north and south. The view thrilled her, not because of the beauty of the scene, but because El Palmar was where the invasion would begin again. Before her lay victory. Before her lay her destiny.

Kylie Harrisford had led quite a colorful life before the soul eater spell had taken her body. High Overseer Shadow Strong had grown to appreciate all that Kylie's wealth, and body, could afford her. Of course, this womanly form was no longer human. The High Overseer had stolen it. For the last two years it had protected her from detection. The human form amused Shadow Strong. She loved draping it in the exotic fashions of this world, not a normal pastime for a Shadow witch. The outfit she wore this evening fit her like a Shadow witch's armor. It made her feel powerful. Every inch of it is perfectly fitted to allow the maximum freedom of movement. The body and the clothes represented the newest weapon in her arsenal. This weapon affected both humans and Shadows in remarkable and powerful ways.

High Overseer Strong appreciated this world's beauty. It was far more beautiful than the dark and dreary world she left behind. Even on the darkest nights, Earth glittered with light. Over time she found that she liked a little color in her life. Of course, she had also found that Earth's beauty was mostly an illusion. Under the bright blue and green veneer, she found an undercurrent of dark violence that, in many ways, rivaled her own Tiarnas. Humans constantly fought wars in far-off places. Crime and terrorism ran rampant everywhere. Disease caused suffering. Governments leaders oppressed their citizens, while living in high places while their people suffered below. Hate, envy, lust, greed, and something called love inflamed the misery. Even with Kylie's memories in her head, the High Overseer couldn't fully comprehend the concept of love. Kylie's life had revolved around caring for herself, her money, and her possessions. That was the extent of it. Yet, humans claimed to love each other, even while they were hurting each other. Humans lived with this terrible reality every day, just like Shadows did on Tiarnas. The humans didn't seem to take much notice of it, though. Unless the violence got too close to home.

Still the humans intrigued her. Some sought out light, while others sought out darkness. The majority, however, the average person, was neither dark nor light. It made her wonder. How do these creatures cope with existence considering the constant philosophical, emotional, and moral contradictions they face on a daily basis? How can one go through life having never chosen a side? Being neither light nor dark, hot nor cold, only gray and lukewarm.

In the long run, these human weaknesses would work to her advantage. Humans were easily manipulated, especially with money or magic.

El Palmar would be her operation center. The Overseer had already gathered the known surviving Shadow witches and re-established military order. Most had already used the soul eater spell for themselves, successfully blending into the community. She would reopen the rift to Tiarnas, allowing a second invasion to occur. Then she would then take her place as an imperial witch, but, instead of returning to Tiarnas, she would stay to rule the earth. With her power she would be like a god to these humans.

Shadow Strong looked down on the lights of El Palmar. She hoped more hidden witches would come forward and join the ranks of her new army. She pulled a shiny black helmet over her head and mounted her sleek, black, rocket-like motorcycle. Turning the key, the powerful bike came to life. Its engine purred with a deep rumble. With a twist of the throttle, she sped off throwing dirt and gravel up behind her. She was a powerful Shadow witch and could just as easily fly, but this human machine was far more fun. The feel of the power between her legs thrilled her.

"Besides," she thought whimsically. "*Why fly like a witch, when you can ride like a bitch?*" Shadow laughed as she disappeared down the road.

Chapter 2

Shadow Rebellion

Shadow dust and blood covered Cooper's magical black battle armor. He took a hard hit from behind. Pivoting away from the blow, he swung his sword up at the larger assailant's two battle axes. The two menacing axes crossed above Cooper, ready to slice through his head, but his blade held them in place.

"Sword burn with fire," Cooper commanded. "As I will, so it will be."

Cooper's sword turned red hot and gave off a flash of magical fire as he thrust his sword upward. The big assailant put too much forward momentum into his attack. Cooper ducked under and to the side, kicking the opponent's legs out from underneath him. The big shadow somersaulted forward. Before he could recover, Cooper's fiery sword burned down through his opponent's head, opening it wide. Burning dust and blood splattered through the air with the downswing of Cooper's sword and then again as he withdrew it.

The Imperial Guards seemed to come at them from every direction. and the battle for the Imperial Palace had proved to be the deadliest and bloodiest battle of all. After considerable loss of life, the capital of Tiarnas was now under the control of the New Republic Army, but the giant Imperial Palace tower had become the last stand for the surviving Shadow Lords and Imperial Witches. Not that Cooper expected the imperial guards to give up easily. These guards had sworn their allegiance to the royal family. That meant every last one of them would fight to the death. He respected their loyalty. They had their duty and he had his. That had always been the Shadow warrior way.

It was breaking his heart to fight against his own kind, but the royals had given him no other choice. They refused to step down, even when all of Tiarnas had denounced them. To free his people, he would have to put an end to anyone and anything that kept the royals in power. That too was the Shadow warrior way.

"I hope the Shadows of Tiarnas truly appreciate and remember the sacrifice of life given for them," Cooper thought. "Maybe... maybe not. Shadows are not known for their long-term memory."

Most of the Shadow population wanted this change of government. Hatred for the royals had been far more universal than even Cooper had imagined. Thus, he intended to bring an end to the royal family's thousand years of tyranny.

Cooper had always thought he hated this world, but, after returning home to defend Shadow rights, he discovered it wasn't true. This was his home and he cared about his kind. He wanted to make Tiarnas a better place for everyone. Like so many others under the burden of oppression, he had never considered that he had the power to make a difference and bring about change. He had felt small and weak. The oppressors in any universe expected the oppressed to remain weak and submissive, allowing the oppressor to enforce dominance. The last two years had taught him much. Self-worth and freedom were an individual right given by nature's god. Fighting for one's rights was a cause worth dying for. Now he realized that it wasn't this world he hated, but the oppressors that ruled it so unrighteously. Destiny had given him an opportunity and a duty to change this world. He vowed to free all Shadow-kind.

Cooper no longer fought alone. He now had an army of over one hundred thousand strong. One thousand of the New Republic Army had entered the palace tower with him. They fought with ferocity as they made their way up to the top of the tower. The remaining Lords and Imperial Witches had barricaded themselves in the Throne Room. Their Imperial Guards came at Cooper and his warriors with a desperate ferociousness. Cooper's Shadow priestesses created one magic shield after another to protect the warriors as they took the palace one floor at a time. The slow pace of the battle had finally turned in favor of the NRA as they took control of the floor below the Throne Room.

Every drop of blood shed, every life lost, every tear shed for lost loved ones would come to an end. Freedom would justify the sacrifice. They had died to make Tiarnas free. Cooper, a most unlikely hero, had become the NRA's standard bearer, leading his comrades into every battle. These brave warriors filled him with pride. If he survived this day, he would sing his song to them, honoring them in the only way he knew how.

The biggest surprise of this rebellion were the Shadow witches of the warrior class. In the beginning Cooper had convinced himself that the witches would never join his cause. Instead, they eagerly joined the rebellion. They wanted to restore honor to Tiarnas.

This was the fulfillment of an ancient prophecy. "The time will come when all will be in darkness." the prophecy went. "After a thousand years of darkness, a warrior, the Great Sign, will rise up and lead the world out of the shadows and into the light. Bringing about a glorious, new millennial world."

For their crimes against the Shadow race, the Shadow priestesses had pronounced a death sentence on the Shadow Lords and the Imperial Witches. For the sake of the new republic, Cooper would carry out that sentence. The royals' crimes were too great. Their unquenchable lust for power was too entrenched in their souls to expect a change worthy of mercy.

One more floor remained. Cooper stood surrounded by the Shadow priestesses. One bold move could bring an end to the killing. The day he stepped back through the rift to Tiarnas, Sam's father had given him two magical devices that had assured his safety. The first made him invisible. The second made him invincible. At the time he had no idea what might be waiting for him when he got home. The image in Sam's mind had been about what might happen when he pushed the button at the end of the one device. There would be an explosion of light for sure, but what did it mean? Sam's mind made the explosion look dangerous, and possibly deadly. Of course, at the time, all that mattered to him was Sam asking him to return to his world and end the Shadow invasion. For Sam he would have done anything. He would even give his life if she required it of him. That was how much he loved her. Love took trust and loyalty to a whole new level. Love transcended all other concerns.

When he stepped through the rupture into the Shadow world, it felt unreal.

Chapter 3

Cooper's Return to Tiarnas

"Who are you," one Imperial Witch demanded?

"That's the little imp that found the rupture," someone pointed out? "The one Magistrate Fire Claws called Little Toe." The Shadows all laughed at the smaller Shadow.

"Why is he here," a Shadow Lord barked?

"Because he is a coward." Laughter again. "The little freak has run away from the battle." More laughter.

But Cooper had remained calm. Their mockery didn't matter to him anymore. He had come to know who he was, who he had become. These fools would discover soon enough.

"The time for change has come my Lords and Witches," Cooper told them. "I have come to make this world free."

They would have laughed again, but Cooper's ludicrous declaration had left them dumbfounded. One Shadow Lord thought angrily, "Kill this imp. Get him out of my sight."

Cooper raised the anti-magic device high, ready to push the button with his thumb. Then he spoke in an audible voice for the first time in his life. "AH-M-KU-PORR! RE-MEMBUR THAT NA-M" He pushed the button.

The effect had been quite dramatic. The anti-magic light spread everywhere instantaneously. Like a powerful tidal wave, it hit the Shadow Lords and Imperial Witches first. The force of the wave threw them back to the walls of the staging area, along with the nearby army. Anyone who lacked magical protection died. The rest fell unconscious. The light wave cascaded over the walls, toppling thousands more Shadow warriors who waited for their turn at battle.

When it was over only Cooper stood. With his back to the rupture, the power of the wave had advanced away from him. He blinked and rubbed his dazzled eyes trying to see.

"Great," he thought. "I survived the blast, but now I can't see." He sighed. "I am as good as dead."

Then a miracle happened. It came in the form of an unfamiliar voice in his mind. "Come to me Ku Por."

Confused, Cooper said, "Who is there?" He turned around blinking.

"My Priestesses will bring you to me, my son," the voice replied.

At that moment he felt the hands of two individuals take hold of his arms. Instinctively he began to struggle. "Please," thought one of the Priestesses. It was a female Shadow. "We are here to help you. Please come with us." Cooper relaxed the best he could as they lifted him off the ground.

Having never been off the ground before, Cooper found the sensation of flying unsettling. The sensation worsened as his eyesight returned to normal. The dark landscape spread out far below them. The robes of the two hooded witches flapped wildly in the wind as they carried him effortlessly over a high mountain pass. As they flew over the crest of the dark mountain ridge the The capital city appeared in all its magnificence. Unlike Far Edge, this city sparkled with rainbows of luminescent light. The streets, the tall buildings glittered with light.

There, at the center of everything, rose the Imperial Palace. The massive structure loomed majestically above the city's skyline. Composed of five outer towers at each point of the palace's pentagram shaped outer wall and a sixth tower that rose up at the center, creating an impressive show of power. The higher central tower rose up into the firmament above. The glossy, smooth black stone surface of the structure gleamed unlike anything found in his rustic home. The word beautiful didn't give it justice. The city lights reflected off the structure and it sparkled and glowed with the colors of magic.

They didn't go directly to the main gate of the Imperial Palace, but to the table top foundation at its base. They landed on a smooth shelf on the inner side of the defensive mote that surrounded the palace. That deep chasm disappeared down into the dark rock below. One of his companions stepped forward and placed her hands on the wall. It opened wide exposing the interior. They led Cooper into a long passageway made of a clean, white stone. His mouth dropped open wide in awe. He hadn't realized that such a stone even existed on Tiarnas. The passageway seemed to go on forever, until it opened up onto the upper level gallery surrounding a wide deep well. The bright light coming up from below was almost as bright as the anti-magic light he had used earlier.

The two Priestesses took Cooper by his arms again and lifted him. The three dark shadows stood out in contrast to the white chamber wall as they floated gently to the floor below. The floor had intricate dark magic symbols burned into the surface. Cooper looked up to see the source of the light. A transparent sphere hovered in the center of the chamber. Whether the sphere was solid or some kind of a magical shield, Cooper didn't know. Dozens of tubes branched out from the top hemisphere and bent upward into a braided column that pierced the ceiling far above.

Inside the sphere stood, or rather floated, a tall, thin being. The being was definitely not a Shadow. What it was, Cooper could only guess. It looked similar to his friends in the other world but considerably taller. Plus, it had wings. The tattered wings hung partly extended. Long white hair hung from the being's head, reaching the bottom of the sphere. Its bony arms and legs hung limp. The being appeared to be either dead or nearly dead.

"Who is this," Cooper thought? He could see that this imprisoned being had magic. Multi Colored particles swirling around the winged being. The particles floated upward toward the tubes at the top of the sphere. The particles separated into hues, each color entering a separate tube "Why is this poor creature imprisoned like this," Cooper thought sympathetically?

"Punishment," a voice replied to his mind.

Cooper turned to see that another Priestess had entered from behind him. Her robe was not dark colored like the two who had brought him here. It was white. The two priestesses bowed to her.

"Unjustly imprisoned by the Shadow Lords," the High Priestess told Cooper

"How long has it been like this?"

"A thousand years," she said.

The shock of such a horrific punishment shook Cooper. "Is that even possible? Are there creatures that can live that long?"

"Yes."

"What a horrible thing to do to anyone," Cooper thought in anger toward Tiarnas' despicable leaders.

Now the being spoke, his voice hoarse but subdued. "The magic that binds me here," the being said, opening his eyes. "It also keeps me alive.

Welcome my dear Kú Pór. I am glad to see you safe."

Although the being spoke aloud, Cooper still understood. He felt a warmth when the winged being spoke. "Who... who are you," Cooper asked?

"I am known as Giver," the being replied.

"Giver? Is that your name?"

"The name the Father of all gave me. My name tells you who I am, but it also tells you what I am."

"Do you mean you give things?"

"I do."

"What do you give?"

"Anything that obeys my will are mine to give. I give hope and peace... courage and power. I can give the power to create or the power to destroy. I am ordained to do these things."

"Who is The Father?"

"The Father gave all life, all living things, the right to exist and to grow within its sphere of influence. Kú Pór, I have magic to give you, powerful magic. Powerful enough to change the world. I give my power to others so that they can save others. That is the power of a Giver."

"No offense, Lord Giver, but you don't look in any shape to be offering much of anything."

"Indeed," the Giver replied.

"Why are you imprisoned like this? If you are so powerful, set yourself free."

"I cannot."

"Why?"

"Because power used selfishly will corrupt my soul."

"The priestess said the Shadow Lords did this to you. I know they are cruel rulers, but this..."

"My crime was having the ability to give them power. I believed them when they said they intended to save their world. But that was a lie. They tricked me. I had always believed that goodness strived in all beings." A grimace showed on Giver's face. "But power corrupts the corruptible, turning potential saviors into dictators and oppressors. As a result of my naive view of the true nature of the Shadow Lords, I have been bound like this. Unfortunately, by the time I realized what they intended, I... Needless to say, their treachery has been without mercy.

"Why would the all-powerful Shadow Lords desire your power? They control all the power in the world as it is."

"That, my son, is the awful secret of the Shadow Lords. They never had... and still do not have... any magic of their own."

That answer stunned Cooper. "That can't be true. They have always had powerful magic. Every Shadow knows that."

"The Shadow Lords are a lie. They had no magic until I gave it to them. Even today, the Shadow Lords have no magic except for what they steal from me." Giver looked up. His eyes flared with anger. "This abominable prison siphons my energy away. Without the power I am forced to give, they would have lost this empire long ago."

This news didn't just shock Cooper. It frightened him. "Who ruled before the Shadow Lords?"

"Shadow witches ordained as priestesses are the rightful rulers of this world. These twelve are all that remain." Appearing out of the walls around him, Cooper saw nine more dark robed Shadow witches step forward. "Shadow witches are the only natural source of magic on Tiarnas. Male Shadows can have a small amount of magic in them, but it is uncommon. Upon seizing power, the Lords killed all witches that dared oppose them. The Lords then destroyed the histories of thousands of generations of noble matriarchs. The truth is lost and hidden."

"The witches... rulers? The witches are as bad as any in the royal family." The Priestesses' subtle reaction to the insult went unnoticed by Cooper.

"The Shadow Lords stole their heritage, erased their history. They lost their purpose. At one time the matriarchal witches were full of light. They used white magic for peaceful purposes. Your race, now known as Shadows, once were creatures of light. Now look at you. I wanted to reward your kind. Instead, I ended up imprisoning you just as they did me." Giver moaned in anguish. "Now darkness rules your world. Shadows have served false kings for a millenia. All because of my foolishness." The priestesses all moaned as they felt Giver's pain.

Cooper was silent for a while, contemplating what he had learned. Then he said, "I returned home because I had hope for Tiarnas," Cooper said. "I want to bring light and freedom to my world. Can you help me?"

"Yes. I will. You are not alone, my son. My priestesses will serve you and, believe me when I tell you, there are millions of shadows who share your dream."

"In that other world, I saw what freedom means. I want all Shadows to know freedom."

"I know your heart and soul, my son. I have watched you from the beginning. I created you, my son."

Cooper opened his green eyes wider than he ever thought possible. "You... created me," he asked? "What does that mean?"

"I mean, Ku Por. You are my son. You are of my body and soul."

Cooper felt a surge of unexpected, mixed emotions. "I have lived alone and afraid for years," Cooper said in a quiet thought. "Why? If I am your son, then why did you not help me. For all those years... I had nothing."

"I am sorry you had a difficult life. As you can see, I am limited in what I can personally do. But trust me, my son, you have never been alone in spirit," Giver declared. "From the moment of your birth, I have watched over you with my mind and soul... but from this prison."

"What kind of father allows his son to starve on the streets?" The Priestesses hissed at Cooper. "When I was being beaten nearly every day, where were you? Even if you had me brought to this place... this prison, I would have been better off than in Far Edge."

The ancient being allowed Cooper's emotions to calm. The young Shadow's reaction had surprised him. Perhaps the years of captivity had dulled his empathy. There was still much to tell his son. So much needed to be done before it was too late. Giver spoke in a soft, kind voice.

"I had to hide you from the Shadow Lords. If they had discovered your true identity, they would have killed you."

"Killed me? Why would they care about an insignificant little Shadow with a name like Little Toe?"

"Because you are not insignificant. You are the fulfillment of a prophecy. The priestesses, the Shadow witches, and the Shadow Lords know the prophecy well. They fear that prophecy and will do anything to stop it from happening. Even a hint that the great *Ku Por* had been born would have led to the deaths of millions of Shadow imps. They would have killed you all just to be sure they killed the right one.

"A prophecy... about me? I have a hard time believing I am the greatest of anything."

Nevertheless, it is true. That forced us to leave you in a harsh world with only your strong mind, your cleverness, and your wisdom to guide you.

"I..." Cooper was speechless.

"My son, have you not wondered why your mind was so much stronger than your fellow Shadows? You saw things no one else saw and understood things no one else understood. Your sharp wit and keen senses made you more in tune with the world you lived in. And you had a kind heart. Did you ever wonder why you were not like Broken Fang and Fire Claws?"

"Yes but..."

"None of this was accidental. You were made to become something greater. You are meant to become like me, a giver."

"A giver? Me?" Cooper felt completely dumbfounded.

"Although I could not be with you physically, I was with you in your mind. I have tried so hard to protect you, to guide you, and to teach you every day of your life. I have wept over your pain. I have felt joy as I watched you grow. I influenced others on your behalf. Even your new name, the one given by your new friends in the other world, is no accident.

"You mean the name Sam called me? Cooper?"

"In my language *Ku* means Great. *Por* means Sign. You are the Great Sign."

"A sign?"

"A sign of what is to come, the fulfillment of prophecy. This is your new name, my son. Use it well. The cruelty of your adversaries was truly unforgivable. I wish with all my heart I could have done more to protect you, but know this, you are now strong and resolute. You are a survivor."

"But still," Cooper thought.

"I am so sorry that you have suffered so much in this life. But is your suffering greater than mine? Imprisoned like this for a thousand years, being drained of my power. Not able to be with my only son. That was the cruelest torture of all."

Cooper felt ashamed. Giver, his father, was right.

"If I hadn't led you to that cave in Far Edge, you would not have found the pathway to a new world. You would not have met your new friends? I concealed the existence of the dimensional rupture until you were ready. Then, I opened it. Now it has led you back home to me and to your destiny."

"I was nowhere near ready for what happened. The whole experience led from one dangerous moment to another."

"Look deeper into your heart. You were ready. Your triumphant return is proof of that," Giver said encouragingly.

A strange sensation filled Cooper with an overwhelming warmth. "What is this," Cooper asked? "This feeling reminds me of how he felt when I was with Sam. Is what you have told really true?" Then, in the blink of an eye, he knew that it was true. There was no doubt. He looked up at being in front of him. "Father," Cooper said.

The twelve priestesses surrounded Cooper. "These, my priestesses, have goodness in them. They swore to serve and protect me. They now pledge their lives to you. Trust them, and please, my son, believe in yourself."

Chapter 4

------- ◆ -------

The End of Tyranny

Remembering all his father told him that day filled him with renewed courage. He and his army would end this battle now, and he knew the quickest way to accomplish it. The anti-magic device Sam's father had given him still worked. The High Priestess had magically implanted it into the armor on his left arm. The device had not only survived his return, but many battles since. He touched the screen and disappeared.

Now cloaked, Cooper reached the Throne Room and found the doors open. He entered just as the doors were closed again. A second device attached to his right arm, the anti-magic light Sam had given him, still functioned as well. Amazing considering how crudely made the device looked. Cooper backed up to the wall facing the throne and reappeared. He extended his right arm and activated the anti-magic light. The powerful rush of energy slammed the remaining Shadows to the far walls of the room. Checking each individual for signs of life, he dispatched the guards to a well-deserved death. The remaining Lords and Witches were either unconscious, dead, or hiding behind the throne.

Cooper spoke with righteous indignation. "In the name of all that is right and true, In the name of the oppressed, I place you under arrest to stand trial for crimes against Shadow-kind. Do not hope for mercy, for mercy will not be given to the merciless!"

One Imperial witch decided to attack. She ran at him with a ferocious scream, but quickly discovered her magic did not work. Cooper sliced her head off in one powerful strike.

"This is over," Cooper thought with firm resolve. "Tell your warriors to stand down or you all will die now."

The sounds of battle ceased. Soon after, the main doors into the Throne Room blew open and the twelve priestesses streaked in and surrounded Cooper. They glared at him and mentally chided him for his reckless maneuver. Cooper smiled back at them and shrugged his shoulders.

"Well it worked, didn't it," he said?

Chapter 5

The Return of the Geeks

Bobby stood alone in the dark with no idea of where he was or how he got there. The darkness around him hid every detail. Even the single, narrow shaft of light coming down from high overhead simply dissolved into the dark void. It revealed little except for the smooth stone floor under his feet. That detail identified this place as either a man-made or a man altered. He couldn't tell if the light shining on him was natural or a spotlight.

Bobby struggled to remember how he had gotten here. *"I was just... uh."* His mind went blank. *"What was I doing,"* he thought.

The clarity of the experience reminded him of the deep sleep dreams and trances he had experienced over the last few weeks. *"This has to be either a trance or a vision,"* he thought.

The subtle differences between the two experiences didn't really matter that much. Although in a trance, he tended to sense pure emotions coupled with an impression of who and where the emotions came from. The first time he had a trance, it was more like a blackout. Those early trances had foreshadowed the Shadow invasion. Since then his traces had become less overwhelming and far more specific. The visions came in the form of dreams. This was a recent phenomenon. Such dreams had a lot of visual symbols embedded in the dreamscape. Bobby had already had three dreams like this in just the last week alone. All signaled a warning, a foreshadowing, that something significant was about to happen. He had learned to pay attention to such things, because the dreams usually warned him about something bad. But, maybe this was just an ordinary dream.

From the column of light, Bobby worked his way out into the dark. If walls existed they lay far from the source of light. The deeper he pushed into the darkness he sensed a malignant force. As his eyes slowly adjusted to the dark, he saw that shapes moved around him. Like sharks in the open ocean, the shapes circled in closer and closer.

"Bobby, be careful," a voice behind him shouted.

Bobby turned to see Sam standing in the column of light. She looked terrified. Jeff stepped forward out of the shadows and stood next to Sam.

"Yeah, be careful, dude," Jeff pleaded.

The silhouetted shape of a tall, slender woman dressed in black entered the fray of shapes circling Bobby. She sauntered alluringly around the space, keeping her face just out of view. Bobby's mind went back to the battle two years ago. The Shadows that flew. This woman felt like them.

"Are the Shadows back," Bobby asked his friends.

"I will win, you know," the dark female figure said. The woman raised her arm and pointed. Another light appeared revealing the presence of Sam's friends, Amy Ross and Delia Bowen. The two terrified girls clung to each other. All the shadowy shapes let out a loud screech as they flew towards the two girls. Amy screamed in horror and buried her face in Delia's neck. They both disappeared.

Sam cried out, "No." She began to sob uncontrollably.

Jeff stood staring in shock. "Amy," he whispered.

Bobby awoke startled. "A vision," he gasped.

Bobby sat in his car outside the city library waiting for Sam. She had spent much of the day researching spells and magic lore - an assignment from Master Maeda. It was Christmas break. But, thanks to Jeff's grandpa, Bobby and Sam had spent every available minute, not having any normal teenage holiday fun, but training. Grandpa Maeda, now known as Master Maeda to them, had insisted they not only continue their training over the break, but he wanted them to double down.

"Time off from school means more time to train," the old man told them. "You are warriors now. There is no time to play."

The year's aggressive training schedule had begun to take a toll. Frustrations led to short tempers. On occasion, short tempers led to hurt feelings. They always forgave each other. No matter what the reason, at least it was time together. Thus far, their relationship had endured the test of time, but could it endure the test of growing up. As far as teenage romances go, theirs had remained relatively uncomplicated. Maybe because they had first established a deep friendship before love had filled their minds with romance.

As Bobby waited, he ran his fingers over the new black leather steering wheel cover he had purchased earlier that day. It felt good. It smelled good too. A little over a year ago, Bobby's dad gave him the go ahead to purchase a car. Bobby soon set his sights on a vintage, meticulously preserved, black Mini Cooper. The one and only owner of this classic car, a friend of his dad, sold it to him for a reasonable price. Newer Minis had lost their sense of uniqueness. The new body design had made them look like every other small car. Plus, the name Cooper had been dropped from the brand. His Mini still said Cooper on the bottom right of the hatchback door.

This car fit him perfectly. He loved it. Later on, he added two neon green rally stripes on the hood. That made the *Shadow 2*, Sam had given the car its name, a fitting memorial to their lost friend. *Shadow 2* soon became the mode of transportation for the couple whenever they were together. Few understood the true heartfelt meaning behind the fanciful name, or, for that matter, why a car needed a name at all. Most thought it silly but not Bobby and Sam. They would never forget Cooper, the true hero of the Shadow invasion.

To Bobby's relief, Sam appeared. Sitting alone in the dark like this made him anxious. He had felt like this for days now, especially with his most recent visions. Sam ran up to the passenger side and opened the door.

"Thanks again for picking me up," she said as she closed the door. "You're the perfect boyfriend."

"I'm glad you think so," he replied smiling. "Shadow and I are here to serve our princess."

She leaned across the car's center console and gave Bobby a kiss. Then she kissed her fingertips and placed them on the dashboard. "A kiss for you too, *Shadow 2*. But, if either of you call me princess again, I'll burn you to a crisp."

"Yes, my lady," Bobby said with a sideways grin. He started the car and they headed out of the parking lot.

"So, have you heard when Jeffrey's plane gets in," Sam asked?

"2:30 tomorrow afternoon," he replied. "So, no training with Master Maeda tomorrow."

"Thank heaven," Sam said.

For the past two years, Master Maeda had worked with the two of them teaching them how to better defend themselves and, more importantly, how to work together with greater unity. The training had made a big difference. It has also led to some exciting discoveries relating to coupling magic. As yet, neither of them had reached their full potential but each had grown significantly. As genetically enhanced humanoids, their magical powers might well be limitless. This realization both frightened and humbled them. As if being a teenager wasn't hard enough.

The last two years had been a reprieve from the violence of battle. Mercifully some of the innocence and everyday normality of youth had returned.

"Jeffrey is cutting it close with the new term," Sam said. "It starts in two days." Then she said thoughtfully, "I must admit I have missed him... even his goofy ways. It will be good having him back home."

"Yeah, me too."

Bobby drove on in silence. He felt uneasy, but still didn't know why.

Sam glanced over at him. "Something on your mind?"

"Huh? Oh, sorry."

"Everything okay?"

Bobby shrugged. "Don't know. I feel off."

"I hope you're not getting sick." She reached over and touched his cheek with the back of her hand.

"Not that kind of off. For the last couple of days, I have felt... uneasy. I can't think of anything specific that might be the cause but something has thrown our world out of balance, toward the negative side."

"Oh great," Sam said. "We just had an election. Everyone is either happy or angry about that. Jeez, I hate politics."

"While waiting for you, I dozed off," Bobby told her, not sure he should tell her about this new dream.

Sam stiffened. A spike of fear increased her heart rate. "Oh?" She took a deep breath. "What was the dream about?"

For the past six months, Bobby had had dreams that later proved to be prophetic. At least they seemed prophetic. The dreams told him things he couldn't have known otherwise. Like the location of a lost kid. Then, a couple days later, rescuers found the kid right where his dream had shown him. He knew the identity of a convenience store robber before the police arrested him. The dreams were that kind of prophetic. At least these dreams had good outcomes. But over time the dreams turned darker and more symbolic. Bobby dreamt of shadowy figures snatching people. Indeed, people had started to go missing. Fortunately, many of the missing returned home after a day or two. Bobby had shared every one of his dreams with Sam. To Sam such dreams were nightmares. They scared her.

"I don't know if I should tell you about this one."

"Why?"

"Because... it's about us... and our friends."

"Jeffrey?"

"Delia and Amy too."

"Do any of them go missing?"

He thought about what to say. "I... don't know," he lied. "I woke up."

"Oh. What happened?"

"The shadowy figures came. It's dark... hard to see who they are, except for one. A tall dark woman. She was dressed in black."

"A woman... dressed in black? Are you sure this is the same kind of dream as before," Sam kidded nervously. This dream felt too close to home and it frightened her.

"Yeah," Bobby grinned at her. "A sexy woman dressed in a black dress." Sam punches his arm. "The woman kept getting closer, but stayed in the shadows just enough to hide her face."

"At least it's a human," Sam said. "I can deal with humans. Would you stop having dreams about shadowy figures? I get more panicky with each new dream. The thought of a repeat of the Shadow invasion is a bit terrifying. If you recall, I don't really like Shadows... except for Cooper of course."

He pulled up to Sam's house. She leaned over and rested her head on his shoulder. "Can you believe this is our last semester of high school?"

"What will we do after graduation," he asked her?

The more Sam thought about it the more she didn't want to think about it, at least not yet. She didn't want to think that far ahead, an unfortunate side effect from two years ago. The Shadow invasion had forever changed their lives.

Sam said, "I guess I should go to college." After another pause for thought she added, "You know, as long as I'm with you, nothing else matters."

Bobby felt a tinge of anxiety. Not that he didn't like that idea, them being together, but lately he felt pressured by Sam's expectations. What if he screwed up? What if he failed her? Sam represented the mature side of their relationship. He had a lot to learn about being a proper boyfriend. High school romances come and go like the summer, or a storm, or lightning. Bobby shuddered. Of course, their relationship was no typical high school fling. They were magically connected. Their destiny meant forever. He loved Sam. He really did. But was he mature enough to handle it. Did their future together include an engagement, marriage and, his face flushed in spite of himself, sex?

Sam looked up and saw his reddish face. "What are you thinking about?"

"That would be a secret," he replied, reining in his thoughts.

"Hmm?"

"I promise to tell you all about it someday," he added, trying to joke away his blush. "And in detail with pictures. I promise."

She kissed his cheek. "Call me tomorrow. We need to make plans for Jeffrey's homecoming." She hopped out of the car and ran into her house, waving goodbye as she shut the front door.

Bobby sighed. It was a good thing he was a shy boy with a mom who had taught him to be a gentleman, because lately his imagination went to romantic ideas previously unexplored. This added further pressure to their relationship. "Besides," he thought. "This girlfriend could fry me if his hands started to wander… uninvited."

Chapter 6

Back to School Surprise

The gang waited together for Jeff to make his entrance. Bobby held Sam's hand. Delia stood next to Sam. Amy hid herself partially behind Delia's left shoulder gripping Delia's left arm firmly. After living two years in Japan, Jeff was finally home.

"This day will shine bright in history," Bobby exclaimed. "Jeff Sasaki has returned. Now we can begin again. Graduation is in sight. We are now on the home stretch. I can see the light at the end of the... uh... high school days tunnel. We've had some of the best days of our lives. But ... uh..." Bobby's mind stalled. This is a new dawn... springs forth... uh...

"Running out of cliché metaphors," Delia snarked.

"Excitement tends to make me ramble on."

"Way over the top, love," Sam said laughing.

"It's just that I want this year to start out on the right foot. You know, put our best foot forward. Sorry, cliché metaphors are easy once you get rolling. But this is our final semester. It marks the end of our... youth-hood," Bobby continued.

"Youth-hood," Delia smirked. "Is that a thing?"

"Yes, and adulthood now looms both tantalizing and terrifying." He laughed.

Delia groaned. "Are you done already?"

In spite of what had happened back in his sophomore year, Bobby still fantasized about his future. After graduation anything could happen. Although the encounter with the Shadow world had somewhat tamed his lust for adventure, he still wanted to discover new possibilities. Sam agreed wholeheartedly. Of course, for Bobby and Sam the past, present and future were an inseparable knot. They were in this together. Their parents had set their destiny long before they were born. In spite of that, they acted as if everything was normal. So, they would celebrate what was left of their senior year and graduate. They had kept their secrets and would continue to do so, at least until the next supernatural crisis occurred.

Cal Phillips, Delia's on and off boyfriend, walked up to Delia and said, "Hey Red." A nickname he called her, referring to her hair. She didn't like it, one of the reasons why he was an on and off boyfriend. "What's going on?"

Amy detached herself from Delia's arm and stepped back out of the way. Cal was quite good looking and she didn't want to look at him too long. He made her blush. She couldn't help being a little envious of Delia, although Delia didn't seem to take the relationship very seriously.

"We are all waiting for an old friend to show his face," Delia said. "If he is the same person he was when he left, his return should prove to be unintentionally entertaining."

"Unintentionally?"

"Just wait. You'll see."

At the end of last year, after admiring Delia from a distance, Cal gathered up the courage to ask the fiery haired girl for a date. It wasn't that he was shy, in fact he was easy going and popular. Delia, however, was constantly surrounded by her tribe of friends. Cal pushed on and asked Delia out. To Cal's delight, the date transformed into an amazing night of fun and laughter. From that night on Cal was around, but not necessarily a new member of the tribe. Mostly it was all about being with Delia. Cal was preceptive. Delia's friends had secrets, Bobby and Sam in particular. Secrets among close friends were dangerous. Time had a way of pushing secrets to the surface. Hopefully their friendships would endure any such revelations.

Amy's envy of Delia and Cal fueled her excitement at Jeffrey's return. Only Delia knew about Amy's crush on the oddball young man. A crush that completely mystified Delia. As Amy's closest friend, she supported Amy anyway. Even if it kind of made her gag a little. Amy had kept close contact with Jeff the whole time he was gone, emailing nearly every week. Sometimes more often than that. Not even Bobby had kept in touch that well. The email relationship had boosted Amy's hopes and expectations concerning Jeff.

Giggles and chatter from beyond the crowd of students drew their attention. Sure enough, it was Jeff making a grand entrance. The tall Japanese boy had changed. Two years of intense training had matured his body and facial features.

"Oh my gosh. Jeffrey is buff," Bobby whispered.

Jeff wore his hair simple, pulled back into a short tail at the back of his neck. He moved with smooth confidence. But the biggest surprise of all was the two, extremely hot Japanese girls attached to his arms. The two girls looked exactly alike in every way, the same face, same hair and same clothes.

Although Jeff had often expressed his love of the beautiful and the sexy, it was important to remember that he was usually referring to two-dimensional characters from anime and games. The old Jeff was essentially afraid of 3D girls, well except for Sam, Amy and Delia. Maybe he was just a little afraid of Delia. She was after all the only girl to actually slap Jeff in the face. From then on he showed her greater respect by staying at arm's length.

Delia turned back to her shy friend. "Amy," she whispered. Amy looked shocked. Delia reached out to Amy, but the girl turned and ran away without a word.

Jeff's familiar voice broke everyone's stare. "Ohayō, guys. Let me introduce you to El Palmar High School's two newest students. This is Asura," he nodded to his right, "and Asuri." He nodded to the left. He looked back and forth at the two smiling girls. "Or is it the other way around?"

The sisters giggled and Asura replied, "You did it right this time." She clapped her hands excitedly.

"Good for you *Senpai*," Asuri added with another giggle.

"We met on the plane over the Pacific Ocean," Jeff continued with a broad smile. "They kept a dreadfully long flight from being boring. Imagine my surprise finding out that they were on their way to the States to be exchange students. Get this... right here in El Palmar... at El Palmar High School. Is that not crazy?"

"Wow," both Bobby and Cal said at the same time.

"Yeah, wow, no kidding," Jeff replied with a big grin. "Their twins. Can you believe that?"

"Yeah, we guessed that," Bobby said.

"Their English is pretty good, a lot better than my Japanese anyway, so feel free to introduce yourselves and ask them anything you want."

Sam spoke up because the boys were still stuck in a stare. Quite a crowd of guys had already begun to gather around. "It is very nice to meet you both," Sam said after elbowing Bobby in the ribs. "I'm Samantha, but everyone calls me Sam. If there is anything I can do to help just ask."

Sam extended her hand to the girls and each shook hands politely with an added slight bow. "You are so kind, *Senpai*," they both replied.

"I told you that you don't need to be so formal," Jeff corrected. "Friends use first names all the time here."

"It will take time to get used to the informal way Americans talk," Asuri said shyly.

Delia spoke next. "Hi I am Delia," she said, extending her hand. "We are all close friends, so please consider us your friends as well." She turned to Cal and gave him a stern nod.

"Oh, sorry," he said, smiling big. "My name is Cal." The twins smiled back and bowed slightly. "I'm on the student council." When the girls heard that they bowed again only deeper this time. "I would be happy to show you around campus and answer any questions you may have."

Delia's red hair had a way of flashing like fire when she got riled. She stepped to Cal's side and grabbed his arm firmly. "Cal's my boyfriend," she said. "For the time being."

The twins looked at each other and giggled.

"Boyfriend," Jeff asked with surprise? "How long has this been going on?"

"A while," Delia said.

Jeff smiled. "Nice to meet you Cal," he said. "You are a braver man than I."

"Just what is that supposed to mean," Delia asked indignantly.

"So, are you denying that you are the toughest girl at El Palmar High School?"

Delia smiled. "Well... that is true."

The twins giggled some more. "You all sound like such good friends," Asuri added.

It was Bobby's turn. "My name is Bobby," he said. And then he quickly added, "I am Sam's boyfriend."

The girls laughed and looked at Sam. "You must be happy," Asura said. "He is so cute." Bobby felt the flush of embarrassment. All the girls laughed. The guys that had gathered around began to laugh, and hoot at him as well. He would be kidded about this all day. He extended his hand to Asura first and she took it. An unexpected jolt of apprehension shot through his mind. His head throbbed as he winced from the pain.

Startled Asura quickly pulled her hand back. "Are you okay," Asura quickly asked him?

"Sorry," he apologized. "I guess I'm not used to being called cute." The girls laughed. Bobby then extended his hand to Asuri. She looked at Asura first and then took Bobby's hand.

"I hope you are alright," she said politely. They shook hands and Bobby smiled as his headache vanished as quickly as it had come.

"It was nothing," he said with a laugh. "I'm fine, really." Asuri and Asura smiled happily.

"I thought I saw Amy," Jeff asked? "Where did she go?"

"Oh," Delia jumped in to explain. "She had something to do. She's sorry she had to go."

"Oh, I see," he said. "Well I guess I'll see her later."

That was interesting, Delia thought. Jeff actually asked about Amy.

The first bell rang. It was time to get to class. The crowd quickly dispersed. Cal and Delia took charge of the two new girls and helped them to get to the main office. They then escorted the twins to class before hurrying on to their own classrooms.

At the end of the day, Bobby and Sam waited for Jeff so they could start catching up on the myriad of things that had happened while Jeff was in Japan.

"Bobby," Sam said. "What was that this morning?"

"What was what?"

"When you took Asura's hand you felt something didn't you."

"Oh... I don't know... maybe. For some reason when I shook her hand I had a strong reaction... but it went away as fast as it came. So, no worries."

"Hey guys," Jeff said as he approached. "Thanks for waiting for me."

"No problem," Bobby said.

"Yeah," Sam added. "We've been waiting for two years. What's another five minutes?"

Jeff gave them both a big smile. "I have missed you guys so much."

"Japan must have been good to you," Bobby joked. "At least you seemed to have finally found your way with the ladies."

"I'll say," Sam laughed. "No offense but that was not the entrance I was expecting."

"Yeah," Bobby added. "To be honest I am not sure if you looked that cool, or if the two girls just made you look that cool."

"Whatever, dude," Jeff said, feigning offense. "I'll take what I can get." He laughed.

"We missed you too," Bobby said laughing. "Good to have you back. But you have got to tell me how you managed to pick up two girls on a plane?"

"I honestly don't know," he said retrospectively. "They were just being nice to me."

"Wow," Sam said. "How unusually humble of you." Maybe Jeffrey had changed more than she thought. "Well, anyway you look great Jeffrey. How was it in Japan. Did you have girlfriends there, or is a plane required for picking up Japanese girls?"

"I dated once or twice, but there wasn't much time for that sort of thing. Not that there weren't girls who were willing, especially when they found out I was in Japan for special martial arts training. That gave them the impression I was... athletic. Unfortunately, they quickly discovered that I was nothing more than a geek, an *otaku* as the Japanese say. Anyway, girls like that aren't my type."

"What about Asura and Asuri," Bobby prodded him. "What type are they?"

"The twins are fun girls," he replied with a smile. "And yes, they are pretty darn hot, but honestly, I don't really know that much about them. I just want to make them feel welcome. To make it better for them than it was for me in my first few weeks in Japan."

"Was adjusting that hard," Sam asked?

"It wasn't that. Don't get me wrong. Almost everyone was nice, but a few refused to see me as anything other than an outsider. In the end, I realized that I just needed to prove that I wasn't there to steal anyone's popularity... or girlfriend."

"Are you going back after graduation," Bobby asked?

"Yeah," Jeff answered. "I had to promise to return, in order to take this break in my training. When that time comes, I will have to fully commit myself. For now, ... I just want to enjoy what is left of my senior year. I guess I got a little homesick. I missed both of you so much."

"Really," Sam asked, touched by his sincerity?

"Of course," he said. "We went through hell together. The three of us...

best friends forever." Jeff made a thumbs up.

Sam almost started to tear up. She gave Jeff a hug. "I missed you too," she said.

"I missed our whole gang," Jeff added. "What's with the new guy this morning?"

"Delia's sometimes a boyfriend," Bobby said.

"Sometimes?"

"Delia can be a handful," Bobby replied.

"Wow, brave dude." Then after a pause Jeff asked, "What about Amy? Uh... does she have anybody yet?"

"Amy," Sam asked? "No one at the moment. I wish someone would come along and realize how incredible she is."

"I know, right? Cute and sweet," Jeff replied. His face flushed a bit. "Well anyway," he added, changing the subject. "How's your training with Grandpa coming?"

"We are going over there this afternoon," Bobby said. "We meet a couple times a week. Nothing like what you have been doing, but it is helping a lot."

"If you are going to Grandpa's place, I'm coming with you," Jeff said. The three of them continued to chat as they headed off toward the parking lot.

As they reached Bobby's car, Sam said, "Jeffrey. Meet the *Shadow 2*. *Shadow 2*, meet Jeffrey."

"Shadow," Jeff questioned?

"Yeah, get it? It's a Mini Cooper, black with neon green stripes."

Bobby added, "Sound like anyone we know?"

Jeff's smile broadened. "Oh, now I see it."

Let's take *Shadow 2* for a ride," Bobby suggested.

Bobby and Sam chatted as they drove out of the school parking lot. Jeff sat quietly, his thoughts drifted. He hadn't seen or talked to Amy all day. Except for a fleeting view of the back of her head as she rushed off earlier in the day. He hoped that she would have been eager to see him, but evidently not. The truth was, if it hadn't been for Amy Jeff's time in Japan would have been unbearable. When he returned home he looked forward to seeing her. He also hoped she felt the same way about him. Maybe he misread her motives for reaching out to him so persistently. Now, he felt disappointed.

Jeff's thoughts drifted again. This time back to the day he made the decision to return home. He had to formally ask his great uncle, Master Maeda, for permission to interrupt his training. Jeff remembered kneeling nervously in the middle of the floor, facing the man who held his future in his hands. Although Master Maeda was grandpa Maeda's cousin, the old man looked twenty years younger. The rumor spreading around the Kanazawa Martial Arts Training School suggested this was the result of some kind of mojo magic. Jeff had to wonder if it was true.

Jeff knelt with his teachers to the right and his trainers to the left and waited for the Master's ruling on the matter. Master Maeda knelt at the front of the room on a twelve-inch raised platform. Master Maeda's Japanese style residence was ages old, but still looked to be in near perfect condition. The training school had several campus structures located not far from the historic Oyama Shrine and the Kanazawa Castle, all well maintained and kept meticulously clean. One hundred and twenty-seven students, including Jeff, lived and trained at the school. Each student had responsibilities for cleaning the buildings daily. Jeff had personally, and endlessly it seemed, hand polished all the wood floors in every building. This was part of their training, or so they had been told. Although Jeff thought it had more to do with free labor, he did his responsibilities honorably. Sometimes it was even fun.

"Jeffrey-kun," the Master said. "You have done exceptionally well in such a short time. Leaving for six months will set back your training. Are you sure you want to do this?" When it came to the school, Master Maeda was tough, hard and unrelenting. But, as a human being, he acted as kind and gentle as Jeff's grandpa, although he noted that the Master behaved in a far more serious manner.

"Yes," Jeff replied, his face downward. "I am sorry, Master, but I needed to take this break."

"Your teachers tell me that you are at a crucial point in your training," the Master continued.

"I understand, Master, but I can continue my training with my grandfather in California. I promise you that I will work hard and return as soon as graduation is over."

"You are enrolled in a very good school here, one of the best in Japan. Many young men would give anything to attend such a prestigious school."

Jeff bowed his upper body low to the floor. "I don't mean to be selfish,

Master. I am still struggling with my Japanese and... other things. I feel a little overwhelmed right now. I have lost some momentum in my training because of this. I thought... I hoped that by going home for my last term of high school to be with my family and friends, I could return to Japan with a renewed commitment." Jeff pushed himself as close to the floor as possible. "I just want to graduate with my friends. That sounds selfish I know, but... I need this. I am sorry," Jeff concluded his explanation. "I need this."

High school in Japan tends to be brutal on newbies. Especially if you didn't understand the Japanese school culture. Jeff's parents had properly instructed him before leaving the States, but even with that advantage, he found the transition tough. Oddly enough, Jeff liked the school uniform idea. He thought it made him look more mature, more serious, and perhaps a little taller.

The Shadow invasion had changed Jeff, just as it had Sam and Bobby. That unique experience had led him to train with the Maeda Clan. This training prepared him to be a monster slash demon slayer and an exorcist. If he wanted to help his best friends, he needed to be a true warrior.

At first, as a foreign newbie, Jeff wasn't sure he could hold up to the Maeda Clan rigorous standards. To his surprise, he had done well. Not that it hadn't been hard work. In fact, it had proved tougher than anything he had ever done. He managed to succeed each step along the way. Far better than anyone expected. It was like it was in his blood... his grandpa's blood. He intended to make his grandpa proud.

Master Maeda remained quiet for a moment. "I see. Still, this is most unfortunate." He sighed. "I will, however, grant the leave of absence." Jeff breathed a sigh of relief. "On this condition, Jeffrey. You must diligently continue your training at home. I would hate to see you lose your position here. That would be very unfortunate."

"Yes Master," Jeff replied, bowing to the floor. "I understand what is at stake. If the Shadows..."

"Silence," the old Master ordered, startling Jeff.

"Sorry Master," he said, hugging the floor.

"You gave an oath to remain silent about such things," the Master chided, showing his gruffer side. "Speak of it only when you and I are alone. Danger exists. Be careful what you say. The enemy has ears."

Several individuals present in the room glanced to the center of the room where Jeff bowed respectfully. From the moment this American had joined them the Master had treated him as someone special. The reason for that was still unclear to most of them.

"Do I make myself clear," Master Maeda said?

Jeff gave a loud reply without hesitation. "*Hi!*"

"Good!" The old man smiled. "Jeffrey. You have searched diligently to find your warrior's spirit. I am proud of your progress." Jeff felt thankful and proud. "Do not lose sight of your goals. Come back to us in good health... with renewed commitment. If you can't do that, then it would be better not to return at all."

Jeff looked up. The Master's caution hurt. What if he failed? What then? In the end all he could say was, "Thank you very much, Master. I won't let you down."

Jeff took a deep cleansing bath that night. Now he would relax and have some fun.

"Bobby, look out" Sam screamed, bringing Jeff back to the present.

Bobby hit the brakes hard and the car squealed to a sudden stop.

Chapter 7

Biker Witch

Shadow Strong, a.k.a. Kylie Harrisford, finished her business in downtown El Palmar. She had established a place of business and a place of residence in a building near the ocean. That meant dealing with humans on a regular basis. Although her lawyer dealt with most of the bankers, accountants, and local and state government bureaucrats, she had to keep up appearances. She wanted to appear to be a normal, but wealthy, human citizen who had taken up residence in a new hometown. Honestly, she wondered how long she could put up with all the nonsense. The High Overseer hated having humans involved in her affairs, but this part of her plan would not take that much longer. Soon she would open the rift to Tiarnas.

Mounted on her black motorcycle, she sped off down the street. Although maintaining a degree of anonymity was part of her plan, today she didn't care. She wanted to ride. It was a great way to burn off tension, so she rode aggressively and loudly. A young woman in black leather sitting on a powerful machine tended to turn heads. She weaved recklessly through the busy downtown traffic headed for anywhere but downtown El Palmar.

After making a quick right turn through a red light, from the inner lane she heard the screech of tires on pavement and the honking of horns. She had barely missed the small black car at the intersection. She zoomed out of sight.

Chapter 8

Trance

Bobby had hit the brakes hard, just avoiding the motorcycle. The three teens were thrown forward hard, their shoulder straps stopping them instantly. They sat stunned for a second.

Sam yelled out, "That stupid biker. He nearly got us killed." Then she yelled out the window, "Idiot!" But the biker was long gone. "Where did that guy learn to drive?"

"That wasn't a man. It was a seriously shapely woman," Jeff told her.

"Are you sure," Sam asked? "The bike went by fast and I am sure the rider wore a helmet."

Jeff let his head fall back. He closed his eyes. "She wore a tight black leather jumper with no logos or visible marking, a black helmet with a dark full-face visor. The bike was a Yamaha FXR 3300 Hornet. That's the hottest new model out this year. Long hair hung out of the helmet and, finally… that body was clearly female. Did I mention the tight black jumper? Besides this is Jeff Sasaki you are talking to. I have special powers when it comes to that sort of thing."

"You got all that in that split second," Sam asked dryly?

"Ninja training," he replied with a smile. "Just a little trick I learned from one of my teacher's."

 more horns honked. Bobby sat frozen to the steering wheel with his eyes closed.

Jeff leaned forward and said, "Ah Bobby. We better get out of the way."

Sam looked over at Bobby's face. "Bobby, are you alright?" He didn't move. "Bobby," she said, concerned.

Sam grabbed his arm and shook him a little. That made him open his eyes. He turned to her and stared blankly. More cars honked.

"Sorry," Bobby said. "I almost hit that biker."

"It was her fault," Sam insisted. "She almost hit us."

A man came up to the window and knocked. Bobby lowered the window.

"Are you guys alright," the man asked. "Is anyone hurt?"

"No, we're okay. Sorry. Just scared me a bit." With that Bobby stepped on the gas and turned in the same direction of the motorcycle.

"That was weird," Sam said.

"When the biker approached, I felt something bad," he explained. "It... she reminded me of the dark figure I saw in that last dream. That's when I blanked out."

"Dream," Jeff asked? "Did I miss something?"

"Bobby has been having strange dreams, sort of prophetic," Sam said.

"No kidding?"

"Yeah. A new ability."

"Hum. The prophet Bobby, huh? Sounds good, dude."

"It has been two years," Bobby said, "but I'll never forget the feeling of the Shadows. Remember the ones that moved so fast through the air. It felt like the biker was one of those."

"Holy crap. Are you sure," Jeff asked? "I am not sure if I should be afraid or in love."

"Well, if not the biker then it was someone else close by. But the biker sure caught my attention."

"Where are we going? Are you trying to follow her," Sam asked?

"That's the idea, but I am afraid she is gone," he said. "I don't feel anything now." They drove around the area for a while longer but found nothing.

"Why," Sam said. "After all this time why would a Shadow show up out of nowhere?"

"Maybe there's another rift," Jeff suggested.

"Maybe some of the shadows from two years ago got trapped in this world," Bobby suggested.

"Dude," Jeff said. "We need to talk to my grandpa... now."

Chapter 9

Giver's Gift

Cooper watched the old Angelic, his father, sleep peacefully. Giver had told him that Angelic was the name of his species. Cooper had finally embraced the idea that somehow this winged being was his father. Cooper knew very little about genetics but it seemed logical, at least to him, that he would at least look a bit like Giver. But he didn't. Not in the slightest. He could see nothing indicating that they were related in any way.

"It would be great to have wings," Cooper thought. "Why didn't he give me wings while he created me?" That thought amused him and he let his imagination go, an indulgence he had denied himself for the last year or so. He imagined flying high above Tiarnas. His wings spread full and wide. His world had been a dark world far too long. Only large cities like Luna, capital city, where the powerful elite lived, had light. The rest of the world lay in hopeless darkness. But Cooper imagined a different future for his kind. A world full of light with lush vegetation growing everywhere, where all villages, towns and cities bustled with prosperity and energetic life.

A vision opened before Cooper's eyes. His mind's eye swooped down into the future Tiarnas and he marveled. Shadows' dark misty bodies had transformed. Inside each individual's chest floated a glowing orb. That light fed the lighted structures throughout their entire bodies. Each Shadow was full of light. It occurred to him that these beings had evolved and probably should no longer be considered Shadows.

Cooper looked down at his own body. He too had changed. "We are beautiful," Cooper thought.

Time quickened. Days flew by like seconds. Cooper watched four generations come and go. Then time slowed to normal. To his distress he saw that many Shadows had lost their light and had reverted to the old ways of hate and violence. The dark Shadows went to war against the light Shadows because they hated light. The two groups met on a great battlefield and the work of death began. For a while it appeared as though the dark would win, but the light stayed faithful. The light in them grew stronger. Believing in the light had preserved them.

"Look," they said, pointing upward. "The light comes to save us."

Cooper looked and saw magnificent beings of light with wings billowed descend from the sky. They were like his father. "Angelics," he thought with joy.

The Angelics flapped their wings toward the enemy. An explosion of light sent a wave of destruction toward the dark Shadows. The concussion wave swept the battlefield free of the enemy. One of the Angelics flew to Cooper and stood before him. They stood face to face.

"Now we are with you and you are with us," the Angelic said.

Cooper jolted back into the here and now. He looked up at Giver. "What just happened?"

The old Angelic, who still remained imprisoned in the magical containment shield, opened his eyes. At present the shield was the only thing keeping the Giver alive.

"You had a vision, my son."

"Was my vision of the future?"

"Yes."

"Was it real? I mean, will Shadows receive the light only to reject it later?"

"If that is what you saw, then that is a likely outcome, but I prefer to believe in free choice, not fate. There are other possible outcomes depending on individual choices."

Cooper hoped his people would appreciate the amazing gift of freedom given them. The vision, however, worried him. Many Shadows had already declared their desire to make him the new Emperor. A truly horrible idea. Hadn't his people learned anything? Tiarnas had a real chance at freedom and equality for everyone. Why would anyone want to put that in jeopardy by putting all the power in the hands of one Shadow, no matter how much they loved or trusted that Shadow. Total power corrupts. Eventually, such power might even corrupt him. Cooper wasn't willing to find out. Instead, he insisted that the original matriarchal order be reestablished. That was the true Shadow way.

Giver smiled at Cooper. "Thank you for coming," Giver spoke softly. "I appreciate the company."

Cooper said, "I know how tired and weak you feel. It's just that I feel the need to report our progress to you and, of course, to ask for your advice. Your enemies are finally gone, father. You are free."

"You have done well," the old Angelic said.

"Our revolution has brought about dramatic changes," Cooper continued. "But not everyone is happy about it. There are still pockets of resistance. There are many who seek power for themselves. Now that the Shadow Lords are gone, a whole new enemy has come forward to challenge what we have accomplished. How do I put an end to the violence without using more violence? This hero stuff is a bit overwhelming. My world needs me. I need to get this right for every Shadow's sake."

"Win hearts and minds," Giver said. "The rest will fall into place."

"It's easy to win over friends but, at the moment, my opponents are not being very friendly."

"Perhaps they need to be taught respect first."

After a couple of minutes of thought, Cooper asked, "Respect is a new idea to most Shadows. They understand fear, but I don't want to be like that."

The old Angelic smiled. "Of course, you don't."

"Perhaps this sounds like a stupid question. I know very little about what is inside me. Do I have a heart? If so, where is it?"

Giver chuckled and pointed at Cooper's chest. "There," he replied. "Right in the middle."

At the center of Cooper's chest an orb of light came to life. Astounded, Cooper put his hand over the orb. The light filtered through his fingers. Cooper's eyes moistened.

"Teach your people that freedom requires sacrifice but it is worth it. Freewill is a right given every creature by their creator. The power to make choices doesn't belong to an elite few. It belongs to everyone. All Shadows have natural rights. Those rights cannot be taken from them by rulers, or magistrates, or anyone else. Make every Shadow declare allegiance, not to government, but freedom itself. Only then will the love of freedom have a hope of surviving in this world."

"What if I fail?"

"Look what you have accomplished, my son," Giver countered. "You will not fail."

"In my vision an Angelic said something to me. He said, 'We are with you and you are with us.' What did he mean?"

"The day will come when Shadow-kind will be like the Angelics. Then you will be one with us. All we have will be yours." The old Angelic coughed. That led to a long coughing spasm. Fluid trickled out of the corner of Giver's mouth.

"My son. I am dying."

"I know." Cooper looked down. "I wish we had a way to heal you."

"That is okay. I get weaker each day but, while I still have enough strength, I need your help."

"What can I do?"

"It is time to use that antimagic device of yours."

"On what?"

"On me."

"But... you said you would die if I did that."

"I will die either way. One thousand years is a long time to live. I have a gift to give you but I cannot give it from this prison."

"But..."

"It is okay. Release me. It is time."

Cooper didn't like it, but he obeyed. He closed his eyes and pressed the button of the tube attached to his armor. The flash of light disabled the sphere of magic that held his father in place. The magic disappeared and the Old Angelic fell to his knees.

"Thank you, my son," he said. "Now I can die with purpose."

Alarmed by the change in magic, the twelve Priestesses flew into the chamber and gathered around Giver to give him support.

"It is okay, my dear friends," Giver said. "I will be fine." He turned to Cooper. "Come here, Ku Por. Stand before me. You have proven yourself worthy of a grateful father's blessing."

As soon as Cooper was close enough, Giver extended his arms and laid his hands-on Cooper's head.

"Ku Por, for that is your new name. You are the Great Sign, the liberator of the Shadow world. By the power of the Creator of Life, I call upon you to receive my gift." The Angelic's heart began to glow from inside his chest. The light traveled down Givers arms to his hands. "The power given to me, I now give to you. Use it wisely, my son." Light transferred from Giver to Cooper. Cooper's eyes went big and round as he gasped at the rush of light within him filling his chest. "For I am with you and you are with me. So, it is ordained."

When Giver removed his hands, Cooper fell forward onto his hands and knees. The light transformed his Shadow body. The orb of light in his chest spread like tentacles of light to his head then snaked out forming fibrous structures throughout his body. Cooper looked at his arms, hands, legs, and feet in pure amazement. He twisted right and then left trying to see his back. There was a moment of disappointment that showed on his face.

"What is it, my son?"

"No wings," Cooper asked? "I was hoping for wings."

In spite of how weak Giver felt, he laughed and laughed. Giver reached out and touched Cooper's head. Two bulges appeared on Cooper's back. Then in an explosion of light, magical wings flashed from the bulges.

"They may not be physical wings, but the magical kind work just as well." the giver said.

Cooper stood. His new body glowed from within piercing even his body armor. He stretched his new wings as if stretching his arms. It felt wonderful. Then the wings retracted and disappeared. The light in his body slowly dimmed, except for the orb in his chest. It warmed his soul.

The Priestesses gently laid the old Angelic on the ground. Giver smiled up at them then closed his eyes.

"Father," Cooper said, rushing to the old Angelic's side. But it was no use. The Angelic was gone, finally at peace. Liquid dripped from Cooper's eyes as Giver's body slowly crumbled to dust. "Collect these remains and bury them in a place of dignity. On the hill above all those that have fallen for our freedom. Raise a monument so all Shadows can remember the sacrifice made for them."

Chapter 10

Grandpa's Dojo

Grandpa Maeda listened somberly as Bobby explained what he felt when the woman in black cut them off in traffic.

"And you say that it looked like a human woman," he asked?

"Jeff got the best look at her," Bobby replied.

Jeff added helpfully, "She wore a helmet so none of us saw her face but that tight black leather jumper left no doubt as to gender."

Grandpa grumbled, "I don't know what we are dealing with. A Siren, maybe. But I associate Sirens with water."

"There is a big ocean out there," Jeff said.

"True, but sirens do not ride motorcycles."

"A feminist, progressive siren," Sam suggested?

Grandpa laughed heartily. "In these times, who knows."

Bobby shook his head. "It felt like a Shadow."

"If it was a Shadow, then somehow they could shapeshift."

"Some supernatural creatures can use magic to create a disguise," Jeff suggested. "At least that's what one of my teachers told us."

"The Shadows we fought had no great magic," Grandpa countered. "Neither did Cooper."

"Maybe so," Bobby said, "but what about that other type of Shadows, the fast ones that flew overhead. They were different. They had the ability to make fire"

Grandpa rubbed his balding head. The years showed on his face. "Something destroyed the military aircraft with ease," he noted. "If they used magic to defeat modern aircraft, then maybe they have the ability to mask their appearance. We may be looking at a creature that can look like anyone or anything. If any magical Shadows got trapped in this world, they would need to hide, maybe hide for years."

"Well this one wasn't doing a very good job of hiding," Sam offered. "She nearly ran right into us with that motorcycle of hers. Bobby sensed her immediately."

"It was our good luck that it was you she cut off in traffic," Grandpa said. "Otherwise we would still be unaware she was even here. What worries me is why are you just discovering its presence? Have you not felt anything until today?"

"Well… for the last couple of weeks I have been feeling uneasy," Bobby replied.

"What about this morning when you touched Asura," Sam remembered. "You felt something weird, didn't you?"

"Yeah, but…"

"Oh, come on. Asura," Jeff mocked? "Asura is all girl, flesh and bone. The only scary thing is her femme fatale vibe. Man, she'd be one scary girlfriend."

"Yeah, I'm with Jeff," Bobby said, shaking his head. "I only felt a weird vibe for a second. Maybe the femme fatale thing got to me."

"Then how come you haven't felt my femme fatale thing," Sam asked with a careful glare?

"I have, but I like your vibe," Bobby replied with a grin. "I didn't like Asura's vibe."

Sam thought for a moment. "Good answer," she said.

Jeff laughed and gave Bobby a little push. "Yeah, good answer."

Grandpa became thoughtful. Ever since the Shadow invasion, the death of his father and grandfather kept coming back to haunt him. In particular, he remembered the siren who killed his father. She had the ability to change her appearance.

"What is it grandpa," Jeff asked?

"The creature that killed my father," Grandpa said, "The surviving witness described her as the most beautiful woman he had ever seen. My father and his men were patrolling the northern end of Biwa Lake near Nagahama. Reports of missing people and animals had had a sudden increase."

"My father and his men combed the forest and Biwa Lake's shore line looking for any evidence of supernatural activity. They found nothing of significance on land, so they took their investigation out onto the lake itself. The first day produced no results, but on the second day a man's body was found floating face down. The man, a tourist who had been reported missing the week before, had been sucked dry of all fluids. The body was dry and brittle as the desert, even though it had been in the water for days. The victim's cracked and wrinkled skin broke away in their hands. It looked like a siren attack, but sirens were extremely rare in modern times. Plus, they lived in salt water. That baffled them. If it was a siren, how had it gotten into the lake"

"My father was a dedicated warrior," Grandpa explained. "No giving up until the job is done. So, the boat took to the water for a third day. My father stood at the bow chanting summoning incantations. They had to bring the creature to them in order to kill it."

"The witness said a woman rose up out of the water right in front of the boat. Her naked skin was like a mother of peril. She had long white hair that flowed down over her shoulders, extending halfway down her body. Her yellow eyes captured all present. The siren enchanted father. He was unable to move or speak. She smiled as she drifted toward him. Mesmerized, he reached out to her. She took his hand and drew in closer and gave my father a gentle kiss. Then she backed away with a smile and transformed into a half woman and half snake. Her beautiful facial features turned sharp and fierce. She let go a piercing scream that broke their eardrums. She coiled around my father and dragged him to his death. More sirens came out of the water and attacked the boat. In the end only one of my father's men survived by swimming to shore. My father might have lived had he not allowed himself to be tricked."

"You never told me that story before," Jeff said in soberness.

"I just want to remind you that beauty is not a sign of goodness. Never forget that. I do not think this is a siren. If this is a Shadow, it is using a human female body as a cover. It may have learned that humans, both men and women, sometimes use beauty as a tool to trap and deceive."

"The second concern," Grandpa continued soberly, "Is it the only Shadow? How many Shadows got trapped in our world?"

"Oh boy," Jeff said with a shudder.

"How could they stay hidden," Bobby asked?

"From what you experienced today, they can hide among us, out in plane sight. Most people would never suspect it was not human."

"I wonder why this one is here now," Sam asked?

"To finish what they started, I assume," grandpa concluded.

"Come on," Jeff said with more than a hint of frustration. "I just got back home. Why can't they just give it rest?"

"I wonder if she knows about us," Sam asked.

"Maybe," Grandpa replied. "Magic is a two-way street to some extent. If you detected it, it probably detected you."

"Just great," Bobby complained. "Just what we need. We haven't even graduated from high school yet. Why now?"

"You three need to keep alert," Grandpa concluded. "Let me know if anything else happens. Oh, and make sure your parents know about this. Don't go handling things on your own again."

"Should we call Master Meade in Japan," Jeff asked?

"Not yet," Grandpa said. "We really don't know anything. No need to raise concerns until we know more.

"Now don't think this new development is getting you out of training today," grandpa said sternly.

"Yes Master," all three replied.

Chapter 11

Witch's Fortress

Shadow Strong turned into a parking ramp that led down to an underground parking lot. With a wave of her hand she opened the gate. That action also deactivated the barrier spell that protected her fortress. Driving on through the gate it closed behind her and the spell re-established itself with a shimmer that only a witch could see. The motorcycle's engine echoed loudly off the concrete walls of the empty parking garage. She pulled to a stop next to the main elevator shaft that led to the upper floors of the old building above. Pulling off her helmet she cautiously looked back toward the entrance gate. She had definitely felt something. There had been at least one magical being, possibly two. Neither were Shadow witches. Preoccupied with the day's annoying errands, she had carelessly let her guard down. The witch, or witches, had been very close. Probably in that car that had nearly hit her. She intended to go on a long fast ride to relieve the stress of acting like a human. As a result of the magical encounter, she had cut her ride short and returned to the safety of the fortress. Now she was in a bad mood. Not that she was in a good mood all that often.

Shadow Strong had discovered the presence of a human witch during the invasion. A human witch caused the debacle of an invasion to fail. The human was an unforeseen threat that needed to be eliminated. The High Overseer ordered her warrior witches to search worldwide for magic makers. They found traces of magic connected to humans in several different countries, but none as powerful as the witch encountered during the invasion. Stupid that it hadn't occurred to her to look in El Palmar in the first place. Considering the power, she had just felt, the human witch hadn't been alone. She sensed the other human had detected her at the same moment she had detected them. She had quickly cast a spell to cover her trail. Of course, that meant she had lost contact with the witch as well. "No worry," she thought. "I will have my spies look for her. They will find her and kill her."

Shadow dismounted the bike and entered the elevator shaft. She had removed the elevator because it served no purpose and it made her claustrophobic. She floated up the open shaft to her personal residence on the top floor. She had had the building renovated for her use, but not according to human standards. The contractors had gutted all floors, exposing the concrete and glass exterior walls and the interior support columns. The top floor provided her with a spacious open loft space. Shadow Strong liked it this way. It reminded her of home. The one-way windows allowed her to observe this world outside freely while remaining in secluded safety.

No furniture existed except for a large, luxurious bed in the center of the loft. Shadow Strong needed nothing else for comfort. She didn't actually need the bed but wanted it anyway. Some luxuries in this world were uniquely glorious. She loved her bed, an emotion that contradicted the Shadow warrior code of conduct. She didn't care. She was High Overseer Shadow Strong who would soon be honored as an Imperial Witch when she returned to Tiarnas.

The only decorative feature in the room floated above the bed. The three-dimensional hologram of the Earth rotated serenely. Points of light appeared on the surface of the globe. These indicated significant locations around the planet such as national capitals, military bases, and any other strategic places. Overseer Strong's witches had used the last two years well, gathering much-needed intel in preparation for the reopening of the rupture back to Tiarnas.

Three floors beneath the bed lay the battle arena floor. Only an eight-foot concrete perimeter remained on floors two and three. These observation galleries were for her Shadow witches to watch training battles fought on the open first floor. The Shadow witches gathered each day to watch their sisters fight. Shadow Strong used these contests to establish a ranking of her warriors. These elite witches represented the best of the best in the Shadow world but, after the rupture closed and trapped them in this world, the witches began to change. The use of the soul-eater spell to establish an identity in this world had an unfortunate side effect. Some human emotions transferred over to the possessing witch. This had caused instability among the ranks. Symptoms presented in a variety of ways from listlessness to uncontrollable rage. The witches only had an eighty percent success rate with the soul-eater spell. That was disappointing. When possible, the High Overseer reversed the spell, returning the affected witches back to normal.

From the floor beneath the arena the witches tunneled under the city in three directions, one led to the ocean, terminating off the coast under the water. The second led to the hills above town. A third tunnel led to the old university campus terminating directly under the Center for Interdimensional Physics where they intended to reopen the rupture to Tiarnas. This final step required a wizard. Fate played into Shadow Strong's hands when she met Theodore (Teddy) Stanley of the law offices of Stanley, Morris, and Fitch.

Chapter 12

Los Angeles
Nineteen Months Earlier

Nineteen months ago, the Overseer, presenting herself as Kylie Harrisford, along with four other Shadow witches, entered a downtown Los Angeles office building for a 10:00 AM appointment. With the unexpected passing of Kylie's father, the grieving daughter now spent her days exploring the many aspects of the Harrisford fortune. Mr. Stanley, the oldest partner in the firm, was not daddy Harrisford's primary attorney. Kylie had been informed by her father's executive assistant that law offices of Stanley, Morris, Fitch were the go to attorneys for the shadier side of business. These lawyers were fixers. They handled everything quietly behind the scenes under the table in the world of dark dealings. This revelation would have shocked Kylie, at least to some extent. But the Overseer was absolutely delighted to find out her late bennifactor was such a scoundrel. As a result, she did not anticipate any trouble persuading the firm to do her bidding.

The five women exited the elevator on the fourteenth floor and proceeded down the hall to the glass doors with the sign - *Law Offices of Stanley, Morris, and Fitch*. They walked with military precision in formation, two at point, Ms. Harrisford center, and two at the rear. The four bodyguards wore black business pantsuits, but Ms. Kylie Harrisford wore a knee length black lace dress with spaghetti straps that allowed the full display of her lean, muscular shoulders and arms, as well as her other female charms. Her long hair hung down over her shoulders stylishly topped off with a wide brimmed black hat. She had discovered that witches in human mythology wore black and the black hat provided an essential finishing touch. All five women wore dark sunglasses which seemed unnecessary as it had been an unusually cloudy day. Of course, even indoors the women didn't remove the sunglasses. It was the eyes. Humans' eyes didn't accidentally flash red, yellow or green when under emotional stress. An odd anomaly caused by this world. The eyes couldn't completely conceal their deceptive intentions.

The first two women opened the double glass doors leading into the law office's spacious ultra-modern reception area. The five women walked forward to the front receptionist.

"Ms. Harrisford is here for her appointment," one of the bodyguards said dispassionately.

"Welcome Ms. Harrisford," the smart dressed woman behind the desk said with a well-used, perfect smile. "Mr. Stanley is ready to see you now. Allow me to show you the way."

They were led down another long, wide hall to another set of double glass doors which led to yet another reception area. Ms. Martin, Mr. Stanley's Executive Assistant, stood to greet the visitors. "Welcome Ms. Harrisford," she said with that same well-used smile on her face. Shadow Strong merely nodded stoically.

Mr. Theodore Stanley waited in his office leaning against the front of a large glossy black modern desk. This new client was a bit unusual. He opened the leather folder he held in his hands and perused the contents. Ms. Harrisford had a platoon of lawyers at her beckoning call. Her father was a former client but she was not. Why was she here?

Ms. Martin led the women through another set of double doors made of rich, dark cherry wood. The far facing glass wall of Mr. Stanley's office provided a magnificent view of downtown Los Angeles. The same dark cherry wood covered the other walls. To the left sat Stanley's large black desk and to the right a seating area with seven luxurious low back armchairs upholstered in soft red leather. The overstuffed arms curled elegantly outward creating a modern style with a classical look. The chairs clustered around a low round table of the same color and texture as Mr. Stanley's desk. If Hell needed a lawyer, this was what the devil's lawyer's office would look like.

The doors shut behind Shadow Strong and two of her bodyguards. The other two remained on the outside of the door. The tall middle-aged Theodore Stanley put on a broad smile and said, "Well, well, well, isn't this a surprise. It is so good to finally meet you Ms... Harrisford?" The two bodyguards moved in front of the Overseer and conjured a magical barrier.

Stanley said, "There is no need for hostility. You surprised me as much as I surprised you. I wasn't expecting three Shadow witches to walk into my office today."

"Five," Shadow Strong corrected. "Two more guard the other side of the door."

"Can I get you some coffee or tea, Ms. Harrisford," he asked politely?"

She said nothing as she sized up the man, or rather the Shadow wizard, standing in front of her.

"You obviously haven't been in this world long," Mr Stanley said. "Are you able to converse in vocal language, or would you prefer the Shadow way?"

The Overseer smiled back. "I suppose communicating verbally would do me good. Practice makes perfect, as these humans often say. No need for coffee or tea either. I don't like human food. Although humans themselves are very tasty. So, what is a Shadow wizard doing running a human law firm?"

"First, please sit," Stanley said, directing toward the chairs. "Ms... What is your Shadow name?"

"I am High Overseer Shadow Strong."

"Oh. You sound so very important. I no longer have a Shadow name. I go by the name Theodore Stanley, as you already know. All my friends just call me Teddy. Shadow Strong sat down in one of the seven chairs, removed her hat and placed it on the table in front of her. The two witches stood at guard directly behind her. Mr. Stanley sat in a chair opposite Shadow Strong and placed his folder on the table. "To answer your question," Teddy said. "I was, in fact, the legal consultant to the Shadow Lords back on Tiarnas. I found it a logical transition, so, when I got to this world... I ate a lawyer."

"And how exactly did you get into this world," she asked?

"Through an interdimensional rupture inside a little cave, but that was a long time ago."

"I see."

"I know the Shadow Empire attempted to invade this world. The humans handed you your backsides, I believe. But, I had no idea some Shadows got left behind."

"The humans got very lucky. That won't happen this time."

"This time?"

"The Shadow Empire lost a battle, not the war."

Teddy didn't like the implication that the war with the humans might begin again. "Well then, High Overseer Shadow Strong, how can Stanley,

Morris, and Fitch help you? I am sure you must have heard about our unsurpassed expertise in all areas of U.S. and international law. Our reputation for getting things done for our special clients is well known. Obviously, whatever your needs, we should be able to fulfill your highest expectations."

"My expectations can be very high, Mr. Stanley," she replied.

"Please call me Teddy. All our clients have high expectations," Teddy clarified. "I suppose, under these circumstances, I should consider you a very special client."

"You are being drafted, Mr. Stanley. I want you to consider me your *only* client."

"Really, Overseer. Such an exclusive agreement is not possible."

"This is not a suggestion, Mr. Stanley," the Overseer barked, raising her voice. "It is an order," Teddy frowned. This was not going well. "Do not worry… Teddy. Your humans will be well compensated."

"Overseer, I have never been a warrior in this world or on Tiarnas. I do not think you…"

"I have little time to accomplish my goals. I need your expertise in moving things along."

"What exactly are your goals?

"I suppose conquest sounds over-ambitious, but that best describes my end goal."

"I see," he replied. "So, you wish to finish the war that the Shadow army started and failed. What makes you think you can succeed with a few Shadow witches?"

"Oh, you have no idea what we are capable of," she assured him.

"These humans are experts at waging war. Conquest will not be easy."

She ignored Teddy's observation and continued. "I have investigated your law firm carefully, Teddy. I came here today specifically because you have an aggressive, self-serving, anything goes work ethic."

Teddy relaxed a bit. "Not that we actively break the law. We do not wish to attract any unnecessary attention from law enforcement. We have, however, often bent the law to our client's needs. Believe it or not, I use magic sparingly. Using magic increases the danger of being discovered. I am sure you understand that."

"Conquest is very dangerous work."

"Do not get me wrong," Teddy assured. "I will always do what needs to be done, but... what you are suggesting will make things far more expensive."

"Understood. You will never want for anything."

Teddy laughed. "I already have everything I want."

"You're a wizard, with Royal Family connections. I expect one hundred percent loyalty."

"I left the Shadow world and the royal family behind. I like it here. To be honest, I am more than a little concerned that you will destroy everything I have biult. Should you fail to win your little war, where does that leave me?"

"I will win."

"So, there is no talking you out of this? I am happy to let Tiarnas die the slow death it deserves. Why not embrace this world as it is? Just enjoy being the richest person on Earth."

Shadow Strong frowned. "It's time to join my war. Your fantasy life ended when the Shadows invaded two years ago. I will accept no dissension. To refuse my orders is treason."

"Please reconsider your options, Overseer Strong. Tiarnas has nothing to offer us anymore."

"Time to choose sides, Teddy. You can either be my new best friend," she explained. "Or my worst enemy."

"I have no desire in being your friend or your enemy," he said bluntly.

Shadow Strong stood. Raising her arm, she pointed at the cowardly Shadow. In the split-second Teddy flew across the office and smashed into the far wall. The Overseer dropped the human illusion revealing her dark, Shadow form covered in body armor.

Mr. Stanley barely managed to dodge a second blow. With his hand outstretched he formed a protection shield. A fireball glanced off the shield hitting one of the thick plated glass windows. The glass turned molten and a large hole appeared as the molten glass flowed down to the floor.

In a blur the Overseer flew toward Teddy. She kicked his magical shield with full force. The shield blew apart, sending Teddy tumbling. With a flick of her hand the Overseer sent Teddy rolling straight through that newly created hole in the glass window. Teddy recovered his senses only to find himself floating helpless fourteen floors above the ground.

"I notice while on the elevator," Shadow said laughing, "that your building doesn't have a thirteenth floor. Are you superstitious, Teddy. I really don't see how skipping numbers to the fourteen makes any difference. It is still the thirteenth floor."

Theodore Stanley struggled. He had lost control of the situation. The Overseer was a powerful witch and he didn't have the skills to fight her. He decided to relent rather than die.

"I see you have me at a disadvantage," he conceded. "Not that this test of wills wasn't fun, but it is a bit windy and cold out here. So, if you wouldn't mind, would you please bring me back inside." Shadow Strong laughed and pulled him back into the room.

It was true, Stanley thought. He had had great success playing human all these years, but his past had just caught up with him. The game was over.

"Let me begin again. Ms. Harrisford, as my only client, how can Stanley, Morris, and Fitch help you?"

"Friends then, Teddy," she said slyly.

"I assure you that Stanley, Morris, and Fitch will stand behind you one hundred percent. We will be fully committed to your needs from now to the unforeseen future."

"Good," she said. "I am so delighted." Shadow nodded to her two bodyguards. "Fix the mess I made."

They immediately repaired the window and the damage to the room and furniture. Within seconds all was back to normal. Then the office door flew open and Ms. Martin ran into the room in a panic.

"Is everything alright, Mr. Stanley," she asked alarmed?

Teddy stood tall and straightened his tie and suit coat. "Everything is just fine, Ms. Martin."

"But the noises... what was...?"

"It was nothing," he said. "Just me jumping for joy over the wonderful opportunity Ms. Harrisford has just given our firm."

Ms. Martin looked confused. Looking around she could see that everything was as it should be. "Sorry for interrupting, Mr. Stanley."

"No problem, Ms. Martin." The woman left, closing the doors again.

Teddy turned back to Shadow Strong. "Before you go, Overseer Strong. I have something you will find interesting." Teddy went to a wall safe and opened it. The safe contained a large package wrapped in cloth. He set the package on his desk and unwrapped it. It was a book, an ancient book from the look of it. "This book contains valuable information and instructions for opening pathways to other worlds. Even more intriguing, the book contains a list of other worlds, including names, descriptions of species, status as to friend or foe, although the information is probably out of date, and... it explains how to get to these other worlds. I found the book in Tiarnas' Royal Library. The book had sat on a shelf undisturbed and covered in centuries of dust. As a scholar of sorts, I recognized the value and rescued it. High Overseer Shadow Strong, if it is the conquest you want, don't expect the Shadow Empire to be of any use to you. With this book you can find far better allies to help you win this war."

The Overseer stood in stunned silence. "You know, Teddy," she said. "This could change everything,"

Chapter 13

Athletes or Soldiers

"As strange as it sounds," Jeff said as the three friends entered Grandpa's backyard through the side yard. "We are now jocks. That's not something I thought I'd ever say. I was a happy geek. What has happened to our world?"

"I wouldn't worry too much, Jeffrey," Sam replied. "We are pretty much the same people. It's just that we've had to grow up a little sooner."

"What does that make me? A jockey-geek," Jeff asked with a bit of sarcasm?

"A geeky-jock," Bobby replied. "I would prefer geeky-jock."

"I suppose so," Jeff sighed.

"We just need to keep a balance," Sam suggested. "Now that you are home, maybe we can get game weekends going again."

At the dojo steps they removed their shoes, replacing them with practice footwear. Bobby, who wore a baseball cap that day, removed his hat and stuffed it into his backpack. At the dojo entrance they each bowed before entering. Jeff went to the weapons rack, chose a *bokken, a* wooden practice sword, and began slicing the air with it.

Bobby took an eighteen-inch-long tubular object from his backpack. The object looked to be a hightech nightstick like the police use. "The funny thing is, I don't even like sports," Bobby said. "Yet, here I am in a dojo three times a week and loving it."

"What have you got there," Jeff asked Bobby.

"This is my new toy." Bobby said.

"It's a *bo*," Sam said, "My dad had made it for him."

"Kind of short for a fighting staff,"Jeff smirked.

"Not when I do this," Bobby said. "Activate." The *bo* extended from both ends dramatically.

"That was awesome," Jeff bleated. "How did it do that?"

"The mechanical parts like the extensions are pretty basic, but this staff does more than deflect blows. This thing is filled with magical tech?"

"Magical tech?"

"Mr. Thomas is an expert in such things. Got it for my birthday last summer."

"Well then," Jeff said with a grin. "Let's have a demonstration, dude,"

Jeff moved toward Bobby, *bokken* raised to an attack. A surprised Bobby reacted, glancing away Jeff's first strike. Bobby retreated two steps twirling the bow into a defensive position. Jeff lowered his *bokken* and laughed.

"Why a *bo*," he asked?

"It's what I started with, remember? So, why not?"

"What else can it do?"

Bobby held out the staff in front of him horizontally and concentrated. Out of both ends of the staff, Crystal clear tips appeared. One had a blunt end and the other had a rather dangerous looking blade. "The blunt end is the lens for a concentrated beam weapon," Bobby explained. "The other end does this." He concentrated again and the blade end flashed with blue fire. Bobby rotated the bo again. The bo created a ring of blue fire light.

"Whoa, dude. It's just liked that new Jedi weapon from latest *Star Wars* movie."

"Mr. Thomas says it will even do magic," Bobby said, "Things like magical spells. I don't know how to do that yet, but Mr.Thomas will teach me."

"Once you learn how to control it," Sam said. "It will be amazing."

"Yeah, dude," Jeff smirked.

"Now I don't just have to stand and point at the enemy. I can fight" Bobby said. "Of course, I can't use it in the dojo. I might destroy the dojo just learning how to use it. But it is cool." Bobby took a pose with the staff. "It makes me look like a warrior in a computer game."

"That makes me think we are more like soldiers than jocks," Sam said. "Our training is a soldier's training. Athletics implies competition. This is not about competition. It's about being prepared to fight."

Bobby reiterated, "I agree."

Just then Grandpa entered the dojo. "You two," Grandpa said to Bobby and Sam. "Time to get to work."

"Yes, Master Maeda."

"Hi Grandpa," Jeff said.

"You get to work too."

"Could we show Jeff what we have learned," Bobby asked.

"Okay then, my young friends," Grandpa said with a mischievous smile. "Let's show Jeffery what you got."

Bobby put his staff away and retrieved a wooden staff from the rack. "I'll go first."

Bobby proceeded to show what he had learned about the fighting with a staff. Although his technique was still a little rough around the edges, the demonstration impressed Jeff all the same.

Sam went next. She went through a progressive set of martial arts moves, impressing Jeff again with the progress made.

"Combining martial arts with your magical abilities will make you unstoppable," Jeff told Sam.

"That is nothing," Grandpa said excitedly. "Jeffery, with your *bokken*, I want you to attack our magical duo here. With the training you received in Japan you should have no trouble handling them both at once. Now don't hold back, Jeffrey. I want you to see what happens."

Jeff nodded and did as instructed. "Okay guys. Don't you hold back either," Jeff said with confidence. "I'll be fine, and I promise not to hurt you too much." He laughed.

"Oh yeah," Sam said? She readied for Jeff's attack. She raised her hand and beckoned him. "Bring it on."

"That's the spirit," Grandpa hooted and clapped.

Jeff moved in for the first strike. Bobby parried, deflecting the sword's blow with his staff. Sam pivoted to the side to sweep her foot behind Jeff's knee but he countered and Sam's kick missed. Jeff swung his sword around making contact with Sam's back. Sam was out. Jeff laughed as he turned again to deflect Bobby's incoming strike. Bobby backed away as Jeff pursued, striking three rapid, hard blows. The staff came out of Bobby's hands and he was out.

The next two matches went about the same with Jeff victorious in both. Then something changed. The harder Jeff fought, the better his opponents got. Bobby's and Sam's moves became smoother, more harmonious. They flowed, countered and balanced together. Its thrilled Grandpa as he watched the magical coupling in action. The obvious awkwardness exhibited in the first two matches disappeared, replaced with an artful choreography, a kind of warrior's dance.

Now it was Bobby and Sam who were getting the strikes. Again, and again they struck Jeff until he put up his hands.

"Enough," Jeff said out of breath. "What... What just happened? How did they do that," he asked his grandpa? "Or were you hustling me in the beginning?"

Grandpa explained, "No,no,no. It was all on the up and up. It's the coupling thing. Once they get going, they become connected in some magical way. They end up fighting as one. After a while, even I can't stop them. Astounding isn't it?"

"I'll say," Jeff replied Jeff, still panting. "What other crazy things have you learn while I was gone?"

"Sam's powers are amazing," Bobby exclaimed. "No kidding. Show him Sam."

"I don't know," she replied. "It's dangerous. I don't want to burn down the dojo."

"I remember the fire blasting from your hands," Jeff said.

"That's only half of it," Bobby added. "Go on and show him the new stuff."

"Grandpa?" She said, asking for permission.

"Sorry, we will need a safer place to experiment with the fire stuff," Grandpa said. "Let's put that demonstration on hold until Saturday."

"We could do the time thing," Bobby suggested.

"The time thing," Jeff asked?

"About six months ago something occurred to me," Sam began explaining. "I don't know why I didn't pick up on it sooner. Back when that ugly fanged Shadow attacked us in the auditorium at school, a strange thing had happened."

"This is the part that is so cool," Bobby interrupted.

"What," Jeff asked as his curiosity peaked.

"Well, out of pure desperation and fear, I yelled, 'Stop,'" Sam said. "And everything did stop, or at least slowed to a near stop." Jeff was still staring blankly at her. "I had actually stopped time."

Jeff stared at her completely dumbfounded. "I don't remember anything like that. Wouldn't I have noticed."

"That's the thing," Bobby explained. "I noticed it, but I was also holding on to her. It didn't last long but it was like in a movie when action goes slow-mo."

Grandpa Maeda stepped in to clarify. "I have heard of this sort of thing before. It is a rare talent. When Sam told me about this, we began to experiment." He thought for a moment. "The best way to explain what we discovered is to show you. Jeff come and face Sam about ten feet apart." They did so. "Now Jeff, attack Sam and she will defend herself. Move as fast as you can, Jeff."

Jeff shrugged his shoulders and got ready to attack. He lounged at Sam. Just as he reached out to grab her, he heard her whisper, "Stop." Suddenly she was no longer in front of him.

"I'm behind you, silly," Sam laughed.

"Holy crap," Jeff jumped and turned. "How… did…?"

"To you as the observer, but Bobby and me, too," Grandpa explained, "Sam simply disappeared and then reappeared behind you."

"Cool, huh? But what is even cooler," Bobby explained. "When I touch her in any way, like holding her hand, I am able to see what she sees."

"Show me," Jeff said.

"Sure," she said.

"Okay Jeff, you stand behind Sam and put your hand on her shoulder," grandpa ordered.

"It will be better if you hold my hand," Sam suggested.

He looked at Bobby. "Is that okay, dude?"

"Don't be silly," Sam said, grabbing his hand.

"This time," Grandpa said, "I will attack. Get ready?" They nodded. The incredibly agile old man launched himself at them, leaping into the air with his foot headed straight at Sam's face.

Jeff nearly lost it and went to pull her away when she said, "Stop." Grandpa Maeda seemed to freeze in midair. There was still some movement. Jeff watched as the foot inched closer and closer to Sam's face. He turned to look at her.

"Time to move," she said smiling. She stepped to the side out of Grandpa's way, pulling Jeff with her. Suddenly time released and the old man flew harmlessly past them. He landed on his feet and turned back.

All Jeff could say was, "Holy cow!"

"Uh-huh," Bobby said.

Grandpa said, "Sam is just beginning to discover her true potential as a warrior. I believe her powers might be limitless. With time, and experience, she will awaken many more abilities."

Sam blushed at that thought. "This may look easy to you guys but it takes a lot out of me. I'm exhausted already." Sam sat down on the floor cross legged.

"What about Bobby then," Jeff asked?

"My skills go in a whole different direction," Bobby replied. "A lot more subtle. You saw earlier how it worked when fighting with Sam. Of course, you already know I can sense things. Mostly the last two years have been about refining my senses."

"Like how," Jeff asked?

"I clearly sense Sam's thoughts and feelings now," Bobby replied. "I sense others more clearly as well. I usually have to be touching them, but if their emotions are strong enough, I feel it anyway. Kind of psychic."

Jeff responded, "That's a good power."

"Not necessarily. We are still in high school. You wouldn't believe the range of emotions, fears and... well everything teenagey that goes on every day. It's a bit distressing."

"The human lie detector thing has been helpful too," Sam added.

"Lie detector?"

"Yeah. Again, I usually have to be touching someone, but I can tell when someone is lying, or at least hiding a secret." Bobby got lost in a thought for a short moment.

Sam noticed the look on Bobby's face. "What is it?"

"I think that is what happened when I took Asura's hand this morning. She is probably hiding a secret. Of course, so are we. I felt nothing from Asuri, so maybe even she is unaware of Asura's secret. Unfortunately, picking up on these things gives me a splitting headache. It usually goes away quickly. The problem is, I don't always have to deliberately touch someone to get a reading. Just bumping into people in the halls can cause an immediate reaction. Again, think of high school trauma and drama. Do you have any idea how many lies, secrets and deceptions there are in the life of the average high school student?"

"I see what you mean," Jeff said, wrinkling his brow. "Your power sort of sucks."

"I'd much rather throw balls of fire around," Bobby concluded.

"Oh, don't be so quick to discount your powers," Grandpa said. "Two years ago, all of us would have been wandering around blind without your sixth sense. You two are a true coupling. You serve each other well. In war victory depends not only on the weapons a warrior has at his or her disposal, but also on good intelligence. Without good intelligence, the nature and location of the enemy, a warrior would be going into battle dangerously handicapped."

"Then there are the dreams," Bobby said. "My newest ability."

"You mentioned that," Jeff asked? "what's that about?"

"They are downright prophetic," Sam said.

Chapter 14

A Meeting of Minds

The next few days were rather normal, even boring. Jeff had easily blended back into an American school. It seemed the rigors of the private school he attended in Japan had given him a decisive edge. Hopefully it would make his final term in the USA a breeze, maybe even a little more personal time.

Grandpa Maeda, however, had a different perspective on how Jeff's time should be used. While under his tutelage, Grandpa intended to drive his grandson hard. The old man began by introducing Jeff to a training schedule that would dominate every spare minute of the boy's life. This was not what Jeff had in mind. So, after a little intergenerational negotiation, grandson and grandpa found a workable compromise. Even so, Grandpa only agreed to the lighter schedule because Jeff mention there was a girl he liked.

"I need some time for dating... girls... well... one girl," Jeff told Grandpa. "That is if she will go out with me. I need time to convince her to go out with me."

That got grandpa all excited at the possibilities for his grandson. "A girl," he said. "Why didn't you say so. Fantastic." The old man hopped. "Jeffrey has got a girlfriend. Jeffrey has got a girlfriend. Does she know how to smooch good? Come to think of it. Have you ever smooched a girl before? I will make it part of your training."

"Grandpa, take it easy. I still have to ask her out. And please don't add kissing to my training. I'll figure it out."

"Well, what are standing here for. Go ask the girl for a date, *baka*."

Amy Ross was the only one of Jeff's friends that had actively kept in touch with him while he was abroad. That had surprised him. It wasn't that no one else made an effort, but it surprised him that Amy would make such a consistent effort. Her letters and little packages had made him feel better. A lot less homesick. Jeff was Japanese by heritage only. Otherwise, he was an American boy through and through. He had missed his normal life back in

California.

Amy had always been so shy. She was cute and Jeff liked her, but he didn't think she like him all that much. Yet, she unselfishly lent him her support. She certainly had no way of knowing how much he needed it. In his time of need, Amy proved to be his best friend. No girl had ever treated him with such kindness, even Sam. Sam mostly tolerated him. Amy on the other hand had treated him like he was special. If nothing else, he needed to tell how much he appreciated it. Ideally, he wanted to tell her how much he liked her. The times she was around everyone else was around. Sometimes it felt like she was trying to avoid him. That frustrated him to no end.

Then there were the twins Asuri and Asura. He understood that he was their connection to home, and he truly wanted to be helpful, but they were hanging around all the time, especially Asura who was acting far too forward for his comfort. Normally he would be flattered by such attention, but he wasn't. It kind of annoyed him. Plus, every time Asura showed up Amy disappeared in a flash. She seemed afraid of Asura.

Asura could be quite aggressive. Asuri on the other hand was nicer, calmer. It was the good and evil twin scenario... kind of weird. Jeff didn't understand why Amy was so intimidated by Asura. As far as Jeff was concerned, Amy was every bit as pretty as the twins. Plus, Amy was a genuine, honest, kind person. The more he hung around Asura, the more he wondered about her motives. She had a weird vibe about her. She didn't seem real.

One night after training Jeff decided to go directly to Amy's home. He wanted to ensure time alone. "Tonight, is the night," he encouraged himself. "I will tell her how I feel. If she doesn't feel the same then, at least, I can stop obsessing about her."

So, he approached her home. This needed to be done right, meaning he needed to keep his mouth under control, think before he spoke... an infamous shortcoming. Approaching the door timidly, he knocked. There was no response, so he knocked again a little harder. In a few seconds the door opened. A very surprised Amy stared back at him. She had changed from the prim and proper school clothes into more casual flop around the house clothes, a pair of jeans and a loose-fitting top that hung off of one shoulder.

"Uh... hello Jeffrey," she said surprised. Her face flushed as she spoke. She tucked her long dark hair behind her right ear, something she often did when anxious or embarrassed. "Why..."

"Hi Amy," he said quickly. "It was a nice night and I went for a walk. Then I thought of coming to see you. Is this a bad time? I can come back another..."

"NO," she blurted out. "No, this is fine. I'm glad to see you." Her face flushed again. She looked back into the house where her family were watching TV. "I'll walk with you," she said. "If that's okay." She pulled the door closed behind her. They walked down the quiet neighborhood street in silence. Amy spoke first. "Are you doing okay at school... since coming home?" She had asked this same question almost every time they got together and she felt stupid for asking it again. Amy tucked her hair behind her right ear again.

"Yes, I'm still doing well," he replied politely.

"Tell me more about school in Japan. Was it a lot different?"

"In some ways, but you'd be surprised. Teenagers everywhere are pretty much the same."

"Was it harder, the classes and homework?"

"Yeah, but honestly, the biggest difficulty was the language. I thought I spoke pretty good Japanese but, when I got into school over there, I didn't understand half of what was being said. The teachers and the students talked so fast. It took a while to get adjusted."

"I can see how it might be a little difficult."

"Yeah," he replied. "I was raised as a pretty normal American boy. Turns out what I knew about Japanese culture was pretty basic. Fortunately, most Japanese teens are just like us. You have your smart kids, your jocks, geeks and nerds as well. There are popular kids and the not so popular kids. One big difference is the strong sense of status and class rankings. It tends to be very formal over there. You don't use people's given names without permission and so on. I made a lot of cultural slip-ups that weren't appreciated by others. Once my classmates got to know me, they started cutting me some slack. I eventually got better at social graces."

"What about studying martial arts? How did that go?"

"The best part of being there." *Here I go again,* Jeff thought, *talking about everything but...* "I wanted to thank you for all the emails, cards and care packages. You didn't really have to do all that."

"But I wanted to," she insisted. "You are a friend and... I didn't want you to forget me." Amy quickly changed that to... "us."

"Well it worked," he declared. "Really, I can't thank you enough. It helped in so many ways. You saved me from loneliness. I just want you to know how much it meant to me."

"Really? I'm so glad."

"That's what I mean." He stopped and turned to face her. "You did something nice because that is who you are. Kindness comes natural to you.

Amy blushed. "I don't know about that, but that's a nice thing to say. Thank you. I'm glad I could help."

"It was so you – friendly, kind, good and beautiful."

That took Amy's words away. She didn't know how to respond to the continuing compliment. Her face felt like it would burn up any minute. "Thank...ah... thank you," she said.

"No," Jeff said with a formal Japanese bow. "Thank you."

"You have changed so much. I am a little overwhelmed by how nice you are being to me."

"Ouch. Was I that bad before?"

"I'm sorry," she said pleading. "I didn't mean it that way?"

Jeff laughed. "It's okay. I used to be so nervous around girls that sometimes I acted crazy. Mainly because I didn't know what to do. A stupid boy thing, I guess."

This time she laughed which made him happy. "Okay," he said. "Here goes. Amy, I like you. I like you a lot and I hope you can forgive the old jerk I used to be and like me too." There he had said it. He was proud of himself because he had handled it like a man. He wasn't, however, prepared for Amy's response.

"Yes," she said, almost jumping up and down with excitement. She lunged forward, threw her arms around his neck. It was a great hug, a fantastic hug.

Holy cow, Jeff thought.

******

Asura hid in the evening shadows watching all this unfold. She had been following Jeff all day, in fact for the last several days. For some reason she couldn't stop thinking about him, so not knowing what else to do about these strange thoughts and feelings, she started to stalk him. But now she felt something new. It was dark and confusing. Her countenance darkened as she watched Amy hug Jeff. Hiding in the dark shadows her eyes seemed to glisten with anger. *What is this*, she thought? *It's more than anger. This must be... jealousy. What a strange sensation.*

Although she didn't fully understand it, she suddenly knew she hated Amy Ross with every fiber of her being. This threat would not go unchallenged.

Chapter 15

———•·•◆•·•———

The Shadow Fortress

Overseer Strong stood at the newly formed book pedestal leafing through the grimoire Teddy had given her. Teddy stood right behind her. "Why," the Overseer asked. "Why had the Shadow Lords never used this information?"

"That is a good question," Teddy replied. "Either they never knew it existed or… they didn't recognize the importance of it."

"Powerful wizards not knowing about such an important resource?"

Teddy and Shadow Strong had worked on the problem of reopening the Tiarnas rift. The grimoire gave them instructions, but it didn't work. The rift remained inaccessible, sealed solid from the otherside. Teddy soon came to the conclusion that, unless someone opened it from the Tiarnas side, the rift would remain closed forever. It was time to give up on the High Overseer's plan to return home. Why she thought a new assault by the Shadow Empire would render a better outcome was a source of pure frustration for him. Somehow, he had to change her mind.

"The Shadow Lords are powerful. That is true," Teddy explained. "But, to be brutally honest with you, they are not all that intelligent."

The Overseer turned to Teddy with her eyes open wide, "Teddy, my friend. That was a treasonist declaration."

Teddy couldn't hold back the laugh. He laughed loud and long, shocking the Overseer. "We are not in Tiarnas anymore, Overseer. It is time to wake up to the reality of our situation. The Shadow Lords are nothing but a collection of short sighted, paranoid idiots."

A stunned Shadow Strong listened to Teddy's less than flattering comments about the rulers of their world. "You should tread lightly."

Teddy scoffed. "Your so-called rulers of Tiarnas will soon come to a violent end. Shadows will rise up and overthrow them. If they haven't done so already. The Shadow Lords allowed themselves to become isolated and irrelevant. At the moment, they are more interested in holding onto power than serving the needs of Tiarnas. There lies their downfall. This book sat in storage at the Palace library for hundreds of years, lost along with other items they must have deemed to be useless and/or too dangerous to be acknowledged. As an imperial member of the judicial system, I had access to such things. When I found this book, a dream of a new life took hold of my imagination."

The Overseer grabbed Teddy by the throat and raised him off the floor. "So, you took the book for yourself. You did not consider our world's needs any more than they did. That was a crime against your people."

"You... may kill me... for saying this, but... I will say it... anyway. Shadows... ceased to... have imagination... centuries ago," Teddy struggled to say. "This knowledge... would be... wasted on them." The Overseer had to admit that was probably true. She dropped Teddy and he fell to the floor. "Overseer Shadow Strong," Teddy coughed out. "I am urging you. Forget Tiarnas. It is a dying world. Look past your years of indoctrination and see the truth. With this book, you can find new allies. Allies who are capable of giving you power beyond your wildest imagination.

"You are right about the Shadow Lords, and all other Shadows for that matter," she thought to Teddy's mind. An alternate plan began to form in the High Overseer's mind. Teddy gave a giant sigh of relief.

Chapter 16

The Center for Interdimensional Physics

Dr. Eugene Miles looked up from his tablet as his driver pulled up to the front sentry gate. The thick concrete walls enclosed nearly half of what had been the old University of California, El Palmar campus. The area was now exclusively the property of the federal government, namely the Department of Defence. What was left of the old campus buildings continued to be used while the new campus was under construction on the hill above the old campus. The campus was famous for its views of the Pacific Ocean and access to the beach. The new campus proclaimed that students could expect even better views.

The D. O. D. officially referred to the invasion two years earlier as the *Shadow Incursion*. Miles didn't care much for the name, but felt it was better than calling it the Demon War as old man Maeda had suggested. The young Dr. Percy McLeod had designated the alien species known as Shadows as Exaterestial Species EX001. Bill Williams and Rich Thomas had told Miles that they believed many more species lived on worlds found on the other side of certain interdimensional rifts. The problem was knowing which rift. The Shadows represented this planet's first encounter of such species. Of course, Mr. Maeda had strongly disagreed that the Shadows were the first.

One of the military guards at the compound's large solid steel gates stepped up to the Miles' car. These gates remained open almost all the time, but were designed to close automatically in an emergency. Miles' driver rolled down the driver side window and showed their ID passes. The guard peered into the back seat where Dr. Miles was sitting, then nodded and waved them on. The car then proceeded to The Center for Interdimensional Physics where Miles was dropped off for the day.

Most of the old buildings inside the compound had either been torn down or refitted to serve the needs of the staff of the Department of Defense facility. There were offices, laboratories, housing, cafeterias and other facilities for the use and comfort of the staff who at times had to stay inside the compound for days on end.

Of course, the original rift was no longer open. Bill and Rich had done all they could to ensure it remained closed, but Bill insisted there was at least a theoretical possibility that the rift to the EX001 world could be reactivated from the other side. As a precaution the Center had the site encased inside a fifty-foot diameter sphere made of specially hardened concrete, steel and magical technology. Half of the sphere was below ground leaving only the twenty-five-foot-high doom visible above ground. Miles professed that a direct hit of a nuclear bomb couldn't crack this sphere open. Bill, of course, hoped that was also true of a magical attack.

Dr. Percy Mcleod pulled up behind Miles' car at the gate and waited his turn. When he pulled forward, the guard took Percy's identification card then returned to the sentry booth and entered the ID number. Unlike Miles, who was driven to work in a sleek black luxury car, Percy had to drive himself in his eleven-year-old hatchback. The paint had faded in the California sun and there was a distinctive dent on the back-passenger side door, the result of an airport parking lot incident four years back. Percy had the money for a new car, but he just didn't care.

Its irked Percy that Miles always got a quick pass into the compound. He, however, always got checked and double-checked as though the guards didn't believe he belonged here. After a about minute the guard brought the card back to Percy.

"Everything looks fine, Dr. McDonald. You can proceed."

"Mcleod," Percy said.

"What is that, sir?"

"Not McDonald's. My name is Mcleod, Dr. Mcleod."

"Oh, sorry sir. You have a good day, Dr. Mcleod."

Percy grumbled as he drove on, "Hundreds of times I have passed by these guards and they still don't know who I am." He looked in the rearview mirror. The guard turned to another guard and laughed. "Sometimes I wonder if they are doing that on purpose. Jerks."

He headed to the Salmur Institute for Biological Studies. The Shadow Incursion the Shadow Incursion had presented Percy with a well-deserved promotion as the Director of the Institute for Biological Studies. The Institute housed all biological research relating to the DOD's top-secret project

Extraterrestrial Biologicals. Benjamin Salmur, the Institute's namesake, had led the first manned Mars mission that discovered the existence of simple forms of life on the red planet. As the first human scientist to study an intelligent alien species, Percy suddenly found himself at the top of a whole new world of opportunities. Unfortunately, the original living subject, the one those kids had named Cooper, was lost. When he accepted his new position, Percy made it clear, to the point of being insufferably annoying, that he needed another live specimen as soon as possible.

The D.O.D. built Percy a newer and better equipped research laboratory located within the campus compound right next to the Center for Inter-dimensional Physics. The old lab remained operational should they capture a new living specimen. This new facility housed EX001 bodies and body parts in cold storage bio-containers. Only two EX001 bodies, mostly deflated tissue and particles, remained relatively intact. Percy preserved them in specially designed hyperbaric chambers. These two large chambers sat in the middle of two separate labs. Each lab had a separate team of scientists which worked independent of each other. Preserving Shadow bodies had proved to be challenging. Most of the EX001 remains had degenerated into a pile of black powder. An analysis of the powder indicated the substance was primarily a carbon-based compound mixed with smaller amounts of a multitude of other components. Some of those components remain unknown.

In the beginning Percy spent most of his time inside his new facility. Miles only saw Percy occasionally. This important work had enveloped both of their lives to an even greater extent than before.

Although Miles' rift research had progressed rapidly, Percy felt his research, hampered by the lack of live specimens, had progressed far too slow. He aggressively advocated for active exploration and species collection. Percy wanted his own extraterrestrial zoo. There were others who supported Percy's position to one degree or another. Even Dr. Miles wanted to move towards exploration someday. But the politicians had grave concerns about the cost. The military worried over the possibility of another confrontation with a hostile alien species. They advocated a more conservative approach. Too many unknowns made the idea of exploration far too dangerous.

Percy resented this short sighted, over cautious approach. Just because the first rift led to adverse circumstances, that didn't mean all rifts would be dangerous. First of all, the probability of another species like EX001 existing beyond every rift they opened was extremely low. Even the great doomsayers, Williams and Thomas, agreed with his assessment. The revelation that life existed through an interdimensional rift offered Percy a research opportunity too important to ignore, a fulfillment of a lifetime dream. It floated tantalizingly at Percy's fingertips. Imagine if the fifteenth century Europeans had decided that exploration was too dangerous and expensive to pursue. What if Columbus and others had just stayed home. That would have worked out better for the indigenous people already here in the Americas, but that was what conquering was all about. Nature is about the survival of the fittest. Somehow, he would find a way to travel through a rift, hopefully through many rifts and get what he wanted. It was the only way for him to move forward. Percy would take every opportunity to influence the process and the ultimate outcome in his favor.

Bill and Rich had agreed to stay with Miles as the rift program moved forward. Although that had not been part of the original deal, Dr. Miles convinced them that they remained an essential part of the team. Mostly they agreed because they didn't trust the Department of Defense. By staying close to the situation, they could monitor any threat to their future. Protecting their families always came first.

As an incentive Miles gave them free reign of the IDR research facility with their own personal, state of the art, research labs. This proved to be fortuitous. Everyone's lives had been dangerously altered by the Shadow Incursion. Bill and Rich had a private agenda that included an escape plan. Should the war break out again, a very real possibility, they would be ready. They doubted this world would be so lucky next time.

Chapter 17

Deal With a Demon

After another frustrating day Percy McLeod left the compound and went home. It had been a long week and he needed some time to think, needed a new strategy for overcoming the objections toward dimensional exploration. Obsessed with the idea, he had argued the issue to the point his colleagues were now avoiding him.

Percy was a young man, far younger than any of his colleagues. But, because of his genius level intelligence and a significant lack of interpersonal skills, he had always had trouble relating to others. He started college at ten, earning a masters and three PhD degrees by twenty-five. There had been no chance to just be a kid, or a teenager, or anything but a student of science. Now, as an equal with much older colleagues, he still felt awkward. "didn't work well with others," as Miles had chastised him earlier today, he truly loved his work. So, work would have to be enough. He didn't need people.

This attitude didn't leave room for a normal life, unfortunately the lack of normality had left him a little confused about life. He found himself wondering. Was he happy? He didn't actually know what happiness was. Were his expectations about life, the future and other people realistic? Were his expectations normal? Considering what he did for a living, what was normal? Having been taught to think outside the box, heck his thoughts were usually outside this universe, he didn't see the world like other humans did. Sometimes he didn't even feel human.

Percy pulled up in front of his two-story condo. He sat there for a minute wondering, *"Am I a good person or a bad person,"* he thought? *"Am I even human?"*

As he got ready for bed that night, he felt restless. He tossed and turned for a while, then slipped off to sleep.

Sometime in the middle of the night something woke him up. There was a noise and... a light. The light on the ceiling above his bed was on, shining in his face. Hadn't he turned his light out? Getting up, he looked around but found nothing. He turned the light off and went back to bed. Before he could fall asleep the bedroom light came on again. Percy turned onto his back and blinked at the light on the ceiling, trying to focus his eyes. His eyes dropped to the end of the bed where a beautiful amber eyed woman, dressed all in black, stood smiling at him.

"It is rude to ignore a beautiful woman," the overseer said.

Now for any normal person this would have caused a frightful reaction, but Percy just stared at her curiously. Then he asked calmly, "Can I help you in some way? Have you gotten lost, because I certainly wasn't expecting company this late?"

Amused, Overseer Shadow Strong replied, "Yes, as a matter of fact you can help me." She crawled onto the end of his bed on her hands and knees until she was directly over him. "Do you like this body," she whispered in his ear? "Human men usually do."

He didn't move, just glanced down to her legs and back to her face. "It is a pleasing looking body," he replied.

She raised up on her knees straddling the young scientist and changed to her natural form. "Or maybe this is more to your liking?" His eyes opened wide at the magical transformation.

"Delightful," he whispered in stunned amazement. "Is this a dream?"

Shadow Strong floated upward while looking down at him.

"You're a Shadow demon," he said breathlessly. "This is truly marvelous." Then he frowned. "I'm just dreaming, aren't I? This is too good to be real."

The Overseer pointed a finger at him and shot a healthy jolt of energy at him. His teeth clenched and his back arched until she stopped. "Are you awake now," she asked, still smiling?" He nodded excitedly. "Good."

"Again," Percy asked, "how can I help you?"

"I understand you want to open rifts and go exploring," she replied. "I can make that happen."

"I can open a rift too, but no one is going to let me go exploring."

"Then someone else needs to be in charge."

"That is something I have believed all along."

"Who do you think should be in charge?"

"I think I should be in charge," he simply stated.

"I see." She transformed back to human. "What if I could put you in charge?"

"That would be nice, but how are you going to do that?"

Since being trapped here in your world, I have sought a way to get home. Unfortunately, I need your human technology.

"You wish to go back to your home world?"

"I did at first, but then I thought, why bother going home? There are numberless other worlds to visit. That is where you come in."

"You can't open rifts on your own?" That caught Percy's curiosity. "I was told Shadows used magic to do such things. Your magic cut through our defenses like butter."

"I have magic, but, this is a little embarrassing, it requires your technology to help us open a rift from this world."

"Fascinating," Percy commented casually. "So, you actually do need our help."

"Yes, I need your help."

"But...Why would I do that?"

"With your technology and my magic, I can open rifts to thousands of worlds. Help me and I will take you along. You can explore to your heart's content. I am also told that you like dissecting strange creatures? I can give you all the creatures you need. Cut them into little tiny pieces if that's what you want. I don't care. I just want to get out of this useless world."

Percy sat up on his bed so that he was eye to eye with the Shadow. "Do you wish to continue the war you started," he asked pointedly?

"Does that matter to you, especially considering I am offering you a way to explore many universes," she asked sweetly. "Be my ally and I will protect you and make that dream of yours come true."

"Are you suggesting I betray humankind?"

Shadow Strong put a finger on her chin. "Hummm," she said, "Yes, that is exactly what I am suggesting. But, considering all your special needs, it will be worth it."

"Point taken," Percy replied. "You have a plan then?"

Chapter 18

Amy's Got a Boyfriend

When Amy arrived at school the next day, Jeff was waiting at her locker. He wanted to see her again as soon as possible. She smiled at him and tucked her hair behind her ear. "Hi," she said. Otherwise she acted like nothing had changed between them. Jeff tried to take her hand but she flinched like a nervous cat.

"I'm sorry," she said quickly. "I'm a little unsure how to act… at school I mean."

Last night in a moment of pure excitement Amy had done something completely out of character. She had hugged Jeff like she never wanted to let go. Today she felt awkward and embarrassed and didn't want too much attention directed at her. Knowing Amy's reserved nature, Jeff understood. Besides, he felt pretty awkward as well.

"Don't worry," he reassured her. "Slow and easy is fine with me."

"Thank you… for understanding," she said. "I just don't want people to make a fuss over me."

"Your wish is my command," he said with a grin. "No fussing."

As Jeff and Amy stood together next to Amy's locker talking quietly, Asura walked by, followed by several other girls. These girls followed the exchange student as if she were a famous celebrity. Asuri follows behind them all. Asure babbled away about some nonsense or another, the girls giggling at everything she said. They were true groupies of the exotic females. Asuri remained quiet but observant as she followed. She didn't like this new attitude of her sister. Asura seemed to have forgotten why they had come to America in the first place. She ignored any counsel Asuri offered. Asura's actions were inappropriate for someone in their position. Asuri worried that things would go bad if her sister didn't snap out of it soon.

Asura paused her ramblings for just a second as they passed by Jeff and Amy. She felt a rush of anger. She scowled at the couple and considered a confrontation right then and there. What was Jeff doing talking so... intimately with this... Amy girl. She decided to let it go for the moment, but Amy better watch out.

Asuri Sensed the animosity building up in her sister's thoughts. Why was Asura acting so strange?

Chapter 19

Just Like Old Times

Bobby, Sam and Jeff spent Saturday morning searching for any sign of the Shadow they had encountered. They started downtown driving slowly up and down each street and around every block. Bobby wasn't sensing anything unusual, but he couldn't ignore the ever-growing sense of anxiety he felt. Following Grandpa Maeda's advice, they had alerted Sam and Bobby's parents. This in turn, triggered one of those special meetings in the Williams' basement. They all hoped this was a false alarm, but an unspoken fear that the Shadows had somehow returned began to trouble their minds.

"This is boring," Jeff moaned. "There has got to be a better way of doing this. We're getting nowhere."

"I am open to suggestions," Bobby replied. "You got any better ideas?"

"Not really," he admitted. "Maybe a divining stick?"

"I have a built-in divining stick, but either my stick is broken or this Shadow is really good at hiding."

"Jeffrey's got a point," Sam sighed. "We can't drive around like this forever. Let's face it, the odds of our paths crossing by accident again are not all that good."

Jeff said, "Master Maeda, that's mine not yours, told me that some supernatural beings have the power to mask their presence with magic. If that is the case here, it will be difficult to detect them."

"Maybe the Shadow will need to drop her magical shields occasionally, to cast spells or something," Sam suggested. "That's when we need to be ready."

"Maybe," Jeff sighed.

Bobby sighed as well. "Yeah, but I will need to keep my senses on high alert all the time. That's exhausting."

Sam had another thought. "Till now we have been searching in a grid pattern, like we were trying to find someone lost in the forest. What we need is some good old-fashioned detective work. The other day was the first time Bobby noticed Shadow's presence, right?"

Bobby nodded, "Yeah."

"So… that means the Shadow may have just shown up in El Palmar. Since she is posing as a human female," she went on. "She probably has taken up residence here in town. There are records of that sort of thing."

"I don't think we have access to those kinds of records," Boddy said.

"But maybe our parents can get access," Sam countered.

"That motorcycle," Jeff suggested. "There has got to be a record of a new license and registration?" Then Jeff started to feel skeptical. "Of course, people who don't want to be found tend to circumvent such regulations. We do, however, have a description of said faux-hot-woman and her cool bike. Surely, we aren't the only ones who have noticed her. She has probably attracted a lot of attention. Maybe we just need to ask around a bit."

"Yeah, good idea," Bobby agreed.

"So, are we done for the day," Jeff asked impatiently?

"Missing your anime," Bobby kidded?

"No."

"Hey, I know," Bobby said. "Sam, let's show Jeff what you can do."

"Okay, good idea," Sam replied. "This search is a waste of time anyway." Jeff looked unsure. "How long will it take?"

"Not long," Sam said.

"As long as I can be home between four and four thirty."

"No problem," Bobby promised.

"Let's go, dude."

Bobby drove to an old industrial park at the edge of town. He turned off the road and drove down between two rows of warehouses. These buildings were a mess with broken windows, debris and trash everywhere. At the end Bobby pulled up to the last building and parked. "This is it," Bobby said.

"This is where you hide the bodies," Jeff asked with a nervous laugh.

"No," Sam said. "This is one of the places where I practice the dangerous stuff."

Bobby smiled. "We bury the bodies after she is finished with them."

"I was wondering."

Bobby led them down a loading ramp big enough for a semi-truck to back down. To one side of the loading dock there were stairs leading up to the loading platform. The trio took the stairs and entered the warehouse through a door clearly marked "NO TRESPASSING". That led them into a typical open warehouse space with high walls and ceiling. Steel posts at regular intervals supported the trussed ceiling above. The windows were all up high, so no nosey onlookers would be able to watch what was happening.

"Creepy... and dirty," Jeff said.

"Okay," Sam said. "Let me get started." She took off her jacket and handed it to Bobby. "I'll start with the simplest trick." She raised both hands out in front of her, one above the other, palm facing palm, at about six inches apart. Closing her eyes, she quietly concentrated. Sam's hands began to glow and a ball of blue light appeared between them. "At night this makes everything glow like the moon. I can make the light engulf me, or anyone near me." She spread her palms apart and let the light spread over her body, leaving her ablaze in light. The warehouse filled with the light. "It's so warm," Sam whispered.

"Beautiful," Jeff said in awe. Sam blushed a little.

"Sometimes this happens when Bobby and I are kissing," she added with a mischievous giggle.

"That would be too much information," Jeff said with a smile.

"The light surrounds both of us and it feels so good," Bobby added.

"Oh ho, ho dude," Jeff replied with a laugh. "I am so jealous. You've got the best girlfriend in the world."

Sam blushed again, but this time she decided to change the subject. "You might change your mind when you see my more violent abilities. Observe the fire bullets."

"Fire bullets," Jeff said?

"On the wall over here, you will see a crudely painted target." The target was pockmarked and blackened by previous training sessions. "Watch and fear me, Jeffrey Sasaki." Sam stood about twenty-five feet away from the wall and target. First, she raised her right arm and formed a finger gun. She pointed her index finger at the target. With her left hand she clasped her right wrist to support her aim. "This has a bit of a recoil, so I have to support my aim." She sighted down her finger. Jeff watched as she tensed her arm. As Sam's hands glowed, she said, "Bang!" A short bolt of energy, about six inches long, left her fingers like a tracer bullet. It hit the target, sending sparks flying everywhere. "Bang... bang...bang... bang!" Each verbal command produced similar tracer bullets and accompanied explosive hits. Sam lowered her hand.

Jeff ran to the target. The concrete wall had five two-inch black holes burned into it. He looked at the holes and then back at Sam with a combination of fear and awe. You're just like *Kitaro* in *Ge ge ge, no Kitaro*.

"I'm a good girlfriend. Just don't piss me off," she said smiling.

Bobby laughed. "A good thing to remember."

Jeff gulped. "And I thought the fire beams you used two years ago were wild. This is... a little disturbing."

"Do the sword thing," Bobby insisted.

Sam held out her hand and a fiery sword appeared. "I first tried the sword thing on the invading Shadows but I have improved the technique. She held it out in front of her with both hands in a defensive position and concentrated. The blade flared red, yellow, and then blue. Sam sliced the air a couple of times for effect. "I can make a real sword flash with fire as well." She let the flaming sword disappear.

Bobby picked up a piece of rusted pipe off the floor. "Here use this instead."

Sam took hold of one end of the pipe and took a defensive position. It only took a few seconds before it blazed with fire. "I can do this to any object I take a hold of. Cool, huh."

"Wow," Jeff exclaimed, unable to contain his excitement. "Sorry Bobby but I think I am in love with your girlfriend."

"You couldn't handle me," Sam mocked. "Dude."

"You are probably right. Any other tricks up your sleeve?"

"Oh yeah," Bobby replied.

Sam took a martial arts position and began to punch and kick at the air. Suddenly her hands turned to fire. With every punch a ball of fire left her hands striking the warehouse wall.

"I'm working on getting my feet to do the same thing," Sam said. "But no good results yet."

Jeff scratched his head. "Why does it burn other things but not you?"

"Honesty... I don't know."

"It probably has to do with the magic gene," Bobby suggested. "The producer of the magic is not affected in the same way as an opponent."

Jeff remembered the time and looked at his watch. "Oh crap. It's almost four. Sorry guys, I have to get going."

"What's up, Jeff," Bobby asked intrigued? "What could possibly be more important than hanging out with us?"

Jeff stammered, "Well, I... a... I sort of... have a date."

That got Sam's attention fast. "A date? With whom? Surely not one of the Siamese twins?"

"Heavens no," Jeff quickly clarified. "Besides, I think that would be the Tokyo twins."

"You know what I mean," Sam said. "Quit dodging the question. Who's your date?"

"Amy, if you must know." The two friends just stared at him.

"Our Amy," Sam exclaimed? Jeff nodded. "When did this happen? I mean without me knowing about it."

"Something I've been working on for a while," was his cautious reply.

"This is so exciting," Sam could barely control her excitement. "Why didn't you say something sooner?"

"Because of the way you are reacting right now," Jeff declared. "Amy doesn't like people making a fuss. You know that. Don't go nagging her about it. You'll end up screwing things up for me."

"I know what Amy is like better than anyone. I promise to be gentle with her, but I am not letting you go anywhere without more info. I will get it one way or another, so, out with it."

"Okay, okay. Amy kept in contact with me the whole time I was gone," he replied. "Which is more than I can say for anyone else." Jeff side glanced at Bobby.

Bobby felt the guilt immediately. "Ah... yeah. Sorry about that. I'm not good at that sort of thing. If it helps, I thought about you a lot."

"I know," Jeff said. "It's okay, dude."

"Yah, yah, yah, it's a guy thing. Can we get back to Amy," Sam said annoyed? "What did she do?"

"She kept me informed about home stuff. Like what was going on with you guys. She was really nice and... I mean she is so quiet normally. I guess emailing, texting, sending pictures and care packages, things like that. We became more comfortable talking to each other. I started to see her in a different way. She stopped being that quiet girl always standing in the background. Now,

I kind of like her... a lot.

"Wow," Sam said, grinning from ear to ear. "I didn't see this coming at all. Has she said how she feels about you, romantically I mean?"

"She gave me a hug when I told her how I felt. If that counts?"

"Really?" Bobby was pleasantly surprised.

"Does Delia know about this," Sam continued probing?

"Oh jeez, I hope not," Jeff replied. "She hates me."

"No, she doesn't," Sam corrected. "It's not like that. She just thinks you're a little... strange."

"Oh, that makes me feel better."

Sam had also thought he was a bit odd, but clearly, he had changed a lot while away. "I'll talk to Delia and prepare her for the shock. She'll be happy for you guys, you'll see."

"Okay, fine. So, can we go now?"

Chapter 20

The Date

As far as first dates go, this one promised to be special. Truth be told, both of the dating novices considered chickening out at the last minute. In the end, the excitement over what they hoped would happen tonight, overpowered their apprehension over what they feared might happen. After a few moments of awkwardness Amy and Jeff began to relax, although nervous ticks continued to manifest throughout the night. Despite the jumbled nerves, they soon were having fun, lots of fun, being together.

Both had been given lots of friendly advice. The best advice on both counts came from Sam and Delia. Sam told Jeff, "Normally I wouldn't recommend you do this, but having said that, I would say just be yourself. Oh, and let Amy be herself." Delia said something similar. Jeff found Bobby's advice to be vague and unhelpful. His advice fit Sam's nature well, but Sam and Amy were not remotely the same.

So that was what the couple was doing. A strong attraction already existed. They just had to let it happen. After a while they were holding hands and sitting close to each other. At the end of the night they even kissed. Amy's house had a porch swing where the couple sat together. They held each other for a while. Then they kissed for a while, quickly became enthralled and intoxicated with each other. These were the first hugs and the first kisses of a perfect match.

Jeff wasn't sure, but it seemed true. This had to be the fastest developing boy/girl relationship in history. Of course, his only examples of such things came from fictitious anime couples, and, of course, Sam and Bobby. His two best friends' relationship had developed glacially slow.

As the couple kissed, swinging on the porch swing, neither realized that Mrs. Ross was peeking out through the curtains. Normally this situation would be a cause for concern for both mom and daughter, but not in this case. The happy Mrs. Ross watched with delight at this new development in her daughter's life. She backed away from the window smiling, hoping this was a positive sign. There had never been a male figure in the home. It had been only her and Amy. Amy's father had died when Amy was just a baby. Mrs. Ross wondered if the lack of a father figure resulted in Amy's shyness around boys.

"Perhaps," Mrs. Ross thought, "by being so against the idea of marrying again, I have denied Amy a more traditional family life. If Amy had had a little sister or brother, would she have grown stronger… bolder." Things like this often worry a parent. "Is it my fault Amy is so shy, Mrs. Ross thought? "Maybe a little, but life is what it is. The future holds hope for us all. "

After leaving Amy at her door, Jeff made his way home with a little extra pep. "Is this love," he said to himself? "Well, maybe not the mature kind of love, but still, at this very moment, I wish I could be with Amy every minute of the day and night, maybe even forever."

When a true geek finds love it's a big deal, a momentous event, epic in nature. If everything turned out the way he hoped, he would remain loyal to Amy to the death. Considering the world in which they now lived in, that concept could easily become more than a metaphor.

He happily sauntered down the sidewalk, paying little attention to anything around him when he was stopped by someone stepping out in front of him.

"Asuri," he gasped, startled. "What are you doing here?"

She bowed slightly. "I am sorry if I startled you."

"No, no. Don't worry about it," he said. "My mind was miles away."

"You had a good date then?"

"Uh?" He was surprised she knew about his date. "Yeah, but how did you know I was…?"

"Oh, everyone knows about you and Amy, and the date," she replied with a shy smile.

Jeff's heart sunk and his face turned red. "Great. Just great. That will make Amy even more nervous."

"Don't worry. Almost everyone is happy for you both."

"I get worried someone will say something mean to her," he said. "Wait. What do you mean almost everyone is happy? Who isn't happy? Do I have a rival already?"

"Do you…love Amy," she asked softly.

Jeff thought about it. "I don't really know yet, but I guess I want to love her. And I want her to love me. You know what I mean?" He started to walk on toward home. She followed.

"Actually I don't," Asuri said. "I wish I could feel what love is like. I do not know anything about love."

"You're kidding me, right? Are you telling me that a girl like you hasn't had a boyfriend before?"

"No. My people would not allow such things."

"Oh, I see. You must come from a very traditional Japanese family."

"More powerful and traditional than you can imagine," Asuri said looking down. "You come from the Meade Clan, don't you? Don't they restrict such modern notions?"

"I don't think so, at least not anymore. Anyway, I grew up here in the States. I am just a new addition to the old family. It's a little different for me."

"Old family?"

"Yeah my grandpa left Japan when he was a young man and came to America."

"Why would he leave such a powerful clan? Wasn't he a good warrior?"

Jeff stopped walking. "Why would you say that?"

"I heard you went to Japan to train in the warrior arts with the Maeda Clan." She looked confused. "I assumed your grandfather would have also received the same training when he was young."

Jeff thought about what to say. "Yeah, but it's no big deal. These days it's not like it was back in the *Edo* period when samurai were sworn to duty or die. He had a choice."

"Edo," she asked. "I don't know that word."

"You know... Edo. The old name for Tokyo?"

Asuri got very frustrated with herself. "Oh, how stupid of me," she stammered. "I thought you were trying to say something else... in English."

"Don't worry, just my bad accent." That was odd, Jeff thought. "Grandpa moved here just after World War II. Grandpa was weary of war. He came to America for a new start. Things got better for him here. He fell in love, got married, and had a family."

"I guess I can understand what he felt like. Since coming... to this place... I have been feeling the same way."

"Why are you out by yourself tonight? Where is Asura?"

"She is doing assigned chores. I got bored and decided to go for a walk."

"I didn't realize you lived around here."

"I don't really. I guess I got carried away and just kept walking. I better get back home before someone misses me."

"You want me to walk you home?"

"Why," she asked simply?

"You know. To make sure you get home safely."

"Oh no," she said quickly. "I am fine." She turned and started to walk away, but then stopped. With her back still turned to Jeff she said, "Thank you for being so nice to me, Jeffrey."

"No problem," Jeff replied, confused by this whole conversation.

"Jeffrey, I need to warn you," she said.

"Warn me? About what?"

"Asura is not who she pretends to be. Neither am I, but I am not like Asura."

"What do you mean?"

"I don't know why she is acting like she is. I think it is you. She thinks you should belong to her... not Amy."

"What the hell," Jeff said, his anger growing. "I don't belong to anyone. Tell Asura I have a girlfriend. She needs to mind her own business."

Asuri turned immediately. "No way I could speak to her like that, and please don't tell her I said anything to you. Please understand. Asura is very dangerous. You and Amy are in danger. Especially Amy. Just stay away from Asura, please. You can't stop what is coming, Jeffrey-san." Realizing she had said too much already, Asuri turned and ran. She was out of sight in seconds.

Chapter 21

Battle Royale

It was a practical matter. The Shadow witch army needed to stay in shape and hone their battle skills daily. Their numbers were far too few. Under the present circumstances, any weakness could mean the difference between life and death. Normally weakness would not be tolerated. She had to continually remind herself that, since their numbers were few, killing the weaker Shadows wouldn't help her cause. Every warrior witch had to serve a purpose. Therefore, the Overseer scheduled warrior tournaments every night to identify strengths and weaknesses of each witch. If a Shadow witch was not strong enough on the battlefield, then they would be used to infiltrate the populace where needed. This process of infiltration had already begun.

There was one other issue of an unexpected nature that had Shadow worried. This world had changed each of them in unpredictable ways. The Soul-Eater spell seemed to be at the center of the problem. The human psyche was far more complex than Shadows. Absorbing such complex minds occasionally causes abnormal behavior. Although the spell had worked well for most Shadows, it didn't for everyone.

The human form itself also presented limitations during combat. Of course, Shadow witches would always have the clear advantage over the humans in a one on one, or even a one on ten, but this world was populated with billions of humans. Mind control spells were effective in creating human allies. The Overseer also discovered money and temptation to be excellent tools for getting the average human to cooperate. What some humans would do for money, power, and fame, surprised her. She would not tolerate such a lack of honor for long.

The training tournaments started with twenty-five individuals. Each night ten new witches replaced the lowest ten from the night before. This continued until all witches had fought. Then twenty-five of the low scorers fought. The top ten returned to battle the best of the best. This cycle continued until each witch had fought a minimum of twenty-five separate battles. As long as a witch won more than half of their rounds, they would be authorized to continue on to more rigorous training.

There were those who scored low every battle. The Overseer did not expect any of her witches to perform poorly. This was an unacceptable outcome for any warrior witch. It displeased her. The tournament produced five lowest score individuals.

The High Overseer faced the five losers. She sat high above them on a black stone throne. The seat of the throne was thirty feet above the floor. The stone base was smooth and glossy. High above her head on the throne back rest was a magical circle. It encompassed the image of two figures. The first figure represented a wizard. His hand rested on the shoulder of the second figure representing a warrior witch. This was the symbol of the Tiarnas Empire to which, until recently, she had been fiercely loyal.

"Weakness is death," Shadow thought to the five Shadows in anger! "Your performance in the arena showed considerable weakness." Shadow bolted from her high seat and landed right in front of the five witches who were doing their best to remain calm. The fact was they had good cause to be afraid. "Under normal circumstances this would mean death," she threatened. "But in this world, I make my own rules. I have only one question for you five. If I grant you mercy, are you willing to turn your failure into a victory for me?"

"Yes Overseer," they each thought!

"Good." She smiled and explained, "You see, not all warriors fight on a glorious battlefield. Sometimes throats need to be cut in quiet secrecy. I have a special mission for the five of you."

"We will do anything you ask, Overseer," said one witch.

"What would you have us do," another asked?

"I need you to infiltrate the local high school. There you will find and kill a human witch."

Chapter 22

Girl's Night Out

Delia and four other girls from school headed downtown led by Asura who skipped happily along in front. "What should we do first," Asura asked in a flourish of enthusiasm.

Delia, doing her best not to be annoyed, just smiled. Asura was hyper beyond any rational reasoning. Delia figured it must be a Japanese girl thing. "I'm hungry," she said, forcing a smile. "How about you girls?"

"I'm starving," said Trista Finley. Trista, and Carla Matson, were cheerleaders. Not girls that Delia usually hung around, but her boyfriend Cal's connections were wide and inclusive. Jo Anna Carlson and Katrina (Kat) Boomer, both student council members. "What sounds good?"

"Let's go to McDonald's," Asura suggested.

"McDonald's, are you sure," Delia replied?

"Yes, yes, yes," Asura said, jumping up and down. "Some real American food."

"You know that McDonalds in the States isn't the same as anywhere else," Delia said.

"I don't care. I want McDonalds."

The other girls looked at each other and shrugged. "Okay, if you want," Trista answered for them all. So down the street they went to the nearest McDonald's.

Asura led them as they entered the restaurant. "Get what you want," she said. "I will pay."

"No Asura," Jo Anna objected. "We can pay for ourselves."

"I insist," Asura said in a tone that almost sounded like an order. Then she softened. "You all have been so nice to Asuri and me. It is what I want to do." Again the girls looked at each other and then then nodded in agreement.

Asura bought a Big Mac, biggie sized. Jo Anna, Carla and Trista had the chicken sandwich, that at least gave the impression of a healthy girl choice. It wasn't. Delia and Kat didn't care if their diet was healthy so Delia got cheese burgers and fries and Kat got a chicken McNugget meal. Asura plowed into the Big Mac like she hadn't eaten in days.

"By the way, Asura," Delia said, breaking into Asura's hamburger heaven. "Where is Asuri tonight?"

"She had something else to do tonight," Asura said, blowing off the question. "I wish Amy would have come though. This would be far more fun with her here."

"Well I'm not supposed to say anything," Delia explained. "But she's on her first real date tonight."

All the girls but Asura reacted.

"Wow," Jo Anna said.

"Really," Trista scoffed?

"I'm happy for Amy," Kat said.

"Who is Amy," Carla asked?

Asura just frowned.

"But don't say anything," Delia cautioned. "The poor girl is shy, she is easily freaked out. I fear that any embarrassment would scare her away from her one chance at true love."

"Where is my one chance for true love," Jo Anna sighed. "Someone tall, milk chocolate, and handsomely yummy!"

"Me too," said Carla. "Although I don't care what color he is." They laughed. "All I seem to find lately are jerks."

"Sorry to hear about you and your boyfriend," Trista sympathized.

"He was a jerk," she replied. "And a cheater."

"Amy is too shy," Asura said. "She needs to… how do you Americans say it? She needs to grow a pair." All the girls, but Delia, laughed at Asura's cheeky comment. Although she had to agree with the sentiment.

"Asura," Kat said, acting scandalized. "You say the funniest things. Are all Japanese girls so bold?"

"Come on girls," Delia said. "Leave Amy alone. It's not her fault she is so shy."

"We know," Kat replied. "She really is sweet, but she is like a scared mouse sometimes."

"Oh if I were a cougar, I bet I would find her delicious," Asura said. "The girls laughed again, again except for Delia.

"Oh, wait. I used the wrong word for my joke," she said a little embarrassed? "I mean cat. In Japanese it is *neko*. An animal that says meow and eats mice. Is that the right word?"

"I don't know," Kat interjected. "A cougar is a big wild cat. Just like me. I'm a cougar." They all laughed this time.

"You got it right, girlfriend," Jo Anna said.

"Amy is probably hoping her date will find her delicious," Trista said.

"You may be right about that," Delia agreed with a giggle of her own.

"Who is it anyway, her date," Trista asked?

"Jeff Sasaki," Delia said sheepishly.

"Jeffrey," said Carla with a dubious look on her face. "Yuck."

"I don't know," Delia interceded on Jeff's behalf. "Since coming back from Japan he's not the same guy."

"He is kind of cute now," Kat said. "In a geek sort of way."

"He would make me a handsome slave," Asura said grinning.

"Asura, I don't think having a slave is funny," Jo Anna said.

"Not real slaves," Kat said. "Asura means metaphorical slaves."

"In that sense I think boys should be slaves to us girls," Carla declared loudly! "I'd whip my boyfriend back into submission. Here's to controlling our boyfriends," she added, lifting her drink cup!" They laughed as they bumped cups together. Jo Anna just rolled her big brown eyes.

They finished their meals, then headed back out on the street to prowl for fun. Next, they went to the arcade. Asura won at everything, so the other girls quickly got bored and wanted to leave.

"Let's see how many college boys we can get to flirt with," Kat suggested.

Asura said. "I have a better idea. Something fun I have discovered."

Chapter 23

The Trap

Asura led the girls downtown to a building that, as far as the other girls could tell, appeared abandoned. "This," she said, "is where I live."

Carla made a face. "You live here? Why?"

"It may be plain outside," Asura explained. "But inside, it is perfect. I love it here."

"It looks a little dead for an apartment building. Does anyone else live here?"

"Yes... many others live here," Asura said, annoyed. "What do you care?"

"Sorry," said Carla. "No offense. Live wherever you want."

"I will." Asura fought to control her mounting frustration. The evening was about over. Soon she would be free of these American girls' stupid comments and questions. "Anyway, I can't wait to introduce you to this lady that lives here," Asura said with renewed enthusiasm. She is a fortune teller. Isn't that wonderful?

"You're sure about that," Delia asked?

"Absolutely. You will see."

They entered the building by a small parking garage. The inside wall had an elevator, or rather an elevator shaft. Next to it was the stairwell.

"where do we go," Delia asked?

"Stairs," Asura said, jumping with excitement.

"Up or down?"

"We go down."

"You live under the ground," Jo Anne

"No. I live upstairs, but the person I want you to meet is down."

"You sure this is the right place," Delia smirked as the girls entered the stairwell.

"Of course, I'm sure," Asura snapped irritably. "I live here you idiot." The girls all looked at Delia surprised. "You will soon see. It will be so worth it."

Down the stairs they went.

"You know what, Asura," Delia said. "I feel a bit uncomfortable. Let's just call it a night. I need to go home."

"Me too," said Jo Anna. She said to the other girls, "Let's go home."

"Don't be silly," Asura said cheerfully. The reached the lower floor. "See we are already here."

Beyond lay a large, dimly lit room. The deeper inside they moved, the darker the room became

Delia yelled "Are you kidding me, Asura? What are you up to."

"I am up to what I said. Have you ever met a real witch? Well, let me introduce you to Ms. Kylie Harrisford."

The light got brighter and Ms. Harrisford appeared as if out of thin air. "Hello girls. How nice to have company."

Asura siad, "Isn't she beautiful?"

The other four girls smiled and nodded politely. Delia didn't like the situation and backed away. Something wasn't right.

"What is she doing in the basement," Kat asked? "This place is as spooky as hell."

"Are you really a witch," Delia asked.

"Yes, she is," Asura said with an eerie voice. "And Kat, it is not like she would have an office on a street corner. She works at night. Her clients are all very loyal."

Kylie smiled at the girls. "Welcome to my parlor." She spread her arms wide.

All of the girls stood there with mouths wide open. "See," Asura said. "I told you she was special."

"You are quite beautiful," Kat whispered.

"Why thank you," Kylie said. "You are all lovely girls as well. Just what I hoped for."

"Excuse me, were you expecting us," Delia asked cautiously?

"Yes," Kylie said. "I want to grant each of you a wish."

"A wish," Jo Anne said. "Where do I sign up?"

"I can give you wealth, power, love and good fortune. I can see it clearly. Your futures are so intertwined with mine. I am a powerful witch and I can make you powerful like me."

Delia laughed, "Okay I'll bite. How are you going to do all this?"

Jo Anna replied, "I don't want to be a witch. I'm a Christian. My mama would have a fit if she knew I was here talking to a witch."

"Then don't tell her," Asura said sarcastically. "It is true. She can grant wishes. I wanted to be a witch too. Ms. Harrisford granted my wish."

Trista laughed. "You are a witch?" Asura nodded.

"Prove it," Delia said.

Asura looked to Kylie, who nodded approval. Asura put out a hand and a ball off light appeared. "See."

The girls gasped. "No kidding," Kat said.

Jo Anna was not sure what to say about that revelation. "Ah... I'm sorry I bothered you ma'am, but I will go home now."

"Me too," said Delia. "Come on girls let's go. I have nothing to wish for."

"Don't be stupid," Asura barked. "You are already here. Listen to what she has to say and make your stupid wish." The girls argued and snipped at each other trying to decide to stay or go.

Overseer Strong raised her voice. "Enough. Take them."

"What is this, Asura," Delia asked, sensing the situation had just changed dramatically. The danger was very real and they all felt it.

Asura backed away. "All of these girls are well known at the school," Asura said with pride.

"Well done," the Overseer said.

The five girls whimpered and huddled closer together. "Asura, what does she mean," Trista asked? Asura ignored the question.

Five Shadow witches appeared out of the dark. The girls screamed at the sight of the terrifying creatures.

"You set us up. Asura, I will kill you," Delia yelled out, trying to sound tough and strong, but she was every bit as afraid as the others.

Asura said. "Too bad Amy is not here."

Delia yelled, "Run!"

The Shadow witches attacked. The human girls continued screaming. Some ran for the exit. Others froze in place with fear. Asura blocked Delia's way. Delia took that as an opportunity to knock Asura to the floor and slam her fists repeatedly into Asura's face. Asura shoved Delia away as the girls were engulfed in a black mist.

Chapter 24

Weird Day

As soon as he walked through the school's front doors, Bobby felt it. "Something's wrong," he whispered as he pulled Sam to the side.

"What are you sensing?"

"A darkness... here at school that wasn't here yesterday."

"The biker Shadow," hissed Sam?

"No, she was far more powerful than this. I passed out when I felt her presence."

"More Shadows then."

Bobby nodded. "And more than one. You know how our parents are always telling us to plan for the worst and hope for the best?" Bobby looked at Sam. She looked confused. "I am sensing maybe five or six right now."

"Why at school? School is just a bunch of ordinary teenagers."

"Not you and me... not Jeff either." Bobby thought for a minute. "When I detected that biker chick, she detected us as well."

"Possibly."

"Maybe... they are looking for us."

"What should we do?"

"Find them before they find us. Then get rid of them. Let's stay on guard."

"We can't fight Shadows in a place like this," Sam said worried. "There are too many innocent bystanders."

"Maybe there is a way to lead them away from here."

"If these new Shadows can look like humans, how will we find them?"

"Normally, I would count on sensing them, but these Shadows found a way to hide. I'm already losing the connection."

"I suppose we look for new faces, at least unfamiliar faces," Sam suggested.

Bobby nodded. "And anyone acting strangely." Bobby sighed. "The problem is, this is a big school and a big town. There are a lot of people we don't know. As for acting strange… what do we consider strange these days?" Sam nodded, then shrugged indicating she had no idea what to do. "I'll find Jeff and let him know what's up." They both head off in separate directions.

The whole day went irritatingly slow. It felt like it would never end. Worry can do that to a person, especially if you are looking for trouble around every corner. The only thing unusual about the day was Amy. At the beginning of the day she acted more open, chatty, and full of excitement than ever before. She was high on love. Then something must have happened because her mood dropped toward gloomy and she retreated back into her old self.

Jeff was beside himself trying to figure out what had gone wrong. He had arrived at school high on love as well. He spent the rest of the day catering to Amy's every need. They were happy. Then everything changed. Amy was no longer happy.

"Did you say something stupid to her," Sam asked later?

"No," he defended. "I mean I don't think so. I had the best time last night. She acted like she had a good time too. This morning she confirmed that it had gone well. She and I had an immediate connection. This morning felt like last night… then…."

"You must have done something," Sam accused. "A girl doesn't get upset over nothing?" Bobby smirked a little too loud. "What's so funny," she said, turning on Bobby?

"I think you are underestimating the average girl's propensity for mood swings," Bobby replied.

"Excuse me?"

"And you are grossly overestimating the average guy's ability to understand why."

"Yeah, well…" She was about to say more, but didn't. "Okay then. What you need to do is carefully press her to express her feelings. Coax it out of her."

Just then Amy appeared. She smiled as she approached.

"Here's your chance buddy," Bobby whispered.

Amy walked up and said, "Hi guys."

"Hi Amy," Sam said. "Are you feeling okay, honey? You seem down this afternoon."

Bobby looked at Sam in surprise. So much for Jeff pressing for answers.

"Hey," Bobby said. "We should get going."

"I'm fine," said Amy. "Really. It was a weird day."

"Okay," Sam said. "Say, have you heard from Delia. I haven't seen her all day."

Amy started to tear up. "Delia is home sick today," she said.

"I'm sure she is just fine. I wouldn't worry about it," Sam said softly.

"I know. I'm sorry." Amy sniffed. "It's not that. It is just that..." She turned to Jeff. "Jeffrey, can you walk me home? I need to talk to you about something."

Jeff's heart sank. Oh crap, he thought. Maybe I did something wrong. "Sure," he said.

"I'll see you guys later," Amy said to Sam and Bobby.

"Of course, we are headed out anyway," Sam said. "Call me later." Amy nodded.

Jeff walked Amy to her house mostly in silence. "Amy... did I do something wrong," he asked. "Because if I did, I am so sorry."

"Of course not," Amy quickly replied. "You have been wonderful all day long."

"Then what is it?" After some probing and pushing, Amy finally opened up.

"When Delia didn't come to school today, I was worried, so I called her." Tears came to her eyes again.

"What... what did she say?"

"She's okay and everything, but she sounded funny."

"Funny how?"

"Not like herself." Jeff looked puzzled. "She asked me about our date. So, I told her everything."

"Everything?" Jeff felt a little defensive. Delia would make fun of him for sure.

"Delia... she laughed at me." Amy kept her head down as she struggled to hold onto her composure.

"I don't understand? Delia laughed at you? That doesn't sound like her."

"I know. Then she said that she had hung out with Asura last night. She kept laughing... like she was making fun of me. That is when she told me Asura planned to steal you away from me, so I better not get my hopes up too high.

She said I was no match for Asura."

Jeff was shocked. "Delia said that?" Amy nodded. Jeff shook his head fiercely. "I promise you that I have done nothing to make Asura think I am interested in her. At this moment I would say that I hate her guts." Then he remembered what Asuri had told him. Was this what she was hinting at? "Listen to me," he said. "I think it would be best to keep away from Asura... and Asuri too. There is something seriously wrong with those girls, maybe even dangerous."

"I doubt she is actually dangerous," Amy said. "Delia said she is fun once you got to know her, but I am not interested in getting to know her... ever. She is nothing but a witch with a broom stuck up her... butt."

Jeff spit out a laugh. This was a side of Amy he hadn't seen before. She blushed and then she laughed too. "That was priceless, Amy," he said. "I wish Delia hadn't said anything to you," Jeff concluded. "It made you worry unnecessarily. Delia is usually more thoughtful than that."

"I wish she hadn't said anything either. Maybe she just wanted to warn me."

"Like I said," Jeff said forcefully. "I don't even like Asura. You are the girl I love, Amy. Don't ever doubt that!"

Amy stood there in shock, her face growing redder by the minute. "You do," she asked in a soft whisper? "You love me?" She was happy, embarrassed, shocked and speechless all at once.

Jeff suddenly realized what he had just blurted out, and he had done so while several other students were walking nearby. They had clearly heard the word "love" and turned immediately to see who had said it. Love was a sacred word in high school and generally was not a word uttered so boldly, not by geeks anyway. There would be no backtracking from his declaration. He had said it, but to his surprise, he actually meant it. There was only one thing left to do. "Yes," he replied resolutely, and then he kissed her in front of God and everyone.

The next day Amy arrived at school ready to face the world with greater confidence. Jeff resolved that this day, and every day, he would defend his girlfriend. Amy's face flushed a little when Jeff met her at her locker. He put his arms around her waist and pulled her close.

"I love you, Amy Ross," Jeff said just loud enough to be heard by those close by. Then he kissed Amy. Jeff wanted Asura to understand the situation.

There would be no doubt. She needed to back off, or he would make her back off.

But Asura's spies had already filled her in about the date and about yesterday's walk home. What especially enraged her was Jeff's open rejection. Jeff had used her name when stating that rejection, embarrassing her in front of other humans. That was more than she could stand. She had vowed to get even.

A red-faced Amy quickly turned to her locker and fumbled with the combination unsuccessfully. She felt so giggly, girly and wonderful. Her life had changed into an amazing fairy tail. Finally, she got the combination right and opened the locker. A strange crackle and a loud pop nearly deafened her. Something in the locker exploded and hit Amy directly in the face. Some kind of green liquid, that smelled awful, dripped down Amy's face. At first, she just stood there in complete shock. Although she felt like screaming she couldn't find her voice. She turned to Jeff to see his horrified face. The look on her face told Jeff that this humiliation was more than she could stand. She looked utterly horrified.

Just then Sam arrived on the scene followed by Bobby. When Sam saw and smelled the green goo, she yelped, "What happened?"

Jeff shook his head. "We don't know. Amy opened her locker door and it just exploded."

"What is that stuff," Sam asked? "It smells horrible."

"A booby-trap," Jeff said angrily. "When I get my hands on Asura...."

"Why would Asura want to do this to Amy of all people."

That was the last straw and the humiliated Amy started to cry uncontrollably. She screamed, "Just get me out of here!"

Sam quickly took Amy to the girl's locker room so that Amy could get out of her smelly clothes and take a shower. The only thing she had to change into were her gym clothes.

Asura and Asuri walked by. "Oh my," Asura said with a smirk. 'Did something happen to Amy? Smells like some rat has been in the sewer." Asura giggled.

Asuri glared angrily at Asura. "What did you do, sister?"

Jeff stepped toward Asura. "Asura, I know you did this. If you weren't a girl, I would beat the crap out of you," he shouted.

Bobby grabbed Jeff's arm. 'Easy, buddy."

"Oh, Jeffrey," Asura mocked. "You are so cute when you are mad."

Sam came back in time to hear that. "Asura," she said. Asura turned to Sam. Sam slapped her face with considerable force. "I'm going to take Amy home now. We will be back in a while. She returned to the locker room to help her friend.

"Why would you do something so mean," Jeff asked?"

"I..." The look on Jeff's face let her know she had lost his friendship. She would never get it back. She was a Shadow witch. Why did she care what this human thought? Still, something hurt inside her chest.

Jeff pointed his finger at Asura's nose. "I don't want to see you around me, or my girlfriend, ever again. I won't forget this. Stay away from us."

Asura looked upset. She didn't like Jeff speaking to her that way. She didn't like anyone, even her sister, talking to her that way. Asura's eyes flashed red momentarily. But then she composed herself and bowed. Before she turned and left she said, growling through her teeth, "Some people do not understand a joke."

Bobby and Jeff watched the Japanese girl walk away. "That is one scary girl."

But Jeff had seen Asura's eyes. Had he imagined it? "That is no girl. Did you see her eyes?"

"Yes," Bobby said. "She is a monster." Bobby had sensed Asura's darkness for a split second.

Jeff was furious. "I can't think of anything worse happening to someone like Amy." Jeff was looking closely at the locker. "And how did the booby-trap work? I don't see any sign of a mechanism. There aren't any bits of balloon lying around - nothing. Just green goo."

"Fortunately, the smell is fading." Bobby had another strange feeling. "Jeff, there is darkness around Amy's locker. Dark magic. Not that strong, but magic for sure."

Jeff asked worriedly, "Bobby, what is going on?"

"I'm not sure yet."

******

Asuri was furious with Asura which was unusual because Asura had always been the dominant twin. Asuri was even a little afraid of Asura. "Why did you do that, Asura?" Asure looked smug. "Jeffrey is a human. He is an enemy."

"Ah, Jeffrey. He is cute, don't you think? He is strong like a warrior."

"I don't understand what is going on with you."

"What are you talking about," Asura snapped back?

"Look I am just saying... I think this place is changing you."

"It is changing you too sister," Asura protested.

"Just don't forget why we are here," Asuri cautioned. "Please leave that boy alone. You are going to get us into serious trouble with the Overseer. We have a mission. We still have not identified the human witch."

"Mind your own business," Asura barked and then walked away in a huff.

"The new rupture will open soon," Asuri said. "We cannot get distracted."

Asuri did not understand what Asura felt. Jeffery belonged to her and only her, and she wasn't about to let a wimpy, nothing of a human female get in her way. "Amy will be very sorry," Asura seethed.

Chapter 25

In Jeff's Tender Care

Sam returned to school without Amy. So, as soon as school was dismissed, Jeff went to Amy's house to check on her. He found her sitting on the front porch swing.

Jeff approached slowly. "Hi," he said.

She looked up. "Hi." She patted the seat beside her and Jeff quickly sat down. "I was hoping you would come by," she said. "I've managed to pull myself together enough to put on a braver front."

"So, you're alright now?"

Amy leaned into Jeff's shoulder. "Now that you are here."

"I told Asura to stay away from you."

"Are you sure Asura did it?"

"Oh yeah. I just can't figure out how she did it. It would be wise for us to stay clear of the twins. There is something not right about them."

Amy sat up straight. "I've decided that I will not be pushed around by a bully."

"Amy, I am serious. Those two girls are not what they seem. They are dangerous."

"I really don't think they're dangerous. They're just bullies. I need to learn to stand up for myself."

"If it were anyone but those two, I would agree with you."

"With all my friends by my side, Asura won't dare bother me again."

"Do I need to start teaching you martial arts?"

"Could you? That would be so much fun."

Jeff laughed. We'll see. In the meantime, please be careful."

Amy turned and wrapped her arms around his neck. "Thank you," she said.

"For what?"

"For being a good person."

Jeff didn't know what to say.

"You know," Amy continued. "I have liked you since... a long time. Long before you went to Japan."

"I didn't know. Why didn't you say something?"

Amy shrugged. "I just couldn't. Besides, you didn't seem interested in being serious about girls. Eventually, I told Delia how I felt but no one else."

"I guess I wasn't ready," Jeff said. He leaned in and kissed her. "But I am now."

Amy cuddled into him. "I'm glad."

They sat on the swing for a while just holding each other. For a geek and a shy girl, this relationship developed amazingly fast. As though they needed to make up for lost time. As though every minute together was precious.

Asuri spied from the shadows. Asura will be so angry, she thought.

Chapter 26

Strangers among Us

An alien entity now controlled Delia's life. It knew her memories, it absorbed her knowledge, even her talents, but it couldn't duplicate her personality. It couldn't be Delia. The same was true of the four other human girls that had been with Delia. The Soul Eater Spell used on the girls, stole all their life's experiences in just seconds. Their bodies were devoured and replaced. Their souls banished. This effective bit of magic allowed a fairly believable replacement of the victim. The spell created the perfect spies, allowing them to infiltrate every aspect of the victim's life. But something had gone wrong in Delia's case. Although her earthly body was gone, her soul was not. Delia still existed, at least in spirit, somehow remaining connected to the thing that had taken her place. Her spirit not only remained connected to the witch, but to her own memories and self-will.

At first, Delia only saw darkness. Her subconscious mind fell into the world of dreams. She tried to make sense of what had happened to her. Something strange had happened. That much she remembered. She was hanging out with... friends... having fun. Then... what? She allowed herself to fade into a dream again.

As far as the Shadow witch knew everything happened as it should, completely unaware of the sleeping and very strong willed soul still present. Delia was no ordinary victim. If she woke up, she wouldn't give up without a fight.

The faux-Delia walked into school and headed for her locker as usual. Amy was there waiting for her with a big smile on her face. That confused faux-Delia. *"Why is Amy happy,"* she thought.

Delia had heard about Asura's boobie-trap. The Shadow scanned her memories and concluded that this encounter required an appropriate reaction. Delia said, "From the smile on your face, things must be going well." Amy nodded enthusiastically. "What about Asura? Aren't you worried?"

"Nope. Jeff put her in her place. She got totally rejected."

Faux-Delia had to admit a certain amusement over this news. Asura was an insufferable witch. "Wow. A lot happened. I only stayed home one day."

"Besides, I know I can always count on a tough girl like you to watch my back," Amy said with so much confidence.

Faux-Delia's mind went blank as a piercing pain stabbed her in the heart. The real Delia had heard Amy's ill-fated declaration and she feared for her friend. That fear and sorrow broke Delia's heart. Then fear turned to rage, emboldening the real Delia. She began to fight back. Faux-Delia clutched her temples and bent over in pain. It was as though someone had stabbed her in the forehead.

"Are you okay," Amy asked, alarmed?

"My head... it hurts so much."

"Maybe you shouldn't have come back to school so soon? I'll help you to the school nurse's office so you can lay down."

"Yes, good idea."

At that moment Asura and her new entourage, Trista Finley, Carla Matson, Jo Anna Carlson and Kat Boomer, and of course Asuri, who was walking a few steps behind, passed. "Hi Delia," Asura said cheerfully. Then she glared at Amy. "Delia if you have a moment I have something to ask you."

"Sure," Delia replied. "No. I am sorry. I need to go home." Delia turned and ran away.

Asura was stunned. "What is with her," she snipped. "Such weakness is unacceptable." The girls all agreed and walked on down the hall.

Sam saw what happened as she approached Amy. "What was that about," she asked?

"I don't know. Delia is still sick, I guess."

"Did Asura say something to her?"

"She wanted to talk to Delia. Then Delia ran away."

"Everyone is acting so weird," Sam whispered.

"Delia is acting strange," Amy agreed. "I assume it's because she isn't feeling well."

"I went over to Delia's house last night," Sam said. "Delia said she felt sick after that girl's night out thing that Asura put together."

"I know about that. For some strange reason Asura invited me as well.

But I had a date with Jeff that night. Not that I would go anywhere with that crazy girl."

"That's just like Delia, going along to give friendliness a try. Listen. It may be my imagination, but as Delia and I talked last night, something was wrong. Delia didn't seem to be our Delia."

Amy was worried. She looked down the hall where her best friend had run away so quickly. Then looked the other way where Asura and the other girls walked away with such an attitude. "I don't know what to say."

Chapter 27

Delia vs. Faux-Delia

Faux-Delia walked home as fast as she could. It felt like something had caught in her throat. She couldn't speak. She brought her hands to her temples and rubbed at the stabbing pain.

"What is happening," the real Delia thought? "Why do I feel so strange?"

"What...? Who said that," a shocked Faux-Delia asked? She looked around expecting to see someone, but there was no one.

"What the hell," Delia barked inside the witches head? "Where am I? I mean... I'm supposed to be at school... I think. That's right, something weird happened... But what? I don't remember... yesterday, this morning... nothing. And why can't I move my body?" Delia panicked and screamed over and over again.

Faux Delia dropped to her knees in even greater pain. "Stop it," she shouted out loud. "Stop it." Her head felt like it was about to split open. The world began to spin, making her nauseous. She ran the rest of the way home, slammed open the front door, and hurried to the bathroom. She made it to toilet just in time to empty her stomach. Instead of food, a black and green goo flowed from her mouth.

"Wait," The real Delia said, recovering her wits. "I remember something. Asura... we were with Asura. Gads, I hate that chick."

"Get out of my head," faux-Delia screamed.

"Your head?"

"Who is that?"

"Me. Who else would I be?"

"What is your name," faux-Delia screamed.

"Don't you shout at me, bitch," the real Delia said. "I'm Delia. So, who the hell are you and why can't I see you?"

The Shadow witch was stunned. This wasn't possible. She looked in the bathroom mirror. "Why aren't you dead," she screamed?

"Dead? Are you threatening me" Then the memories came rushing back. "What did Asura do to me... us?"

"You're dead. Go away!"

"I'm not dead. I... I'm right here." Shock began to set in as Delia remembered the horrifying attack, the seething hate of Asura, the choking black mist, and then blackness. *"I died? You... you killed me?"*

"Yes," faux Delia said. "So go away. You are dead."

"Why would you kill me," Delia asked, struggling to process this revelation? "I don't even know you. Wait. Am I a ghost?"

"Shut up, shut up, shut up! Leave me alone," the faux-Delia screamed!

"I..." The real Delia went silent.

Faux-Delia searched her mind for the other voice, but it was gone now. "The Soul Eater spell...."

"Delia," Asura shouted through the open front door.

Faux-Delia panicked. She didn't dare show any weakness in front of Asura. She wiped her face. "I'll be right there." She hurried to the door. "What are you doing here?"

"I was going to ask you the same thing," Asura said. "You left your post. What is wrong with you?"

"I am sorry. I got confused. The Soul Eater spell is messing with my mind."

"Don't be stupid," Asura said uncaringly.

"I'm sorry," Faux-Delia said. "Forgive my weakness. This is the first time I have used the spell. I wasn't expecting...."

"Get yourself together. You have work to do." She paused and remembered passing Amy in the hall earlier in the day. "Amy did not look unhappy," Asura scowled. "What did you say to her?"

"I told her you were her rival," Faux-Delia replied, recovering her thoughts. "That you said Jeff was your boyfriend. Yesterday she cried. Then you did that stupid thing with her locker. That just made Amy and Jeff grow closer together. You made a big mistake."

Asura's eyes flared with anger. She raised her hand and released a pulse of magic at faux-Delia's chest, throwing her to the back of the foyer. The witch crashed into a side table that sat next to the wall. The wood table splintered into many pieces. The large vase of flowers sitting on the table exploded in all directions.

"Are you crazy," faux-Delia shouted. "What if the human girl's mother had been home?"

"I would kill her," Asura said calmly. "And if you ever speak to me like that again, I will kill you too. We have a human witch to find. Stick to the plan."

Faux-Delia thought about Asura's plan to find the human witch, using Amy as bait. "Why are you so convinced that Jeffrey knows the human witch? The human Delia's memories are very unflattering toward him. They give no indication that he or his friends are anything but regular human teenagers."

"He is a warrior of the Maeda Clan," She growled. "Of course, he knows her. They would be allies. Why else would his Master have sent him back to this place? Jeffrey is here to protect the human witch."

Faux-Delia saw the flaw in Asura's logic. Humans didn't work by the same rules as Shadows. This Jeffrey boy wasn't that important in the human world. He had little respect among his peers. Asura had this all wrong. Then she realized that this might be more about getting rid of Amy. Asura wanted Jeffrey all to herself. Not like a warrior witch at all. If this Jeff thing got out of control, it would endanger their mission. Overseer Strong would not be happy. They would all be blamed. Still Asura was dangerous. Although she wasn't acting like it, she was a far superior warrior. They were all afraid of Asura, including her sister Asuri. Faux-Delia decided to go along with anything Asura wanted.

Asura commanded Delia, "Set it up for Friday night. We can't wait any longer. Let's make the human witch reveal herself. Then, after we capture her, I will kill Amy and take my trophies... Jeffrey and the High Overseer Strong's praise."

Chapter 29

Percy's Coup d'etat

The long dark car pulled up to the gate and a guard stepped forward to identify the visitors. The two individuals in the back were expected. The driver handed the necessary documentation.

"Please open the rear window, sir," The guard ordered.

Sitting in the backseat was the beautiful Ms. Kylie Harrisford, wearing a black dress and dark sunglasses as usual. Mr. Theodore Stanley sat next to her. His attire was a complete contrast to hers. He wore casual pants and a cream cardigan sweater over a cotton shirt. Teddy ignored the guard and continued texting on his phone. The guard noted the large, ancient looking book sitting on the seat between the two V.I.P guests.

"What is that between you," the guard asked, indicating the object?

Mr. Stanley lifted the book and feathered the pages. "This is a gift for Dr. McLeod," Teddy replied smiling. "He loves old things like this."

The guard nodded. He said nothing more, waving them forward.

Harrisford Enterprises had recently become a generous benefactor of the Salmur Institute for Biological Studies. As new benefactors, Eugene Miles had agreed to giving a personal tour of the CIDP facility. The benefactors also insisted on meeting with both him and Percy. It annoyed Miles that this schmoozing event had interrupted his weekend plans. Miles understood the need for a little butt kissing from time to time, but why did it have to be on this Friday evening. He had tried to get Percy to reschedule for a later date, but both Percy and Ms. Harrisford had insisted on no delay. Miles also tried to pass this responsibility on to a subordinate, but the benefactor demanded that Miles be in attendance. Since none of this new money would benefit the Center for Interdimensional Physics, Miles thought this to be a monumental waste of his time.

Percy couldn't wait to meet these visitors. Miles thought this was out of character for Percy who normally hated dealing with the money lenders. Percy didn't understand regular people because he was not a normal person. Abnormal best described Percy. Not that Ms. Harrisford and Mr. Stanley were normal people. They represented the very rich, eccentric, and powerful one percent. As far as Miles knew, neither of the two visitors had any kind of scientific background. What would Percy even say to them?

Percy acted unusually nervous as they waited in the Center's front lobby. He had been annoyingly present all week long, hanging around the IDR control room every day. He frequently talked quietly with some of the other scientists and technicians in the Center. Miles knew Percy. He was up to something.

Percy felt a little uncomfortable with what he was about to do. Whether his decision was right or wrong, depended on one's point of view, this path led to success for both he and Eugene. Eugene would see that... eventually. Percy felt certain that his friend and colleague would see that there was only one logical way to proceed. The resulting scientific discoveries alone would surely outweigh the cost. They just needed to focus on the tasks ahead. The door to a real-life fantasy was about to be opened. That the door probably would never be shut again. His future would be forever changed, but in the end, he would be justified. Percy readied himself for an angry debate once Eugene realized that this Coup d'état was already underway.

Chapter 30

The Hero's Return

Cooper stepped through the newly formed rift into this world followed by his father's high Priestess, still wearing her white robe. Eleven loyal warrior witches stepped through next. The warrior witch clans now wore armor that reflected the new republic they had helped to form. The colors of the New Republic of Tiarnas are black for the Shadows' body, white for the heart and soul of the Shadows, and silver for the republic's bright and shining future.

After crossing through the rift, they stepped down into an existing tunnel, undoubtedly created by magic, that led away from the rift. "The smell of witch magic hangs heavy in the air," the Priestess thought.

"The abrupt end of the Shadow invasion must have trapped several Shadows in this world," Cooper thought. "The Shadow witches are probably the danger my father spoke of."

"They tried to open the rupture from this side," the Priestess noted. "Tried and failed."

Cooper looked down the long passageway that turned and disappeared out of sight. "They left this place unguarded, but the witches may return soon. We should move on."

"These are corrupted witches," the Priestess thought with a vocal hiss. "How unfortunate. We cannot allow any of them to return to Tiarnas to stir up trouble."

"Agreed, sister," Cooper thought.

The Priestess immediately established a masking spell that created a cover over the rift opening. This illusion tricked the eye, but the accompanying forcefield would also trick the body.

"Move forward." Cooper waved them on. Two of the warrior witches took the lead. As they approached the end of the passageway, the witches came to halt. "We detect at least four or five enemy witches up ahead," they reported. "They do not know we are here."

This time Cooper took the lead. A sword magically extended out from his hand. What a different entrance this was compared to his first accidental step into this world two years before. He was no longer that tentative little Shadow. Now, clothed in magic armor, he commanded this clandestine team of Shadow witches. These two contrasting life events did not go unappreciated. He was thankful for the control and sense of purpose he now possessed.

The Priestess conjured a holographic map. "Up ahead is a great open chamber," the Priestess told Cooper. "Two witches stand at the entrance of this passageway. Two more are on the far side of the chamber guarding two more entrances to the great room."

"Since no one knows we are here," Cooper thought. "Let us make this fast. Take out the four guards."

Four witches left his side. In a blur of silver and black they darted away. The four enemy guards didn't have a chance. The team moved into the great circular chamber. Cooper looked up at the ceiling formed above his head.

"Impressive work," he thought. "But why did they make this place?" It was a rhetorical question, so he didn't expect any of his team to answer such a question. He was just thinking out loud. "And why are there only four witches on guard? Where are the rest of the Shadows?"

A shadow witch thought, "Maybe, there are no more?"

"No," thought the Priestess. "I sense many more. They are just somewhere else."

Two more openings breached the circular wall. These openings lay opposite to each other. Cooper approached and entered the first. He found a horizontal shaft that led straight up to other floors. Dim, almost imperceptible, light escaped through several openings in the dark shaft. The other opening on the opposite side did the same. Black lines, burned into the floor, formed a pentagram. Several concentric circles lay inside the five-pointed symbol. Each point of the pentagram centered on each of the five openings in the chamber. The Priestess darted to the openings to sweep for magic, as well as more enemy Shadows.

Pointing into one of the open tunnels on the far side of the room, she thought, "At least two more Shadow witches are at the far end of this passageway, although not close at the moment."

The priestess pointed at one of the horizontal shafts. *"There are more through there... maybe two floors up."*

"Five of you, watch these access points," Cooper thought. "Two of you enter the tunneled passageway and eliminate the two Shadows. Everyone else... follow me." Cooper walked to the horizontal shaft where the Priestess detected more witches. "We will eliminate any witches above us," He ordered. Cooper's magical wings unfurled and he flew into the horizontal shaft.

Cooper and his squad of warriors had no idea how fortunate they were. Overseer Strong had only left eight warrior witches to protect the fortress. Afterall, the magically shielded complex was immune to attack. The Overseer's plan was in place. She assigned the rest of her Shadow witches at strategic locations to the Center for Interdimensional Physics.

Chapter 31

Crazy Girl

Jeff thought about the booby trap in Amy's locker. Then he remembered that Asuri had warned him about Asura. In fact, she said Asura was dangerous. He, and Bobby as well, had sensed something odd about Amy's locker incident. It felt unnatural. For some reason Asura had focused her evil intentions on Amy of all people. Everybody liked Amy. Jeff worried about what that crazy girl might do next. Asuri had also told him that her and her sister were not who they seemed to be. That thought had made Jeff feel more uneasy every day after that. The twins were not just two ordinary high school girls.

"So, if not ordinary high school girls," Jeff said. "Then who are they?"

They were just ordinary high school girls until..., Jeff thought as he laughed to himself. That simple phrase was the first sentence in almost every description of the typical anime series. Jeff sighed. The twins had flattered him. They made him think that somehow, he had become cooler. He loved the attention and the boost to his ego, so he had ignored the danger the twins had brought into his world.

As if I were that special, Jeff thought. He wondered if this was his fault. *Man, what an idiot I've been.* It embarrassed him that he had made such a big deal of it on that first day of school.

One thing he now knew for sure, they had not met on the plane by accident. It suddenly occurred to him that, since he was so deeply involved in the Maeda Clan, he might have become a target of the Clan's enemies. No one had warned about that possibility.

"Asura is acting jealous and possessive... like an outright creepy stalker. I mean, I met a gorgeous stranger on a plane and she fell in love with me - too unbelievable. A crazy girl falling for me, that was believable. He needed to talk to Bobby and Sam. But that would have to wait. He had a date with Amy in an hour.

Jeff finished getting ready and drove as fast as he dared to pick up Amy. The car belonged to his dad. His parents were so pleased that their son had actually found himself a real girlfriend, his dad had offered unlimited access to his *special* car, an older model Jaguar coupe. Until now, Jeff's dad hadn't even let him touch it, let alone drive it.

"I will not have my son picking his girlfriend in an ordinary family car," Jeff's dad had said. "How would that look? You are an important man in the Meade Clan now." That was when he handed Jeff the keys to the Jaguar.

Jeff pulled up in front of Amy's place and trotted eagerly to the front door. He rang the bell expecting Amy to appear immediately. Instead her mom answered the door looking a little confused. "I'm here to pick up Amy, Mrs. Ross," he said politely.

Mrs. Ross looked surprised. "I'm sorry Jeff. There seems to be some sort of mix-up. Amy's already left."

"What? Where did she go?"

"Well…," Mrs. Ross didn't know what to say. "Delia came by. She said you sent her to pick Amy up. I guess there has been a misunderstanding. Do you want me to call her?"

"No that's okay," he replied. "I've got my phone. She must be over at Delia's or back at my house. Don't worry. We will find each other soon enough." He ran to the car. Mrs. Ross yelled, "Good luck," and shut the door.

"That was weird," Jeff told himself. An uneasy feeling flooded his mind. "Why would Delia lie like that?"

First, he tried to call Amy, but she didn't answer. Then he tried Delia, still nothing. He called home to see if the girls had gone to his house. They hadn't. That left Delia's house. He drove even faster, getting there in a few short minutes that felt horribly long. Anxiety overpowered his senses.

Delia's mother answered the door. "Oh, hi Jeffrey," she said. "Delia said you might be coming by looking for Amy." She then took a sealed envelope from a side table in the foyer. "She said to give you this when you got here."

"Thanks, Mrs. Bowen," Jeff said with a sigh. "Hopefully this will tell me where those two girls have gone. Do you know what's going on?"

"Sorry, not a clue," Mrs. Bowen laughed. "I bet they're taking you on a wide goose chase tonight. Good luck. You will find them soon, but be prepared. With Delia involved, anything could happen."

Back in the car Jeff opened the letter and read it. "I don't understand," he whispered. "What is going on here?" He read it again.

"Master Jeffrey Sasaki of the great Maeda Clan, the ancient tribe of monster slayers. I challenge you to a duel. If I win you will be mine forever. If you win, you can have Amy back."

"Since I am quite sure you can't beat me, then you may choose a champion to take your place. There is a human witch in El Palmar. As a soldier of the Meada Clan, I have no doubt you know who she is. Bring her with you and I will allow her to fight for your honor... and your mousey girlfriend's life. You will find us in the high school's gymnasium at midnight tonight.

With perfect intentions, Asura."

"Who does Asura think she is?"

Jeff sat in silence in his car for a moment. The clock and it said 8:30. The only people he knew who had witchy-like powers were Sam and Bobby. No doubt Asura is talking about Sam. This led to a thought that made his blood in his veins go cold. His hands began to shake as he started the car. He pulled his phone from his pocket and speed dialed Bobby. "Bobby... listen, there is no time. Where are you and Sam? I need you right away!"

Chapter 32

The Fortress Falls

Cooper calmly came up behind the two Shadow witches patrolling the upper floors of Shadow Strong's fortress.

"Greetings," Cooper thought. The two Shadow turned startled. They stared in stunned disbelief at the unknown male Shadow. He let out a gruff laugh and smiled. This big toothy grin had become a legend on two different worlds. "I am Grand Overseer Ku Por of Tiarnas. Sorry to burst in uninvited, but I will take over from here on." The two witches were seized and bound. "Sorry about this," Cooper thought. "But I need you to tell me what is going on."

One of the two witches extended a thought of relief. "Grand Overseer, we have waited so long for word from Tiarnas.

"Thank you for returning for us," the other witch thought. "High Overseer Strong, has led us with honor up until now, but you can lead us on to victory."

"Overseer Strong," Cooper asked, turning to his Shadow warriors?

"High Overseer Strong is the highest authority among all the warrior clans," he was told. "Many consider her to be next in line to become an Imperial Witch."

"Oh dear. I see."

The enemy witch said with excitement, "The progress the High Overseer has made since the rupture closed, will please you. We are ready to resume the invasion."

"How many others are there," Cooper asked?

"There are now thirty-seven battle ready witches still living. We have enslaved humans to help further this cause."

"No other Shadows are in the complex, "Copper asked?

The prisoners shook their heads. "No, only us and the four guard's downstairs."

"Where are the others now," Cooper demanded?

"Most have infiltrated the place where the rupture had once connected our worlds. Others have assimilated into the local community."

"Assimilated?"

"The Soul Eater spell," thought the Priestess. She had just entered the shaft.

"Yes, Royal Priestess."

"Soul Eater," Cooper asked?

The Priestess considered for a minute before thinking out, "It is a way to steal the body and mind of others. A type of possession."

"What happens to the victims?"

"They die when the soul leaves the body. If these witches are good with shielding magic, it might prove difficult to identify who is human and who is Shadow."

The two captured witches looked confused. "Why would any of us need to hide from you," one witch asked?

"We are not here to help you. We are here to stop any further attack on the humans. You are now under arrest."

"What is this," the other witch demanded. "We serve under the order of the Shadow Lords and Imperial Witches."

"I am afraid the Shadow Lords are no longer among us," Cooper told them. "I am your Grand Overseer. I order you to stand down... or die."

"Only a traitor would give such an order."

"We take our orders from Overseer Strong. No one else."

Cooper sighed and looked away. There was no time to deal with hostile prisoners. "So be it."

One of Cooper's warrior witches stood behind the captives. She stepped back and lowered her staff, pointing it at the prisoners' backs. Another warrior witch stepped up in front of the prisoners and pointed her staff at them.

"Surrender to my authority or die," Cooper said again. "You only have two choices."

The two captives looked at each other, closed their eyes, and thought, "Overseer Strong, hel...!"

Blasts of magic blew the prisoners to dust. Cooper didn't like this part of the war. The necessity to kill. But he had learned that changing the mind of an enemy was much harder than one might think. Unfortunately, killing was a simple fact of war. A bitter pill for someone like Cooper to swallow. Killing was never a good thing.

Chapter 33

Chamber Magic

Doctors Miles and McLeod met the V.I.P. guests at the Center's front entrance. "Welcome to Center for Interdimensional Physics, Ms. Harrisford," Miles said. He extended his hand.

The Overseer looked down at the hand dispassionately. She ignored the hand and said, "Thank you, Dr. Miles."

Rich people can be so rude, Miles thought. "And you must be Mr. Stanley."

Teddy reached out and shook Miles hand. "Please call me Teddy. We will start working together, so we may as well use first names."

Percy stepped forward. Excited, Percy asked, "Is that the book?" Teddy nodded. "Let me look at it... please. I need to see it, touch it."

Teddy looked to the Overseer for permission. She gave a nod. Percy nearly grabbed the book out of Teddy's hands. "Be careful," Teddy cautioned. "This book is one of a kind and older than you can imagine."

"Yes, yes. I know," Percy replied, impatiently taking the book in his hands. He ran his hand over the cover carefully. Then opened it and thumbed through the first few pages.

Miles looked sideways at Percy. "Have you two met before?"

Percy nodded and whispered, "Yes." He was only half answering Miles' question. His reply was more about being in awe of the book.

"Are you going to keep me in suspense," Miles said? "What is the book about?"

"Oh... marvelous things. From what I have been told, this is an ancient grimoire. Only this one supposedly tells us how to open rifts to other worlds... inhabited worlds."

"Wait," Miles said incredulously. "Are you saying this is a book of magic?" Miles smirked. "Let me see that..."

Teddy interrupted Miles. "May I suggest we go somewhere more private? This thing is extremely valuable. I am sure you understand."

"Of course," Miles replied. "This way."

Miles lead them to the nearest conference room. Percy pushed several chairs aside and laid the book on the table. Percy and Miles examined the book. The symbols and drawings left them baffled.

"Percy," Miles said. "I am no expert in ancient artifacts, but this book looks real. How old did you say it was?"

"I didn't," Teddy said. "I suspect it is tens of thousands of years old, but there is no way to know for sure."

"What about carbon dating," Percy asked, not looking up from the book?

"Oh, I had it tested. The report came back as 'Unknown'."

An enthusiastic Percy said, "Teddy says the book is for opening rifts. This could give us the answers... lots of answers."

"Come now, Percy," Miles said with a chuckle. "The artifact may be real but that doesn't mean the information inside it is real. I mean... a grimoire? Really?"

Teddy spoke up. "I assure you it is very real indeed."

"And how would you know that?"

"First of all, I can read it," Teddy said. "Secondly, I have used it before."

"What do you mean?" Concerned, Miles stepped back.

"I mean just what I said. I have opened a rift before." Teddy grinned. "That is how I got to this world."

"You...?" Shocked by this revelation, Miles stood speechless. "Who are you people?"

Tired of this pointless conversation, the Overseer stepped in to clarify her intent. "Dr. Miles, I am here because of your marvelous machine. I am impressed by human technology. It is so shiny and purposeful. Although magic is generally much simpler to use, some magical spells require considerable power to get the desired results. Your rift machine has the power I need. With Teddy's book and you and Percy's help, I will open a rupture to another world. Rupture is what we call your rifts."

"What do you mean by *we*," Miles asked, afraid of the answer.

"We are Shadows," she declared. "When you won the battle two years ago, did you think the invasion was over, silly man?"

Percy sheepishly spoke, "Sorry Eugene, but this is the only path forward for me. I need specimens, live ones. Let the Shadows have what they want. Ms. Harrisford promised to leave you and I alone. We will be free to continue our research unimpeded by government interference. This is the chance of a li...."

"Percy," Miles began with a shaky whisper. "What have you done?"

"No, Dr. Miles," the Overseer said. "The question is, what will you do?"

Miles said nothing as paced toward the head of the conference table. He sat down. His face showed the shock and outright fear he felt. He could not let this happen. Under the edge of the table was a button. Pushing it would set off a silent alarm causing security to appear. It would only take seconds for this to be over. He had sat down with his hands on his lap. With one hand he felt the underside of the table for the button. Finding it said, "Screw you." Miles pushed the button.

"Teddy," the Overseer barked! "Take him." Teddy leaped into action, changing to his Shadow form as he flew toward Miles. A black mist swirled around Miles, overpowering him. Teddy vanished as Miles' face dropped to the table.

"Percy screamed out, "What are you doing? I need him. He is the interdimensional rift expert."

Overseer Strong laughed. "Now Teddy is."

Security guards blew into the conference room with weapons raised. "Dr. Miles," one shouted. "Is everything okay?" The terrified Percy backed up to the wall wishing he could disappear. Miles sat up abruptly.

"Sorry, gentlemen. False alarm," Miles said with a smile.

Chapter 34

A New Rift

The huge monitors on the front wall showed a display of the IDR chamber area. This new chamber differed in many ways from the old one. The large room was empty except for six metallic, arched posts that extended from floor to ceiling in a circular array. Overseer Strong marveled at the simple beauty of the machine. Until she saw the pattern laid out on the floor. "What does the symbol on the floor do," she asked?

"Miles did not fully understand how the symbol worked," said the faux-Eugene Miles, also known as Teddy. "Miles' memory tells me that two colleagues designed it as a failsafe to ensure control of any rift remained on the human side of the rift. After what happened two years ago that makes sense. Let's take a closer look." He pushed a button and an overhead view of the chamber appeared. "Well, will you look at that? It is magic for sure."

"We have looked for magic users everywhere," Shadow exclaimed. "We found very little evidence that magic is used in this world. How did the humans do this?"

"Ah," the faux-Miles said. "That is because the aforementioned knew some magic."

"What," the Overseer shouted? "Are you sure?"

The faux-Miles frowned. "High Overseer, it is what Miles believed."

"I need to get inside that chamber."

"It is a delicate and expensive piece of technology," Teddy cautioned. "I hope you are not going to do something we all will regret."

"I said... I need in there. Now!"

"It is okay," Percy chimed in. "Show her the chamber."

"If you say so."

All but three individuals in the control room ignored this exchange of words. Those three sat amazed. This rich lady came in and began giving orders like she owned the place. What really shocked them, Dr. McLeod told Dr. Miles to do whatever she wanted. In fact, Miles bowed to Mcleod's order. The world had just tilted the wrong way.

Miles led them out of the control room, down some stairs that led to an unusually long underground hallway. The hallway ended with a set of security doors. Faux-Eugene placed his hand on a wall panel that scanned his hand print. The doors open inward. The Overseer quickly pushed past and went into the IDR chamber. She removed her dark glasses and concentrated on the magic in the room. It was nearly perfect. The room was the perfect height, width and depth. The base of the array of posts formed a perfect magic hexagram star which was embedded in the floor.

"Someone," she barked, "who knows a lot about magic made this chamber."

Faux-Eugene nodded. "That would be Rich Thomas and Bill Williams." Teddy delved into his new host's memories. "Oh, my," faux-Eugene said. "Thomas and Williams told Miles that they came from another world."

"Another world? You mean like we came from another world?"

"Exactly. At least that was what Miles believed to be true."

"This magic is designed to not only contain the rift, but anything that comes through it." Overseer turned angrily to Percy. "What is this Percy?"

"What is what?"

Turning her hot amber eyes toward Percy, she asked pointedly, "You didn't tell me about the Magic, Percy."

"Sorry," Percy replied with a smirk? "I am a scientist, not a magician." Percy stared into Overseer Strong's fierce glare. He quickly realized she wasn't in the mood for sarcasm. "I mean... how was I supposed to know?" He pauses to take a deep breath. "Is that a problem?"

"Yes, you idiot."

"I didn't know there was magic," Percy explained nervously.

"Where are they now," she demanded?

"Who? Williams and Thomas," Percy asked? "Well..."

"They work in this building," faux-Eugene said. "I don't know if they planned to work tonight or not."

"Find them," the Overseer shouted. She swatted faux-Eugene away like an annoying fly and crossed the room toward the exit. He ended up landing on his head and fell unconscious.

"Why did you do that," gasped Percy? "Don't break him. We need him."

"No, what we need are the two men who designed this chamber," She yelled. "Get them here, now."

Percy ran back to the control room. "We need Mr. Williams and Mr. Thomas here, a.s.a.p."

A young woman who had just started in her position that week, started making calls immediately even though she was shaking with fear. There were only three humans in the control room. She knew that everyone else had changed in some way or another. Something about this situation alarmed her, and rightly so. Bill Williams didn't answer his phone, even after several tries. Rich Thomas, however, was still in the building, working late in his lab. "Mr. Thomas, this is Kate in the control room. Dr. McLeod needs your help."

"Percy? What does he want?" Rich asked. "I'm kind of busy."

"Sorry to bother you sir." She turned her back on everyone. "There is trouble in here. Don't..." Her words were cut short by a fiery bullet through her back.

Shadow stepped up to the dead woman lying on the floor. Picking up the phone, the Overseer said, "Just get in here or everyone dies!" She dropped the phone.

"Would you stop killing people," Percy pleaded. "We... I needed her too."

"There are only two individuals in the room that are not already mine," she said. "You know who you are, if you want to live another day, do as I say." Everyone turned to the two humans. The two terrified team members backed away from their desks.

Shadow shook her head, "I need to break the binding magic. I don't wish to accidentally kill anything coming through the rift. We don't need any more enemies."

"You better time it just right," faux-Eugene cautioned as he entered the room rubbing his head. "Are you sure you want to do this tonight?

She glared at him.

"Okay." He shrugged. "I guess tonight is a go then."

******

Rich didn't know what this was about, but he had stayed on the phone long enough to hear a woman's voice say, "There are only two individuals in the room that are not already mine. You know who you are, if you want to live another day, do as I say."

He hung up and called Bill. No Answer. Then remembering that Bill was out with his wife tonight, and date night being somewhat sacrosanct, Bill would have turned off his phone. Rich left a troubling message with little explanation attached. All he said was, *"The Shadows are back and have taken control of the IDR control room. Activate the emergency plan. If I don't make it out here. Do what you have to do to save our families. And tell Anne and the kids I love them."* Rich had considered leaving for home, but the idea of the people in the control room left in danger left him conflicted.

Rich walked out of his office and made his way to the control room. If this was what he and Bill feared would happen. He hoped he would survive to see his wife and kids again. Opening the control room door, he entered. He scanned the room of technicians all standing and waiting for him. The woman who had called him lay on the floor in front of him, dead. Next to the body stood Percy, who had this ghastly, sheepish look on his face. Behind Percy stood a woman he did not know and Eugene. He looked to Percy, then to Eugene, expecting an explanation.

Percy fidgeted a bit and spoke. "Sorry about this Rich, but things haven't gone as planned."

"What was the plan then, Percy?"

"Well..." Percy started to reply.

"Eugene, what is going on," Rich demanded?

A tall dark woman walked around Percy. "Once I found out about you and your friend, I knew I didn't really need anyone else. Just you two. Well for now, just you."

"Percy," Rich let go of his anger! "Is this your doing?"

"I couldn't move forward without opening another rift. I won't let anyone keep me from my important work." He stood tall and said, "Ms. Harrisford and her associates are willing to help me, so I..."

"Oh, do shut up you little worm," Shadow Strong said, getting annoyed. "At first, I tried to open the old rift but it would not respond, so I decided to use this facility to open my rift. It is quite remarkable isn't it Teddy."

"Yes, it is, Overseer," the faux-Eugene replied.

"I can't tell you how surprised I was to see the chamber had a spell around it," she went on. "Tell me Mr. Thomas. How do you know so much about magic?"

"Actually, I know very little about magic," he replied. "This is just a trick I learned from fighting creatures like you."

She raised her eyebrows. "So, it is true. You are not from this world."

"I have also read a lot of documents on magic and have learned how to use technology to produce magic. I call it magic technology. It is a hybrid of the two. Put those two things together and they can throw quite a punch."

"I am a Shadow witch. I can handle magic with far greater skill than any human," she answered knowing what he was getting at.

He looked at her, doubting her claim. "You are not like any of the Shadows I have met."

"I am a warrior witch and the Overseer of many," she said. "But don't let this body fool you. This is just a magic spell." She transformed into the tall thin and muscular Shadow she had always been. Her shiny armor flashed reflections in the room's light. "Shadow females are born with magic, unlike the males that are best used as cannon fodder in a battle… and, of course, as genetic providers." She looked back at Teddy who had also transformed. His weakling body had gotten thin and useless. "Take Teddy here." She shook her head in disgust. "Teddy you really have let yourself go, but you do have quite a brain. That alone makes you worth saving, good genetic material. Do you understand me, Mr Thomas?"

"Where is the real Dr. Miles," Rich asked?

"Gone. What was Miles is now my dear Teddy."

"Look. This is ridiculous. Even with this new chamber we created," he pointed out. "We cannot open a rift to any specific location. You can't go home this way."

"Actually. I decided not to go home," she said blandly. "Why would I when I have this world and all its charms? No, I intend to open rifts leading to many new worlds."

"That's where I come in," Percy said. "I am helping her… so she will help me."

"Like I said. We don't know how to open any specific rift that leads to another world," Rich replied, hoping to stall her. "What we do here is completely random."

"By the way, help will not be coming," she said, tapping her head. "I am an official visitor tonight. The guards outside are unaware of what is happening here."

"And we don't need you to open the rifts to new worlds," Teddy added smiling. "We have the addresses right here in this book." He held the old book above his head.

"We need you to undo the magic spell you created in the chamber," Shadow added.

Rich was afraid. More afraid than he had been in the last two years to be exact. Once again, this world got caught with its pants down. "I don't know if I can undo the spell," he said. "It is built into the floor structure."

Shadow drifted to him menacingly, "You better, or these humans and everyone in this town will die."

She meant that, and Rich didn't doubt it for a minute. "I didn't say I wouldn't try. This magic stuff is difficult. My partner, Bill Williams, is the expert on magic, but he isn't answering his phone. I guess I am all you got."

Chapter 35

---◆---

We Need a Plan

Cooper now focused on High Overseer Shadow Strong as the true target of their mission. She was well known, one of the most powerful witches on Tiarnas. Stop her and the other enemy witches would give up. But he was worried. They had discovered Shadow Strong's plan. She had already taken control of a human facility that housed a device capable of opening ruptures to other worlds. Cooper already knew the humans had this kind of magic but, evidently, they had developed far greater capabilities since his last visit to this world.

"The question is why," Cooper thought to himself.

"Why what," the Priestess asked, understanding his thoughts?

"Why take control of the human's rupture magic?"

"We can only speculate," the Priestess replied. "But since she failed to open the rupture to Tiarnas, I suspect she needed an alternative escape plan."

"She does not know about the end of the Tiarnas Empire," he added. "I would rather she did not go home."

"Well if she does open a new rift to Tiarnas, she will find out soon enough," the Priestess answered.

"We need to stop her before she does," Copper asserted. Not knowing the Overseer's intentions, he worried she could cause considerable trouble for their new republic. They needed a plan. But any plan of action needed to include Sam, Bobby, Jeff, and Grandpa. Cooper considered what had happened the first time he visited this world. He did not want things to get any worse.

The Priestess and the Shadows witches he brought with him would stay hidden in the fortress for now. The Priestess cast a spell that she hoped would trick the enemy witches into returning to the home base. They could eliminate them as they entered the complex. Cooper left the witches to that task and headed out to find his friends.

Chapter 36

Asura's Tantrum

Jeff showed Bobby and Sam the note from Asura.

"Is this some kind of stupid, sick joke," Bobby said?

"Asura is so weird at times," Sam added.

"Asura and Asuri are complete opposites," Jeff said. "Asuri warned me that her sister might cause trouble. Now I am really worried. What is Asura up to?"

"Delia's involvement in this makes no sense," Sam said. "Delia would never agree to a stunt like this. And why threaten to harm Amy. Delia has always protected her."

"Something is wrong," Jeff said. "It was Delia who told Amy that Asura planned to steal her boyfriend... as though I have no say in it. Whatever Delia said to Amy, it hurt her feelings. Asura has lost her freaking mind. That much I know for sure."

"Like you said, none of this makes sense," Bobby agreed. "But the letter disturbs me. The part about the human witch. Sam, I think she's talking about you... your powers."

"Why would she know anything about that," Sam asked? "Not even Delia and Amy know about us."

"Exactly. If they know about you... us, then this situation might be a lot more dangerous than we think. My sixth sense is screaming at me right now. What if this duel thing, and the threatening to harm Amy, are not meant as a joke. If we meet these girls at midnight, like the letter says, then... we better go armed and ready for anything."

Jeff nodded in agreement.

"Maybe we are overreacting," Sam said. "If we get caught on school grounds with our weapons, we will be in a buttload of trouble."

Bobby insisted. "We will need to defend ourselves. I am sure of it."

"And I will defend Amy with my life," Jeff said, more serious than he had ever been in his life.

"Okay," Sam said. "Let's do this."

At 11:30 the three friends headed for the school. Bobby pulled into the parking lot next to the gymnasium. There was only one other car in the parking lot… Delia's.

Jeff got out of the back seat with his sheathed katana in hand. The scabbard had arm straps fitted for mounting it onto his back. He slipped it over his right shoulder and fastened the chest straps Bobby took the shortened fighting staff out of his backpack. Sam stood quietly looking at the gym front. Things went fuzzy and distorted.

Sam said, "I think something is happening."

" Yeah, I sensed it as well," Bobby said. "It feels bad. Be careful."

When the three young warriors reached the main sidewalk leading to the gym's front entrance they froze. The world around them suddenly altered before their eyes. The school's interior lights and the outside walkway lamps went out. It was as though a blanket of darkness had draped over them. Even the stars in the sky disappeared.

"Oh, crap," Jeff said

"Double crap," Sam said.

Bobby nodded his head. "Make that a triple," he said. "Well this confirms our suspicions. What are we dealing with?"

Then something else crazy appeared, it took them a minute to process the bizarre scene. Standing tall in front of them was a Japanese torii gateway arch. Behind it sat another torii gate, and then another, and another, and another. The first gate was bright red, but each gate in succession became a darker shade of red until the gates appeared as black.

"What the…" mumbled Bobby.

Jeff visibly shuttered. "This is like something out of a Japanese horror movie. The entrance to the underworld where the dead…" He decided not to finish that thought.

Sam whispered, "Well, I guess we weren't over reacting."

"What do you want to do," Jeff asked?

"Amy is in there somewhere," Sam reminded him. "We need to get her out of there."

Jeff's continence changed from confusion to determination. "Let's go get

Amy." Jeff took the lead and entered the torii lined portal. Sam and Bobby followed.

Considering they were only twenty feet away from the front doors, for some reason it took nearly ten minutes to reach the end of the torii gates. As they exited the portal, they stepped onto the gymnasium floor. The bleachers were pushed back against the walls on both the bottom and the top levels. The only light came from the upper left side. An emergency light cast harsh, weird shadows across the gym. At the far end they saw seven girls standing in a semicircle under the basketball hoop. Each girl held a raptor staff.

Then Sam saw Amy. They had stuffed Amy in the basketball hoop with her arms outstretched to the sides. Her hands tied to the glass backboard like someone's sick idea of a crucifixion. She was unconscious.

"Amy," Sam screamed out.

"What kind of sick joke is this Asura," Jeff barked angrily. "Get Amy down now or I'll..."

"Or you'll what, Maeda Clan boy," Asura called back laughing.

"This isn't funny," Sam said. Sam's hands got hot and fireballs appeared as Sam prepared to attack.

Asura laughed. "You," she said. "You are the human witch? Look Asuri. Look who the witch turned out to be. She was right there under my nose."

"Did you just call me a witch," Sam protested? "Listen here you...!"

Bobby stepped forward. "What is this about? Asuri, Delia, this is not like you at all." Suddenly he knew why. He sensed all seven witches at the same time. Bobby stumbled back, his hands clasped to the sides of his head.

"Well, look at that," Asura continued. "The boyfriend is a bit of a witch too. The Overseer will love this. Right Asuri?"

"Yes," she replied with her head down.

Sam went immediately to Bobby. "What is it?"

"None of these girls are who they seemed to be," he said, pushing the pain of darkness from his head. "They are all Shadow demons. I don't know how they did it, but they hid themselves from me." He looked at Delia again. "Sorry Sam, but that is not Delia."

"So, the two hot girls I flew home with were Shadow demons," Jeff squawked? Then he thought about it. "Of course, they were. Just my luck."

"Baka... We are not demons, Jeffrey," Asura screamed. "We are Shadow witches."

"Delia," Sam yelled at the girl that looked exactly like Delia. "Where is Delia?"

Delia stepped forward into the light. "Delia is dead, Sam," she said calmly.

"How," Bobby said," now fully recovered? "How are you able to look like people we know?"

Asuri answered, "It is called a Soul Eater spell."

"Shut up, Asuri," Asura ordered.

Just then Amy opened her eyes. "Delia," she called out in pain. "It hurts so bad. What is going on? Please... help me."

Delia turned to look up at the pleading human, "I told you..." Delia grabbed her head and staggered to the side, leaning against the bleachers. "What? Not again." She looked up at Amy and spoke in a completely different tone of voice, "Amy? What are you doing up there?" Delia clutched her head again. "No," the Shadow witch yelled. "This can't happen!"

"What is the matter with you," Asura barked, annoyed. "You are spoiling my dramatic scene."

"The human's soul, it is not gone," Delia struggled to say. "She is still in my head."

"Ah, ha, ha, ha, ha," Asura cackled! "This day has been full of so many surprises."

"Help me," Delia screamed. "I can't see. This is all wrong."

"You are so useless," Asura said, waving her arm violently at Delia. The Shadow witch flew against the bleachers hard and fell to the floor where she lay motionless.

"Sam... now," Bobby yelled.

Sam aimed at Asura and let go with everything she had. The first fireball barely missed Asura. Then the second flew toward Asuri. They hit the concrete gym wall. The two explosions left big round black holes in the wall. Concentrating Sam began shooting fire bullets at the Shadow witches. Firing one after the other in rapid succession. The witches scattered. Asura threw up a shield in time but the shield pulsed red from each impact.

One of the witches dove for Sam, but Jeff drew the sword and sliced her head off. The head and black dust fell to the floor. "Still think the katana was a bad idea?"

"Just fight," Sam yelled. Bobby extended his staff and readied for an attack. Jeff backed away, keeping an eye on the five girls left standing.

The remaining witches, except Asura and Delia, leaped into the air. They circled above in a blur of black. The trio of human fighters came together back to back in the middle of the court waiting for the next blow to come. They didn't have to wait long. A witch slowed for a second. She pointed her staff and a line of fire shot out, scorching the floor right in front of Bobby. He raised his staff and the fire hit his staff. It absorbed the energy.

"They are going to set this place on fire." The wood floor smoldered and sparked with fire everywhere.

Sam yelled, "Asura is mine. You two stop the others."

Another Shadow emerged from the swirling mist. She swung her staff fiercely at Jeff's head. Bobby blocked the raptor staff and glanced away the blow. The scary looking raptor head on the witch's staff swung inches from Jeff's nose.

Bobby whirled around and blocked the witch's staff with a loud, "Crack." The witch lost her hold of staff and it fell to the floor. She tumbled out of the air onto the floor. Before she could recover, Jeff sliced through her head. The witch burst into a cloud of dust and shadowed body parts.

Jeff took a deep breath and said, "Thanks. Nice moves."

Sam and Asura Continued to exchange violent volleys at each other. Asura's shield protected her while Sam had to use her powers to deflect Asura's attacks. The stalemate frustrated both combatants to the point that neither could restrain their rage. Amy still sat unaided tied to the back stop. The outrage Sam felt went far beyond anything she had ever felt, but her strikes were not enough to overpower the witch alone.

"Bobby, I need you," she shouted.

"Oh... does the human witch need her male to save her," Asura said with a psychotic laugh. Asura leaped behind Sam so fast that Sam barely had time to turn and protect herself. a flared ring of protective fire encircled Sam, but Asura's attack hit so hard it threw Sam across the room.

"Bobby," Sam pleaded.

"They are moving too fast to even see."

"Go help Sam," Jeff yelled. "I can handle this."

Bobby rushed to Sam's side. He grabbed her hand, lifted her up and pulled her out of the way a split second before another magical blast struck the floor. The blast didn't hit either of them, but the accompanying concussion knocked them up and away. They both managed to land on their feet, although still sliding backwards from the force.

Jeff looked up at the circling ring of black mist. He had an idea, a desperate idea, but an idea that might work. He quickly climbed up the bleachers to the top and turned to the circling witches. Closing his eyes, Jeff took a deep, calming breath. When his eyes opened, he focused on the flight paths of the two remaining witches. From this new position he saw that inside the circling mist two denser moving objects stood out. He watched as one of the dark objects changed its course to move in his direction. Before the witch could come into view, Jeff leaped into the air toward the approaching witch. His katana sliced the air making contact. The witch exploded in pieces like the others. Jeff fell to the floor in a not so graceful manner. He did manage to tuck and roll at the last moment, ending up face down. The katana ended up a few feet away.

"Sister," Asura screamed.

"I am here sister," Asuri said, coming to a stop at the top of the bleachers. She jumped to the floor to stand next to Asura.

"Well done, Jeffrey. That is why I must have you. Do you not see? I can make you even stronger. Join me and serve me. I will withhold nothing from you in return." She reached out with her hand and sent a magic line toward Jeff. It wrapped around his leg before he could react. Asura yanked back on the line and pulled Jeff toward her as hard as she could. A little too hard in fact. Jeff flew across the floor and knocked Asura off her feet. The impact loosened the magic. Jeff recovered and backed away.

"That hurt," Asura yelled. "You idiot, just give up and I will set Amy free. I promise."

"We can't fight in here," Jeff yelled. "We need to get outside. Get her away from Amy." Sam and Bobby nodded and they ran to the exit.

"Get back here you cowards," Asura screamed. Asura let go an explosion of power. Sam threw up the ring of fire again. It deflected Asura's attack but the concussion knocked Sam backward into Bobby and Bobby into Jeff. The blast made a ten to twelve-foot hole in the gym wall. Unfortunately, it destroyed the portal leading directly to the outside. The dibre blocked the closest exit.

The only path left led down the hallway. Running down the school halls wouldn't be any better than staying in the gym, but they needed to find an exit, get outside, and rethink their strategy. Sam fired bullets at the twins as the retreated.

Asura exploded with fury. Asuri joined her sister and fired back. Fire bullets and lightning like fire flew everywhere. The gym was now burning in several places. The human trio ran.

"I can't believe I ever thought those two girls were hot," Jeff yelled back as he ducked around a corner.

"Hey," Bobby said. "When did you learn how to throw up a shield like that?"

"I didn't know I could… until now."

Asura and Asuri looked at each other and then took pursuit. The other witches had been completely useless. They were better off on their own. The sisters spread out at the end of the hall. Sam met them with a salvo of fire bullets. They took flight. Asura dove above the bullets along the ceiling and Asuri below just above the floor. They blasted past the humans, knocking the trio down in the process. The two witches stopped several feet down the hall and turned for the final assault.

Sam reached out and said, "Take my hands boys. I need a rest."

"A rest," Jeff said, gulping for air?

"We need time on our side," Sam insisted, extending her hands to them.

They grabbed her hands just as Sam yelled, "Stop!" They stood there in the silence, breathing hard. "Now what," Bobby asked.

Jeff stood up straight still holding hands. "What will happen if I throw my katana at Asura right now?"

"I don't know," Sam said, finally catching her breath. "You could lose the sword, but what the heck, try it."

Jeff pulled the sword overhead and threw it with all his might at Asura. As soon as it left his hand it froze in the air. "That was disappointing," he said.

"No," said Bobby. "A body in motion tends to stay in motion. Right?"

"Yah, so," Jeff asked?

"So." Bobby extended the blade hidden at the one end of his staff. He held the staff like a javelin, sharp end first. As soon as he found the balance point, Bobby threw it directly at Asuri. Like the katana it stuck in the air. "This way, they won't see our weapons coming."

"Ah," Jeff said. "Assuming we hit something."

"That would be the intention," Bobby said, shrugging. He looked at Sam. "This will be the *Hail Mary pass* of all time. A little prayer might be wise. Use the religion of your choice."

The three stood together hand in hand, side by side. They were forever friends, a friendship that might end in a few seconds if this didn't work.

"Go," Sam whispered.

Bobby's staff shot through the air toward Asuri. Jeff's katana flew blade over hilt, spinning gracefully towards Asura. The staff penetrated Asuri's shoulder. She spun and fell. The katana's sharp blade struck Asura in the forehead. The spinning blade easily sliced through her head and body. Asura stood stunned momentarily. Her eyes rolled back and her human form disappeared. She fell to the floor dead.

Asuri slid across the floor to her sister. Sam raised her hand, but Bobby said, "Wait.

She is not going to attack us."

"You must go for the kill," Jeff insisted. "She is a Shadow demon... our enemy."

"Cooper is a Shadow demon and he is our friend. I've had enough killing."

Asuri, overwhelmed and distraught, said, "I tried to tell her not to do this, but Asura... She never listened to me. Now look at what has happened. Poor Asura." She looked down at what had been Asura and then back at the three humans. "Just go away. Leave me alone with my sister."

"Oh crap, Amy. We need to get her down before the gym goes up in flames," Jeff said.

Jeff recovered his katana and the trio ran down the hall to the gym. The bleachers were now on fire as well as anything else that could burn. A choking smoke filled the air. Finally, the sprinklers sent a deluge of water dousing everything.

Delia was still out cold, so Sam sat next to her and watched her. To be safe she was ready to react, in case it wasn't Delia that woke up. She didn't know what to do if that was the case. Could she kill someone who looked exactly like her friend?

Bobby and Jeff got a tall ladder and climbed up to Amy. They untied her hands and gently helped her down the ladder to the floor.

In spite of the fact that he had plenty of reason to worry about Amy's condition, the ensuing battle hadn't given him the chance to be worried. What she had just been through was horrible and she was in shock. They all were in shock, and very wet. "Can you stand," Jeff asked her?

"Yes," Amy said. "If you hold me. Please, just hold me."

"Okay, sure," he said softly. He would hold her for a long while. He had nearly lost the girl he had come to love.

A voice came from behind them. "Asura was a terrible sister in every way," Asuri spoke over the splatter of the waterfall. She had Bobby's fighting staff in her hand. "She was always mean to me, but only because she wanted me to be stronger, as strong as she was."

"Shoot, she's got my staff," Bobby said.

"But she was my only sister. Surely you understand that. Shadows don't usually have siblings, let alone twins. That made us special. You killed the only thing I had in the world," she said. "The only thing that made me special. My sister was special." Her eyes brightened. "Jeffrey. Remember what I told you the other night. I told you that I didn't know what love was... but that was not true. I loved my sister."

The next part she said only to herself. Had any of them heard it they would have moved sooner. *"You killed something I loved,"* she thought darkly. *"I will kill something you love. That's only fair. Do you not agree?"*

Bobby realized what Asuri wanted to do. "Look out, Jeff!"

The witch was lightning fast. Jeff and Amy parted. Both he and Bobby lunged for Asuri and the staff, but they missed. Asuri didn't. Her true Shadow form appeared a second before she drove the blade end of Bobby's staff deep into Amy's Chest.

"AMY," Delia screamed. She had awoken just as the horrible scene reached its tragic conclusion. She launched herself at Asuri. Having no idea of how strong her Shadow body was. Delia hit Asuri with savage rage. She grabbed Asuri by the neck and slammed her into the bleachers. Asuri didn't fight back. Delia twisted the witch's head with everything she had, separating it from the body.

Jeff cradled Amy in his arms. "Amy, please. Look at me Amy. Please don't go."

Bobby and Sam hugged him and Amy as life drained from her. And then she was dead. Sam cried uncontrollably. "This is wrong," she screamed. "This is not how this is supposed to end."

Delia was sobbing too. She fell at Amy's feet. "I am sorry, Amy. I am so sorry! I couldn't get control of that thing inside me in time to save you. I am so sorry!" She continued to say sorry over and over again in a pained whisper. Sam came to Delia. They hugged and cried together.

Bobby got to his feet wiping his eyes. Taking out his phone, he called his dad.

Jeff pulled the staff out of Amy's chest. He picked her up, cradling her in his arms. He started to walk away.

"Jeff," Bobby said. "I am so sorry."

Jeff stopped, but didn't turn around. "The gym is still on fire. We better go." He started walking, then stopping once more. "Bobby," he said, choking on his emotion. "This is why, in a war with demons and monsters, you go for the kill. No matter who they are! So... so the wrong person doesn't end up dead." He walked out through the wreckage carrying Amy into the night. The night, no longer lined with ghostly torii gates, flashed with red and blue lights from the fire trucks and police cars.

The back doors into the gym behind them banged open, knocked off the hinges. A fuzzy black creature appeared. His green eyes looked so sad. "My Sam," Cooper vocalized loud and clear.

"Cooper," Sam yelled as she ran to him in despair. She threw her arms around his big neck and hugged him as hard as she could. He held her gently, patting her back. "Sorry, my Sam." He had seen what she saw, had felt what she felt. If only he could have gotten there sooner. He scooped Sam up and carried her from the smoking building.

Bobby retrieved his staff. He retracted it. "Delia," Bobby said. "Take this and hide it for me. You need to hide as well."

"Where do I go?"

"Follow the big guy carrying Sam. You can trust him with your life."

"What are you going to do," Delia asked?

"I'm going after Jeff."

Chapter 37

There is Trouble

After listening to the voicemail from Rich, Bill's first impulse was to go to the Center and help his lifelong friend. But Rich was right. The first priority was getting their families to safety. Helping Rich had to wait.

"What is it," Sarah asked?

"We need to get home," Bill said. "That was Rich. *There is trouble*." That was a code phrase the two families devised after the Shadow invasion had caught them off guard two years earlier. It meant, *get to the safe room as soon as possible*.

Sarah looked at her husband. "Are you sure?"

"Rich was dead serious." Bill did a quick U-turn and headed back toward home.

"What has happened?"

"Don't know. Rich didn't elaborate."

Sarah pulled her phone out her purse and pushed the speed dial. "Anne? This is Sarah. Bill got a message from Rich. *There is trouble*," she said with clear emphasis. We will be home shortly."

"Rich is at his lab," Anne said over the phone. "Did he say what the trouble was?"

"Sorry, no details. I'll see you in a few minutes." She ended the call. "I'll call Bobby." Bobby's phone went to voicemail immediately. She left the message, "*There is trouble. Come home.*"

They pulled into their driveway and found Anne and Sam's little brother, now twelve, waiting for them.

"I tried to call Sam," Anne said. "It went to voicemail."

"Same for Bobby, I'm afraid."

"This is so typical."

Then Bill's phone rang. "It's Bobby," he said, relieved. "Bobby, where are you?"

They all heard Bobby's voice over the phone. "Dad, *there is trouble - terrible trouble.*"

******

Bill and Sarah waited in the police station lobby for Bobby to be released. Jeff's parents had gotten a call as well. Concerned, Bill talked with the Sasakis. Bobby had kept his phone call short, so no one knew anything as yet.

Then Mrs. Ross came out of a private office. Amy's mom was crying. A police woman comforted her. The strain of the situation weighed heavily on Mrs. Ross' face. The officer led her downstairs to the morgue. "This looked bad, very bad." Sarah Williams said. "Something must have happened to Amy." The police were beside themselves. What the investigating offices saw at the high school had greatly disturbed them. This was no ordinary school fight. They found remnants of bodies, inhuman creatures in the gym and in a school hallway next to it. It brought back horrifying memories from two years ago. Nobody closely involved in that night believed the terrorist story, but the alternative was too unbelievable.

Eventually Bobby appeared escorted by a police officer. Jeffrey was not with them.

"Mr. and Mrs. Williams," the officer said. "We are releasing your son into your custody. He is free to go now."

"Wait, what was this about," Bill asked? Mr. and Mrs. Sasaki moved closer.

"A young lady was killed," the officer replied. "Your sons were witnesses."

Sarah felt a surge of dread. "Amy Ross?"

The officer nodded.

Mrs. Sasaki gasped, "Oh no... oh no."

Mr.' Sasaki interrupted, "Our son Jeffrey, where is he?"

"Your son is being charged with the possession of a lethal weapon," the officer told them. "A Japanese sword."

"Are you saying you think my Jeffrey killed Amy," Mrs. Sasaki said fearing for her son.

"No ma'am. The sword has already been ruled out as the murder weapon."

"Dear God," Jeff's mom whispered. "Murder?"

"In fact, we do not have a murder weapon yet. There were several strange staffs lying around that your boys told us belonged to their attackers. Look… your boys told us quite a story. We are not saying that we don't believe them… Especially after what we saw inside the school but Jeffrey admitted he used his weapon to defend the girl."

"That sounds like our boy," Mr. Sasaki said.

"Jeff has been through an awful trauma," Bill said. "Can't he just go home with his parents? He's a kid. He won't go anywhere."

"We need time to sort this out, folks. Unfortunately, Jeff is eighteen and he brought a weapon to the scene of the crime."

"But…"

"Jeff," Bobby called out. Jeff, in handcuffs, came had come out of a room down the hall. He ignored all of them as the police officers took him away. "What do we do dad?"

"Don't worry son. We will get to talk to Jeff soon."

"Dad." Bobby pulled his dad to the side and whispered, "I need to tell you about what happened."

"That can wait till later."

"No, dad. Listen. Sam and Delia Bowen were with us tonight. They are in trouble as well."

"Where are they now?"

"Well… believe it or not… they are with Cooper."

******

Bill and Bobby pulled up to the security gate. Bill intended to tell the guards what had happened inside the Center, but then thought better. If the guards went into the control room with guns blazing, no telling what would happen. First, he needed to get Rich out safely. He drove directly to Rich's lab. This was not how he expected to spend his date night.

After parking, Bill grabbed a duffle bag from the back seat, then he and Bobby proceeded to Rich's laboratory. Inside a locked room in the lab, Rich kept several devices designed to provide greater safety for their families. All these devices were tech-magic. Some were designed specifically for Bobby and Sam to enhance their powers. An updated version of Bobby's fighting staff now included a magical shield, so he wouldn't have to rely on Sam as much. This high-tech staff had a narrow-beamed version of the anti-magic device at one end and a particle beam weapon at the other. The staff was made of a lightweight polymer that was hard enough to break skulls and bones.

"Here Bobby, this is for you," Bill said, handing the new staff to him. "Rich will have to show you how to use all the new features later. First, I have to get him out of here. You will love the added tech-magic."

"Cool." Bobby took the retracted staff and extended the ends to full length.

"No playing yet," his dad said. "We don't have much time. I have a couple more devices to explain to you." Bobby retracted the staff. "These high-tech looking gloves are for Sam. The gloves will protect her hands while fighting, but, more important, the gloves will help her better focus her powers. Again, Rich will have to explain everything later." Bill handed Bobby a duffel bag he took from the trunk of his car. "Put the devices in this bag." Bobby put the staff and the gloves in the bags. "This last tech-magic device is a wrist mounted cloaking shield."

"I remember. You use these when you try to rescue us from the DOD agents."

"An earlier version, yes. Here." Bill handed his son one of the cloaking shield devices. "Put this one on your wrist." Bobby did as told. "There are a total of seven of these, one for each member of our families. I will wear this one. It is the master control for the other six cloaking shields. Rich usually wears this one but... well, it is my turn to save him." Bill attached the device on his wrist. He stuck another in his pocket to give to Rich later. He tossed the remaining four devices in the bag. "Take the bag home as quickly as possible. Hand them out. I hope to be home soon... with Rich."

Bobby looked at the one on his wrist. "How do I make this thing work?"

"Once I turn the master on, it contacts the other devices and activates automatically. As long as you are within a mile radius of the master it will remain activated."

"What will happen? How do I tell if it is working?"

"Your device will turn green. You and I, for all intensive purposes, will disappear. But remember, you are still physically in the world. The device merely keeps others from recognizing your presence. If someone runs into you, they will feel it. Fortunately, the magic also makes sure the person immediately forgets about it. Sneak quietly past the guards at the gate. Just stay away from them or anyone on the street. By the time you get home, you will be out of range and will reappear."

"Okay, I got it."

"Good, everyone is counting on you."

"Don't worry. I won't let you down. Oh, and dad. Be careful." Bill smiled and activated the cloak. Bobby took off on foot toward the security gate.

******

Rich frantically studied the problem, scribbling numbers on pads of paper, searching through lines of code in search of a way to cancel the built-in warding magic so individuals could enter or exit the chamber circle freely. More than anything, he was stahling. Perhaps some solution would appear and bring this situation to a peaceful end. He knew that the hexagram within the circle wasn't there to aid in opening a rift. It was there to avoid what happened two years ago, to keep anything from slipping through an open rift. This secret he would keep to himself for now. The last thing he wanted was to actually remove the warding spell. The fact was, he knew of no way to disconnect the magic without breaking the chamber columns. Without even one of the columns, a rift couldn't be formed.

"There is one possible option." Rich told the faux-Miles. "Remove one column after the rift was open. However, this idea will only work if any visitors coming through the rift have the capability to keep the rift open themselves. Only then can the column be removed." Rich was pretty sure removing was near impossible. At least he hoped that was the case.

"Timing will be everything," he told them. "You don't want to do anything until someone or thing has taken control of the rift inside the circle. That way, after the chamber is breached, it won't matter what we do to the chamber after that."

The Overseer said, getting annoyed with the technical talk. "Just do it."

"That's the problem," he replied. "I don't have a way to remove a column like that. The lower portion of the columns are buried deep inside the concrete floor. I doubt even a bulldozer could break through one of these columns."

"Teddy," she said. "Do you understand what he needs?"

"Yes, I do," the faux-Eugene, a.k.a. Teddy said. "Use magic to remove the column. You, my Overseer, can make it disappear easily." He turned to Rich. "Very good Mr. Thomas. I believe we are ready to go."

That was not what Rich wanted to hear. He needed to stop this, or at least delay it. He needed to escape if he wanted to survive this insanity.

"Let's get our pathway open," Shadow demanded.

Rich looked worried. "Like I said before. I can't open a specific rift to a specific world. This technology is not that advanced."

Teddy explained, "The book tells us how to get the address we need, or the phone number, whatever." Teddy went down into the room that housed the IDR chamber while Rich started the process to open a rift.

Bill Williams stood outside the control room door. The plan was simple. Walk in unseen, hand a cloaking device to Rich, and walk out. He would notify the guards of the situation after they reached safety. Of course. Bill had no idea what he was walking into. He took a deep breath, opened the door slowly, and slipped through unseen. Standing as still as possible, he waited.

The Overseer lifted her head and sniffed the air. Something had changed. She turned to the main door. It was closed. She sniffed the air again as she walked toward the door. Touching the door, she turned to the side and stared at the wall.

Bill held his breath as the Shadow stood inches from him. If she reached out, she would discover him. Sweat trickled down his face.

"Overseer Strong," Teddy said over the comm. "I am in place… so… ready when you are."

"Alright, Mr. Thomas, let us begin."

"Stations everyone," Rich ordered. "Reports?"

Each station acknowledged, "Ready."

"The Rift event will begin at ten…" He counted down to one. "And engage." The rift chamber activated with a snap and whoosh. Teddy began reading from the book.

Chapter 38

A New Rift

A rift formed.

Teddy read, "Creatures of distant worlds, we seek a pathway to you. To you, great and powerful Fomorians, we ask for your favor and acceptance. Reach through the open space we provide and make yourselves known to us."

The rift didn't respond. On the main screen at the front of the room, they watched Teddy read the incantation once again. Again, nothing happened.

Overseer Strong lost her patience. "Teddy, why is nothing happening?"

"I think the rift chamber is interfering with the incantation," Teddy replied.

"Well, what are you going to do about it," she shrieked? "I want the pathway opened... now."

"I have an idea," Teddy said.

"Spit it out then, you bottom feeder," the Overseer shouted.

"Someone needs to read the incantation from inside the rift chamber. While the rift opens."

"I can't guarantee anyone's safety," Rich cautioned. "Like I said. This technology isn't that advanced. I don't know what would happen to the person inside the chamber. It would very likely kill them."

"Oh nonsense," the Overseer replied. "Teddy won't have any trouble doing it."

"Me," Teddy protested. "It should be one of your minions. I am too important."

"I want you to do it," she demanded. "Any problem with that?"

Teddy glared back angrily. "This plan of yours just keeps getting better and better," he said, not hiding his sarcasm. "No. No problems at all, High Overseer."

"Good," she said. "Now get my rift open!"

Rich shut down the system and the rift disappeared. "Okay, Teddy," Rich said. "The chamber is clear. You can go."

A nervous Teddy moved inside the circle and readied himself for what might happen next. "Okay," he said. "I'm ready."

Rich called for reports again. Then engaged the rift chamber.

Within the chamber circle, Teddy held the ancient grimoire up to his face as though he hoped it might protect him in some way. The chamber activated. The columns resonated with a low frequency hum. Teddy backed away from the center of the circle until his back almost touched the circular perimeter. Soon a tiny gleaming light appeared at the very center. The rift began to form, Teddy's cue to begin his incantation. He stared at the forming rift with both fascination and terror.

"Now, you idiot," Shadow said entering the rift chamber room behind him. "What are you waiting for?"

Teddy ignored her and chanted the words, "Creatures of distant worlds, we seek a pathway to you. To you, great and powerful Fomorians, we ask for your favor and acceptance. Reach through the open space we provide and make yourselves known to us."

According to the book the Fomorians were a powerful warrior race that had conquered thousands of known worlds. Of course, that was thousands of years ago, so who knows if they even exist anymore. Teddy kept repeating the incantation. This interdimensional handshake flowed through the rift. They waited for the other side to reach out and shake it.

The light at the center flickered twice, then started to pulse in a random pattern for several minutes.

"It's working," Shadow gasped.

"Assuming someone is home," Teddy replied.

"If they aren't, then we will try another address," she replied. "Keep at it."

The pulsing stopped. Now they would wait.

During this time of considerable distraction, Bill, still invisible, moved to Rich's side. He laid the cloaking device down on the table right in front of Rich. As soon as he let go of the device it became visible. Thankfully Rich looked down at that moment. He grabbed the device and hid it in his lap. Looking around to see if anyone was looking. Carefully, he slipped it on his wrist and disappeared.

Bill motioned to the door. Rich hugged the wall as Bill opened the door enough for them to slip out. They moved down the corridor and out of the building.

"This is rather reckless of you," Rich whispered. "Still, I am glad to see you."

"What are they trying to do," Bill whispered? "Contact their home world?"

"No." Rich shook his head. "That is the worst part. She seems to be looking for new allies. I gather there is another warrior race out there somewhere that is better suited to her needs than her Shadow comrades."

"She?"

"I think so. If the human form she chose is any indication of gender," Rich said. "At least that's what Percy implied. She is a Shadow female."

"Why is Percy here," Bill asked?

Rich said with more than a hint of sarcasm, "Percy just became humankind's newest Judas."

"That little worm," Bill sniped.

The rift started reacting to Teddy's call. The rift grew larger and brighter, then snapped, whoosh. Something or Someone had answered their call. The rift opened upward over the floor's magical circle, parallel to the floor.

"Get me out of here," Teddy shouted. "Overseer... Mr. Thomas, anybody... get me out of here."

"Where did Rich Thomas go," someone in the control room asked?

Almost everyone in the room stood, alarmed at the realization that a rather important hostage had escaped without anyone noticing. The High Overseer would be furious. A Shadow witch ran out of the room and all the way outside the building. She changed to Shadow form and took off into the air. From an advantage point above the facility, she could see everything. A car had just left the compound. She watched it as it drove away into the city.

Part II

The War of Wars

I am reminded of something a great Twentieth Century leader, Winston Churchill, once said. "One ought never to turn one's back on a threatened danger, and try to run away from it. If you do that, you will double the danger. But if you meet it promptly and without flinching, you will reduce the danger by half. Never run away from anything. Never."

From the journal of Robert James Williams (2069)

In our universe there is light as well as darkness.
There is good as well as evil. And, just as a person can embody the essence of godliness, so can they also embody the essence of inexplicable wickedness.

Chapter 39

The Fomorians

When the first four creatures appeared, Teddy let out a cry of fear and desperation. Walking on four legs, the creatures moved around the circle with a cat-like stealth. Actually, the front legs looked more like long arms with human like hands instead of clawed feet. They were about twice the size of the average male lion, only they were hairless and pale with almost white skin. Their rib cages had a pronounced hungry look. Sunken eyes set deep in dark holes gave them the gaunt look of death. Each creature had a glowing blue-collar ring around its neck. Connected to the collars were blue whip-like lines of light that led back down into the rift. They climbed the chamber's circular walls and ceiling, looking for an opening. Finding none, they turned their attention to Teddy.

"Overseer," Teddy whelped. "Let me out of here."

"Not just yet, my friend," she replied. "We need to greet our guests first."

Teddy fell to his knees and prostrated to the ground. "It's okay. We are all friends here. You be good boys." he shouted hoping that that message got through to the creatures, who appeared to be nothing more than wild animals. Bending over Teddy, they sniffed and growled. He was scared to death. "Nice doggies," Teddy pleaded.

Four new beings appeared. These ones stood erect, about ten to twelve feet tall. They too had pale skin, except for what appeared to be blue tattoos that covered their bare chest, arms and legs. Each had a long mane of white hair. Armor covered the groin area. Each carried a long sword-like weapon that glowed. The other end of the blue leashes that bound the first four creatures wrapped around the right hands of the four warriors. Two took position to the right and two to the left of the rift center. They stood quiet and motionless.

The shaking Teddy stayed down low on the floor. Overseer Shadow Strong looked on in awe. This was the stuff of fantasy tales told to imps. Only this wasn't a tale. It was real. Beings on other worlds do exist. The Tiarnas

Empire would no longer be an isolated world.

The other Shadows and Percy in the control room stared at the monitors... captivated. The only humans left in the room saw the chance to leave. They quietly moved to the wall and made their way to the exit. They opened the door only to come face to face with the returning Shadow witch who was in a very bad mood.

Back in the rift chamber a new visitor entered the center. He was a giant of a being, dressed in full, shiny armor made with peculiar craftsmanship and style. Several weapons hung from his waist, arms and legs. His blue tattooed face was large and angry looking. "If you wish to be friends," he growled. "Why is this magic binding us here?"

Shadow kneeled and bowed low. "Forgive me, my lord. Weak human magic had to be used to ensure control of the rift. Please be patient as I remove the shield." She looked up and thrust her hand against the nearest column. She said, "Be gone."

The four guards reacted immediately to her action moving between their Lord and the Shadow. Once they realized that the Overseer had created an exit, they relaxed.

"I am Overseer Shadow Strong of the Tiarnas Empire," she announced. "I welcome you."

"Tiarnas Empire, huh? Never heard of it," the giant said, mocking her. He looked down on her with arrogant disinterest. "You are a Shadow. What does a Shadow want from a Fomorian?"

"Forgive me, my lord. I wish to serve you, my lord. As a token of my goodwill, I offer you this world, which is called Earth. The lords of the Tiarnas Empire declared war on this world, but then ran like cowards from the humans. They stranded my army of witches in this world without support. We remained ready to fight for Tiarnas with honor, but it seems our leaders have no honor and have abandoned us. This is unforgivable and cowardly. I have summoned you, my lord, because the great Fomorians are known as warriors of honor and valor."

"Is that so?"

"Yes, my lord. My army of witches are fierce warriors. They deserve to live and die as warriors. I commit myself and my army to you and entreat you to restore our honor by leading us to victory. Once the Earth is crushed into submissions, I will give you Tiarnas as well. There are millions of able-bodied Shadows to enslave. They don't deserve such kindness considering their cowardly treachery against my brave warriors, but you can do with Tiarnas as you please."

The giant said nothing at first, considering what the Shadow had told him. "Why did your lords attack this... Earth," the giant asked?

Shadow looked up and smiled. "Because Earth is filled with abundant resources, but... to be honest... because humans taste delicious, my lord" she replied with a wicked smile.

The giant's glowing eyes flared. He laughed heartily. "I am General Balor, Lord of the Realm, the son of the Fomorian king. I will take your offering and place it before our supreme leader, the Royal mother. But first I must take a penalty from you. Binding royal blood, even for a good reason, is an unforgivable offense," General Balor declared. "I will require a life as penance for this affront." He pointed at Teddy. "Therefore, this one must forfeit his life."

Teddy looked up in shock. "What... wait," he started to say. That was all the time he had left before the leashed creatures ripped into him. It was over in seconds.

"The offense is forgiven."

The wide-eyed Overseer Strong thought, "I guess that makes one less mouth to feed."

Balor stepped out of the circle. To Overseer Strong, who was still prostrate on the floor, he said, "Rise and show me this world," he ordered.

The Overseer rose but kept her head low. She raised her right hand in a cup shape in front of her. A glowing blue-green sphere appeared in her hand. She then moved her left hand to the top the ball and touched it at the apex with a finger. As she raised her hand the ball grew. When done, a perfect model of the Earth, about four feet in diameter, floated in the air.

"From everything we have learned thus far, Earth is rich. Vast amounts of land and water with countless precious minerals for power and energy. A wide variety of life covers the planet. It is, as the humans themselves say, *ripe for the picking*. Over seven billion humans live on this world and they procreate quickly. As livestock, these humans are the greatest resource of all."

"Hum," the giant said thoughtfully. "Are we on the surface of the world right now?"

"Yes, my lord," the Overseer humbly replied.

Balor raised a hand toward the ceiling. A concussion wave of magic blew a section of the chamber roof away. He looked up at the early morning sky.

No exit path large enough for these giants existed. Shadow pointed at one of the exterior walls and said, "Create according to my mind and will so will it be." A large section of the wall crumbled inward. The rubble organized into a perfect ramped path to the surface above. "Bond as one," she said, turning the debris into one hard stone. "After you, my lord."

The Fomorian ascended the ramp out into the open air. Shadow followed closely behind. Balor looked around casually. "This world stinks of strange smells."

"The smell is the humans and the organic environment that grows nearly everywhere," Shadow explained. "All it needs is a little fire."

Balor laughed heartily. Just then, around the corner of the building, ran several military guards, responding to the explosion and falling debris. The soldiers reacted as you would expect. They open fire. The rounds struck General Balor's armor, ricocheting away. Annoyed, he drew his weapon and lunged forward. His flaming blade of energy struck the soldiers, incinerating them instantly. "How many of these insects did you say inhabit this world," he asked turning to Overseer Strong?

"Over seven billion," she replied. "As you can see their weapons are not magical. Very weak, ineffective tools."

"And yet you say they beat you in your first battle with them."

"It wasn't these weapons that beat us. It was the magic of a powerful human witch. The Shadow army allowed her to penetrate their defenses. The witches closed the only pathway back to Tiarnas. That rift remains closed. Shadow witches will not be so easily compromised."

It is true Sam and her friends had been enormously lucky that night. Plus, it wasn't Sam and Bobby's abilities alone that had defeated the Shadows. The main factor in the Shadows' humiliating defeat had been bloodlust. The Shadow males, whose job it was to pound the enemy to dust, had become so intoxicated by human blood that they lost control. A mindless feeding frenzy began. The Shadows ended up killing each other more than the enemy. Coupling magic and human technology did the rest.

"Where are these witches now?"

"My Shadow witches have found and killed her." This was not true, but this was no time for honesty.

"Human magic will not be a problem for the Formorians, Balor said arrogantly.

The Overseer made the model of Earth appear again and waved her hand over the globe. It spun around. Several points of light appeared. "The green points of light indicate locations of major population centers. The red points indicate major military complexes. Fortunately, the Earth is divided into many different countries with their own governments. No single ruler presides over the Earth."

"Easier to divide and conquer."

"To serve such wise and powerful military leaders is a true honor, my lord.

"I will summon the Royal Mother. We need her blessing," said Balor. From his armor he took a device. He raised it high and pointed straight up. "Activate shield." A beam of light shot upward. High above them, the air exploded with a bright flash. The entire area went instantly dim as a shimmering dome appeared covering the campus and much of the city. The dome sealed off the surface at the dome's perimeter. Later, in quick jumps, it would expand in size. Once sucked inside the dome, there was no way out. Once solidified in place, the dome was impenetrable. Only during the dome's expansion, could the shield be breached. The magic became plastic as it engulfed new territory. This technique for capturing territory had been used by the Fomorians for thousands of years.

The ultimate goal was total dominance. Power could only be achieved through dominance. Those willing to submit to the Fomorian rule had a far better chance of survival. Those who had value might even be given a small piece of the power. Those with no value became slaves of the empire until death released them from the world. Those who resisted were executed.

"We must protect the Royal Mother," said General Balor. "Kill every human creature who dares to resist. Release the *crainn*." The blue leashes that held the animal-like creatures disappeared. The four *crainn* darted away to seek out the enemy. The four handlers followed close behind. More creatures emerged from the rift. Soon screams were heard from not that far away. The work of war proceeded from that moment.

The Shadow witches from inside the control room exited the building with Percy in tow. They brought him to Overseer Strong. "What will you do with this human," one witch asked.

"Leave him with me. He is my pet now," she replied. "Where is Mr. Thomas?"

"Forgive us, Overseer, he escaped," the witch replied bowing low before Shadow.

"How," she growled.

"While we were busy opening the pathway, he disappeared from the room. No one saw him leave."

Overseer Strong screamed in fury. "Find him."

Chapter 40

------◆•••◆•••◆------

No Time for Grief

Jeff sat on the narrow cot in the cell with head in hands, his grief more than anything he had ever felt before. More than anyone else could understand. His heart was broken. Amy ended up in that gym because of him.

"If I hadn't gotten so close to her." The words fell out of his mouth with a gasp. "Yet how could I not get close to her?" His heart felt like Asuri had stabbed him instead of Amy. His thoughts carried on. *If I had just played along with Asura's... crush... obsession, maybe she wouldn't have turned on me like that.* That thought deserved a full-fledged smack in the head. *Asura was a freaking Shadow demon, idiot. Mad crazy rage seemed to be a regular Shadow thing. I... no one could control that.*

Then there was Asuri. She was alive because he had let Bobby's sense of merciful justice overpower his common sense. The enemy was evil. Mercy had no place when fighting evil. Master Maeda, not his grandpa but the one in Japan, had warned him about this. "In battle with an enemy demon, monster or evil spirit," the master had said. "Always go for the kill. Otherwise the wrong person, a friend, a comrade, or a loved one, may end up dead."

Jeff knew he couldn't blame Bobby either. Bobby was still learning how to be a warrior. Asura and Asuri were far more complex and skillful than the Shadows they fought before. Bobby had no way of knowing they could mask themselves so well. Everything about Asuri indicated she was done fighting. Asura, the real threat, was dead.

Jeff's mind shifted from guilt to shame and back to guilt. "I am the only person," Jeff expressed painfully. "I am responsible for Amy's death."

Jeff's grief got much worse. He hadn't cried for Amy yet. He was too numb. The buzz in his ears, the pain in his chest, and the confusion in his mind left him without a path to a coping mechanism. He just shut down. A self-induced coma became the best option for protecting his hurting soul.

Jeff wondered if this was what his grandpa felt like back when he lost his father and others in his family. "Grandpa made a choice," Jeff murmured. "He walked away from the horror of our family's business. Maybe I should do the same."

His mind brewed in this dark mood for most of the day. He heard nothing and saw nothing. He curled up in his little cell. The only detail that broke through his mood was the lack of light coming through the small window in the cell wall. *Was it so dark outside because I feel so dark inside*, he thought? *Stop thinking, idiot.* He must have called himself an idiot a thousand times since last night.

Jeff was unaware that a giant dome had appeared over most of El Palmar. The dome's dense dark surface appeared solid, as hard as diamonds. When it appeared, it divided land, businesses, and homes. Structures along the perimeter of the wall were neither crushed nor damaged. The wall simply penetrated all objects as though they weren't there. The bottom edge hugged the ground. Family members sitting in one room of a house suddenly found themselves on one side of the wall, while others ended up on the other side. All reported attempts to get through, inside the dome, had been unsuccessful. Imagine the panic of a parent or a child being suddenly and inexplicably separated by this strange phenomenon. The police, fire and rescue personnel started receiving phone calls for help. Most officers had left the station to go assist the fearful population.

All of this had happened while Jeff sat brooding in his cell. His cell was against an outside wall on the first floor of the El Palmar Police Department. Without warning, a large section of the wall collapsed outward. When the dust settled, Jeff saw his grandpa, Delia, and a familiar large black shape.

Cooper had pulled off an old-fashioned jailbreak worthy of any movie western. He had grabbed the bars on the outside of the window and pulled. Evidently these bars were an integral part of the overall structure of the wall. Strong enough to keep any human from escaping. Keeping a Shadow out was not part of the building's original specs.

"Cooper," Jeff said, stunned? "Grandpa what are you doing?"

"Getting you out of here," his grandpa replied.

"You can't do this. It's against the law. You'll get into a lot of trouble."

"They were going to let you go anyway,' grandpa said. "But we couldn't wait. There is another kind of trouble going on... big trouble."

"Well you will have to take care of it without me," Jeff said, shaking his head. "I am through with fighting."

"We don't have time Jeffrey," Delia said. She stepped through the hole in the wall. "I lost my body and my life. We all lost Amy. Instead of sitting here feeling sorry for yourself, come help me get vengeance."

"Asuri is already dead."

"But not the Shadow witch who sent Asura and Asuri into our school. Not the Shadow who ordered Asura to find and capture Sam at any cost. Not the Shadow who ordered Shadow witches," she indicated her present body, "to kill me and four other girls. So, get up, Jeffrey. There will be time for grief after this is over."

"But..."

She grabbed him and dragged him out of the cell. "Come on, kiddo. Let's go. We need you to be back in the game."

Grandpa Maeda handed Jeff his katana. "You will need this."

"How did you get this? The police had it locked up."

"That was why they were going to let you go," grandpa said with a smile. "Your katana was not the murder weapon."

"Grandpa, I don't know if I can do this."

Grandpa grabbed Jeff by the shoulders. "Listen to me, my favorite grandson. Years ago, I ran away from what I feared. I turned away from my family hoping to find a life of peace and safety. But look what happened. It seems I ran right into the cradle of everything but peace and safety. I was wrong to think I could run away from destiny. Don't make the same mistake I made. This is our destiny. It is in our blood. We are warriors. It is time we both started acting like it."

******

When Sam walked through the door, they all breathed a sigh of relief. They were all home safe for now. But a decision about the future had to be made. The arrival of this new alien race had turned their lives upside down. This was why so many different cultures referred to these creatures as demons, monsters, or sometimes vengeful gods. The creatures were unpredictable and almost always out to destroy everything that was good.

"What should we do, Bill," Sarah asked?

"What do you want to do?" Bill directed this question to everyone present. "Do we stay and hope this invasion will fail like the last one, or do we run."

That surprised Bobby, "Run? Run where?

"Yeah," Sam said. "Where could we go, except maybe a deserted island or something?"

"Our lives are here. We haven't even graduated from high school, for heaven sakes," Bobby complained.

"And what about our friends," Sam said, fighting the tears back? "What happens to them?" The past few hours had been full of tears and grief. "Amy is dead. Delia is dead, her soul alive in the body of a Shadow. Jeff is in jail facing charges. All of this is because of me, the human witch. But, if I remember correctly, didn't they burn witches in this world. So, what future do we have?"

"Honey," her mom said. "None of this is your fault. We don't know where the current situation will lead. Maybe it will end soon and our lives will go back to normal."

"Whatever the case," Bill said. "If this gets worse, we need to be ready to leave at a moment's notice. I am sorry, but we must consider the worst-case scenario. Domes like the one above us could pop up all over the world, leaving nowhere safe."

Everyone was quiet, soberly considering the options. Bobby broke the silence.

"Then I say we fight. If we want to bring this to an end... then, just like two years ago, we fight with all we've got."

"You may be right," Bobby's dad said. "But there has to be an escape plan. Over the last two years I have searched for possible escape routes. There are at least three separate worlds we need to consider."

"Worlds," Sam asked?

"The problem is," Rich said, "there has been no time to prepare a landing sight. Our move to this world was calculated. We had identities and money. We don't have time to set up new lives elsewhere?"

"Wait," Sam said. "Are you saying we may need to leave this world? What about our friends? Do we just leave them behind? Abandon them to these monsters?"

"Sam honey," Rich replied. "I don't know what to tell you. We may have no other choice."

"Sam," Bobby added. His gut wrenched because of what he was about to say. "From what I sense going on out there, this is about to get very ugly, very fast. We may have no choice.

Chapter 41

The Royal Mother

"Kneel to the Royal Mother," Lord General Balor ordered.

The Fomorians, the Shadows and Percy, possibly the only human left alive under the dome, knelt with heads down. The Royal Mother lifted up through the rift and rose up majestically out of the IDR chamber building.

Percy couldn't resist taking a look. He had to watch this historical moment. When Percy saw her, his mouth dropped open. She embodied the meaning of magnificent, exquisite, even angelic. She was even taller than the Lord General Balor. Her flowing silken robes shimmered of pastel rainbow gently swirled with energy. Her face was long and thin with two large pearlescent eyes and a delicate nose and mouth. Her skin was pure white like the other Fomorians, but without the blue tattoos of her soldiers. Of course, as the Royal Mother, she wore a spiked crown on her head. This moment justified his betrayal of the human race. He was in heaven, or at least he thought until he felt the strong hand shove his head to the ground with a painful thud.

"Do not look at the Royal Mother, low one," the soldier ordered. "You are here only because the Shadow Overseer protects you."

Stars flashed in his closed eyes as the pain of his impact with the ground rushed from forehead to spine. Fortunately, he had chosen a grassy area to kneel.

The Royal Mother spoke, "Which is High Overseer Shadow Strong?"

the Lord stood and beckoned Shadow Strong to rise. "This is her."

"Show me this world you have discovered," the Royal Mother ordered in a pleasant, melodic voice. Shadow quickly conjured the holographic Earth for her. The Overseer spread her arms and the globe grew in size in front of the Fomorian Royal Mother. "This is it," the Royal Mother asked?

"Yes, my Royal Mother. All we have learned over the last two years is in this image."

"The beings of this world are bound to only this one orb?"

"Yes, my Royal Mother."

"Good," the Royal Mother responded. She raised her hand and touched the image of the Earth with her index finger. The fingertip absorbed the image. The Royal Mother then lifted upward to the highest point of the dome. An opening appeared which allowed her to move up into the outside world. She paused. After taking a 360-degree view, the Royal Mother turned to face the Pacific Ocean. Spreading her arms, the image of the Earth reappeared in front of her. Then she placed her palm on the sphere. At the speed of light, the sphere spread to fill the entire horizon. An immediate flash of light filled the horizon all around her, resulting in a full scan of the Earth. The Royal Mother closed her hands together with a clap. The light returned to her and formed an updated image of the Earth.

******

The fighter planes darted toward the creature as soon as it appeared at the top of the dome. The military had responded quickly this time. Lines of tracer rounds shot through the air as well as the fire trail of missiles. Massive explosions engulfed the alien figure, but when the fire and smoke cleared, the Royal Mother remained unmoved and unharmed. Guided cruise missiles traced over the coastal hills toward the target. The being and the dome were hit hard again. The explosions rained down fire on the area surrounding the dome. Fire scorched the landscape. Everything around the dome was on fire. The military gave no warning of the incoming attack. Just as it had done two years previous. People outside the dome fled in fear. Many saw the unusual being emerging from the dome. This time no one believed this was another act of terrorism. These beings were extraterrestrials.

When the fire and smoke dissipated, the Royal Mother still floated above the undamaged dome. Witnesses from far to the north and the south saw the fireworks. Those close enough to see, watched the Royal Mother as she raised her hands above her head. A spiraling line of light left her hands, encircling her and then the dome. The light grew brighter and split into several fiery lines. Each line of fire rocketed away toward an identified target. The trails of fire hit the jet fighters like missiles. The planes went down fast.

In this moment between attacks, the Royal Mother raised her hands again. A spiraling line of fiery light appeared and split into many more trails of fire, but this time they flew up and away in all directions. The new targets included major cities, national capitals and major military bases on every continent. Countries had no warning of the incoming attack. No technology know to humans could have detected the incoming missiles of fire. Upon impact, each explosion opened a new rift. Over each point of impact, a new dome formed. These domes protected the rifts, as did the first one in El Palmar. At this stage of the attack, all domed rifts would remain unchanged. Worldwide war loomed as world governments reacted. The armed forces of Russia, China, Europe and the United States sat at the highest alert.

Thankfully, no one could determine the source of the attack. The Fomorians had nearly tricked the humans into starting a devastating nuclear war.

The Royal Mother retreated unharmed, unfazed by the human attack. Still she was pleased that these humans had shown aggression so quickly. Maybe this world would put up reasonable resistance. Not a huge challenge for the Fomorians, but more than the usual. It had been a long time since an enemy had fought with any strength or courage. Strong warriors made stronger slaves.

She floated back to the rift. "Begin," the Royal Mother declared. The El Palmar rift spewed out soldiers led by the magically leashed crainn like angry fire ants defending their colony.

The black dome began to expand. Within minutes it encompassed the entire city, the residents taken by complete surprise. No matter what the police, fire and rescue tried, the dome now trapped everything and everyone on the inside. The U.S. Air Force attacked the outside of the dome with a vengeance, but to no avail.

Chapter 42

Safe Room

With the dark dome now engulfing the city and much of the surrounding area, the Williams and Thomas families now had a full-fledged emergency. From what they had learned so far, this new enemy, the Fomorians, were ancient beings with, if not the power of ancient mythical gods, they had the arrogance. The alliance between the Shadows witches and the Fomorians made the situation far more dangerous.

The two families agreed they only had three options at this point. First, hunker down in the safe room shelter and wait for conditions above ground to improve. Second, go out and fight. Third, leave the planet in search of a safer place. This third option would be a one-way trip. None of these options felt like a happy solution.

They retreated to the safe room that lay beneath the hydrangeas in their backyards. The safe room provided safety, plus room for extended living and sleeping. They had stored enough water and food for the two families to live up to six months. Still, this place was no ordinary underground shelter. It was an interdimensional transport. If it came to that, they had a way out. Unfortunately, this situation required them to jump to a new world blind. The ship could send them across multiple universes to multiple possible worlds. The problem was, would there be a place to land.

The final decision was made. They would leave. Bill and Rich prepared the transporter while everyone else finished preparations for travel which included health screenings and vaccinations for each of them. Not knowing the actual conditions at the end site, this had to be done. Something as simple as a common cold could be deadly to them, or to the population on the new world.

Finally, they were ready. They each strapped on their wrist mounted cloaking devices. Then strapped into seats located around the perimeter of the saucer-like ship. Poor Kevin had this whole shocking news thrown at him without time to process it, let alone prepare the twelve-year-old for the change that was coming. He was terrified and, understandably, angry.

Bill started giving instructions. "Okay everyone, check your cloaking shields. They should all be green.

They all replied, except for the bewildered Kevin. His mother sat next to Kevin, she replied for him.

"When we arrive at the landing site we may need to transport immediately to a second location, so keep your seat belts buckled until I give the word." Bill paused. He struggled to keep calm with all the adrenaline coursing through his veins. "I'm sorry. I really am. I love you all." Then he said quietly, "Let's go."

"I can't go," Bobby declared abruptly.

"Bobby, we..."

"No. I am sorry dad, but this is not right," he said. He had been brooding about it all day long. With the invasion underway, his senses were on high alert. The more he thought about it the more knew that this was not what they were supposed to do. This was his parents' protocol in case of this kind of emergency, not his. Maybe running away made sense when he and Sam were kids, before their powers awakened, but now it felt like they were running from their obligation and duty. "If we are just going to turn and run every time there is danger, it seems like we are wasting our gifts. Even danger of this magnitude needs to be faced."

"Bobby's right. I'm not going either," Sam said. "We have a way to escape, but our friends do not. Seven billion other people do not have a way to escape."

"We can't run and leave Cooper, Jeff, Grandpa, and all our friends to fight alone," Bobby pleaded. "This feels wrong."

Their parents sat quietly. Bobby was right about this.

Bill finally spoke, "So then... we stay and fight."

Sarah said, "For our friends."

Anne added, 'For our home."

"For everyone," Rich said.

Without saying another word, they all released their seat belts.

Chapter 43

Gathering the Troops

Cooper returned to the captured Shadow fortress with Delia, Mr. Maeda, and Jeff. Sam had gone home. Cooper's little army prepared as best they could for the coming battle. When he decided to return to Earth, Cooper expected to encounter and mop up the few remaining Shadow troublemakers. But then nothing had gone the way he expected.

Cooper thought out to his comrades. "We came here to put an end to the conflict between Shadows and humans. But Shadow Strong has escalated the conflict. By allying herself with non-Shadows she has endangered this world, Tiarnas as well. That is the crime for which she will die. We know nothing about this new enemy, but we have felt their power. It is..." What should he say? Underplaying this threat would do no good, but neither would an honest, frightening assessment. "Honestly, these Fomorians' power terrifies me," he thought. "I must stand with my human friends and fight to defeat this new enemy, but I cannot ask you to do the same."

One of his warrior witches pointed out, "Is the enemy the humans' enemy, or are they our enemy as well?"

Cooper's forever loyal Priestess, replied, "By allying herself with another species, the High Overseer has become a traitor to her kind. We must do what it takes to undo the damage she has done. Shadow Strong is dangerous to our new republic because she desires to rule over us. I am convinced that, once she is done with the humans, she will turn on Tiarnas."

"I agree," thought another warrior witch. "We fight now, here on Earth, or we fight later on Tiarnas."

The Priestess agreed. "The fate of the Shadow Republic lies in our hands."

"Then we fight," thought all the witches at once.

"Thank you. All of you," Cooper thought. "I am honored by your support. Before he passed away my father blessed me. In that blessing he told me his power was now my power. His magic is now my magic. I do not know if it is as simple as that."

"The magic is yours to use," the Priestess told him. "But you but must have faith in your magic. Imagine what you wish to accomplish, whether it is to command the elements, form a shield of protection, heal sickness and wounds, or even transform space and time, by your faith it will be as you wish. There are infinite possibilities."

"All I have to do is believe in it?"

"Always say to yourself, I desire this according to my faith."

"According to my faith."

"That is right. You must truly believe in the power given you. You must have faith that your father's gift is real. Only then will the magic work. Master," the Priestess added softly. "Your father was a miraculous being. He could perform miracles. Now you can perform miracles."

"I can call for anything I wish?"

"There are limitations. The laws of nature can be controlled and manipulated, but not altered." The Priestess explained. "You cannot change the black rock of Tiarnas to gold. That is impossible. The elements must be in harmony. You can, however, change a certain black rock found on Tiarnas into diamonds. That is because the two are related by possibilities. Other limitations are self-imposed, such as right and wrong, justice and mercy."

"*I see,*" Cooper said in deep wonder and thought.

"One more thing. All actions, whether for good or evil, have a reaction. Sometimes the reaction presents you with unintended results. You must live with those results."

Cooper wondered about her words. "I understand how a bad decision would have consequences, but why be concerned about a good decision?"

"I am afraid you will have to discover that for yourself, Master," the Priestess said. "You also have the ability to endow power to others, or strengthen the powers someone already has."

"Good. I want to bless my friends like my father blessed me. I want to bless you all."

"The possibility of magic exists in all living beings, we do not know to what extent it will affect others, but that is a wonderful idea, Master. Remember, the power you give can be used for good or for evil. Choose who you endow with power wisely. Your best intentions does not limit the free choice of the recipient of your blessing. Remember, your father's misguided trust in the Shadows led to a thousand years of imprisonment."

"*I see,*" Cooper thought. He trusted his human friends with his life, but they were still growing. The Humans he had thus far encountered had it within them to be good or evil, in fact very evil. This new adversary would be far more dangerous than Shadows like Broken Fang and Fire Claws. They all needed to be stronger, so he would give them strength.

Cooper turned to the humans, Jeff, his parents, and his grandpa. Grandpa had rescued his daughter and son-in-law earlier that day. "We need Sam and Bobby," Cooper vocalized.

Jeff pulled out his Phone. Thankfully, the phone service actually worked inside the dome. He speed dialed Bobby.

******

Jeff's phone call gave Bobby, Sam and their parents a more honorable path to follow. Jeff told them about the fortress and the magic shield that protected it. There was a safe place to gather and come up with a plan, so they decided to join Cooper and Jeff as soon as possible. The new enemy had probably spread throughout the dome by now. Fortunately, each of them had a cloaking device. As long as they stayed together, getting to the fortress would be relatively simple. At least, they hoped so.

Bill explained, "When we get there, we will need to turn off our cloaking devices long enough to call Jeff and let him know we have arrived. They will need to shut down the shield momentarily in order for us to get inside. This will leave us and them vulnerable to attack. So, when we arrive, we need to move fast. Be ready for anything."

Is everyone ready," Rich asked? They all nodded. "Then let's go." He activated the cloaking devices.

Rich and Anne took the lead with Kevin in tow, followed by Bill and Sarah. Sam remained at Bobby's side all the way to their destination. Bobby carried his new and improved staff, the only physical weapon with the group. Of course, Sam's weapons were far more powerful. With cautious stealth, it took a little over an hour before they arrived at the fortress.

On the street directly in front of the fortress building, the group reappeared. Bobby phoned Jeff immediately.

"We are here," Bobby said. "How do we get in?"

'The parking garage entrance," Jeff said. "Hurry, you've got company."

"What?"

"Run, guys," Jeff yelled into the phone.

Evidently the magical shielding on the fortress may as well have been a giant neon sign saying, the enemy is in here. Several Fomorian warriors, attracted to the magic, had hid themselves nearby. When the seven humans appeared, the leashed *crainn* creatures came out of hiding and ran towards the humans. The *crainn* encircled them like wolves.

"Everyone down," Sam yelled as she produced a blade of fire. To Sam's amazement the new gloves produced a precise blade extending from her outstretched fingers. The blade had a slight arc and a visible cutting edge. It looked solid and glistened with the extreme heat of blue and white flames. Sam swept the blade 180 degrees, quickly killing three of the beasts. Bobby, who stood at her back, blasted two more with the beam weapon in his staff. Fortunately for the members of the two families, seven Shadow witches appeared next to them and flew them into the parking garage to safety. The shield was restored.

They had a happy but short reunion. Sam's and Bobby's parents were pleased to see that everyone was alright. Martin and Shelly Sasaki looked bewildered and were probably in shock at the revelations the day had brought. Evidently, Grandpa with Delia's help retrieved the Sasakis from their home. It hadn't been easy. Mrs. Sasaki had been quite upset to find out her son had broken out of jail, and that her father had been behind the escape. No talk of monsters and demons seem to make any difference until Delia ended the lecture by transforming into her Shadow form and then back again. Mrs. Sasaki screamed but said nothing more afterward.

As soon as Jeff saw his parents, he hugged them as hard as he could. He didn't want to let them go. His grief for Amy's death came flowing over in the form of tears. Jeff sobbed. "I am glad you are... safe." Jeff said, trying to rein in the tears.

Delia watched this scene in anguish. In her new Shadow body form, she didn't seem capable of crying, at least she couldn't make it cry. But as Delia, she wept. She too had lost Amy. At that moment, she needed her mom more than anything else. Delia needed to hug her mom the way Jeff hugged his. But what would her mom think when she saw what Delia had become.

All of Delia's friends had their families with them now. Earlier Jeff asked Delia if she wanted to get her mom as well.

"I want her safe," she had said. "But look at me. I'm a monster."

"What happened to you was terrible," Jeff pleaded. "But you're not a monster. The body you control is an alien species, the same species as these Shadow demons who are helping us now. If they are able to choose good over evil, then they are not monsters. Besides, you can still look like yourself, your mom will never know. Unless you want to tell her."

She shook her head. "She wouldn't understand. How do I explain what happened to Amy... my part in it? She will hate me?"

"She's your mom. She loves you no matter what."

Delia shook her head again in protest. "Delia is dead. I am a living ghost. She will be afraid of me. I couldn't bear that. I want her safe, but the reality of this new world will be more than she can stand. It is better if she thinks I am dead." In her heart though, Delia didn't believe what she said. She did want to see her mom at least one more time. Delia came back to the moment. She looked around. Everyone had a purpose, a goal. She needed to get her act together.

A voice in Delia's head said, *"I am sorry."*

"What," Delia asked?

The Shadow voice said, "I was forced to take your body." I am, or was, a warrior. I had to follow orders."

"You had to follow orders? So many humans have used that same excuse after murdering millions of innocents."

"I'm not a murderer. I am a warrior. I hate what they made me do. You don't know what it is like in my world, Tiarnas. There is no such thing as free will on Tiarnas. I would have been killed if I hadn't done what I was told."

"What gives you the right to decide your life was more valuable than mine?"

"That's not what I mean. I didn't understand what human life was like, to have choices," the Shadow voice said. "You value the life of others. Shadows... I... have never..."

"Well now you know. I am in control now," Delia asserted her will.

"I... I understand," the Shadow said. "I will go now... if that alright with you."

"Why should I care whether you come or go," Delia seethed in anger. She hid her face away from the others, shaking with anger, with fear and with sorrow. Sam saw her distress. She left Bobby's side and went to Delia. The two girls looked at each other and then embraced. Delia's new, glowing green eyes began to shed tears.

Copper spoke vocally, "Share what you know... Please."

Rich told them about the Shadow he knew as Kylie Harrisford and how she had gained control of the rift chamber. How one of his colleagues had betrayed his own kind. Then he told them about the ancient book that gave them the addresses to other worlds and how with that book, the Shadow had opened a rift to the Fomorian world.

"Where is the book," Cooper vocalized?

"I assume it is still at the Center," Rich replied.

"We need a book," Cooper insisted. "We destroy book."

Bill and Rich looked at each other. "That's a tall order," Rich said.

"Book must be destroyed," he insisted. "Protect your world and mine."

"I agree," Bill said. "Cooper, if you can get us there alive, Rich and I can get us into the center quietly."

Cooper was worried about their open rupture to Tiarnas. Was it vulnerable? Magic could hide the rupture, but probably not for long. If he closed it and bound it. They would have no means of escape from this world. He and his Shadow Priestess discussed the situation at length. With his new power, Cooper could close the rupture, but it needed to be bound from the other side by someone else. There wasn't a lot of time. The Shadow Republic needed to be warned and made ready in case they failed. Shadow Strong had to be stopped. That was the only option. Closing the rupture would have to wait until they had the book and traitor witch was dead.

Cooper insisted that the Priestess and four warrior witches stay in the fortress with the humans who were unable to fight.

The Priestess protested. "I will never leave your side, dear Master. I have given my life to serve you. If you die, I will die too."

The three mothers also protested, worried about their children, but Cooper insisted. "Warriors need to fight with clear minds. They cannot worry about you and fight well." Cooper glanced at the Priestess who had indeed followed him at his side since his father's death. He smiled at her tenderly. *"Do you understand,"* he asked the Priestess in thought.

"She looked down. *"Yes, Master."*

"What about me," Martin Sasaki asked? "I may not be a soldier but surely there is something I can do to help. It doesn't feel right staying here out of harm's way while my son and my father-in-law fight those monsters."

Grandpa understood how his son-in-law felt. "I suggest that you come with me. We'll avoid the big guys together."

"But what should we do," Mr. Sasaki asked. "I have no training, and you are, forgive me father, a bit old to be a hero?"

"Excuse me?" Grandpa said annoyed. "I can still kick your butt."

"Father, you always could kick my butt. I'm a lousy fighter. I'm even afraid of your daughter. But are you able to kick those monsters' butts? They are pretty damn big."

Grandpa Maeda spoke quietly to his son-in-law, "Well, we are not going to stand around doing nothing while others risk their lives."

"Listen," Martin said. "I have an idea. These tunnels, where do they go? What are they for?"

"I assume they must be escape routes"

"So why don't you and I find out," Martin suggested? "Maybe there is a way to go under the dome wall."

Cooper smiled and nodded in agreement. "Good idea. Explore tunnels." It was settled.

Before they departed, Cooper wanted to level the battlefield for the humans. One by one he blessed them after the manner of his father. To Jeff, he gave the power to use magic according to his own will and faith. To Bobby and Sam, he blessed them that their magic would fully mature with power and purpose. To Bill, Rich, Martin and Grandpa, he gave the power to protect with magical shields.

Then Cooper came to Delia. "I can make Shadow witch go away," he told her "You want me to?"

Delia's first thought was to say yes, but then she remembered what she had said to the Shadow earlier. *What gives you the right to decide your life is more valuable than mine?* "No," she said. "The two of us will just have to work this out... somehow."

The Shadow voice said, *"Are you sure?"*

"Yes... I guess... I am sure."

"But..."

"It is a fact of life for both of us."

"Thank you, Delia."

"By the way," Delia asked, "do you have a name?"

"Shadow Child," she replied.

"I will call you Child, then."

"I like that." Then to Cooper, Child thought, *"Please give us the strength to work together with courage and harmony."*. Cooper nodded. He laid his hand on Delia/Child's head and gave them what they needed.

Now they were ready to go on the offensive. Cooper's little army of seven witch warriors, seven humans and one-half human Shadow left through the worried tears of those left behind. He had fought with fewer than this at times and had come out on top. So why not again?

Chapter 44

Rewards and Punishments

The Fomorian Royal Mother stood atop Percy McLeod's building, the Salmur Institute of Extraterrestrial Biological Studies. The architectural design of the building exhibited the purse holders desire to give the architect a free reign. The result bordered on an ultra-futuristic and science fiction fantasy, both above ground and below ground. Being the tallest building in the complex, it made sense to make it the Royal Mother's choice for an earthly throne. but the irony didn't escape Percy. In fact, he was thrilled by her choice.

"Thank you, Royal Mother, for honoring me," he said only to himself. The Fomorians were way too touchy about class protocol. He no longer cared what the Fomorians did. He was on his own journey into science fantasy. Finally, his driven curiosity was rewarded.

Shadow Strong knelt before the Fomorian Royal Mother.

"Overseer Shadow Strong, you have made a wise choice allying yourself with me," The Royal Mother proclaimed. "I am pleased."

"Thank you, my Royal Mother," Shadow Strong replied. "In doing so, I pledged myself and my army of witches to you. We will serve you and die doing so."

"Indeed, you may, but for now you live to serve me. I will reward you with two crainns for your defense. May your life be long with these loyal beasts at your side."

"Crainns, my Royal Mother?"

"Those slave creatures that serve my warriors, dreadfully ugly creatures but quite useful, and expendable. To own one Crainn slave is an honor. To own two means you are of the highest warrior class."

"I am deeply honored, my Royal Mother. I shall use them well."

"Crainns may look like animals, but they are somewhat intelligent and bound magically to their owner for life. Of course, that means your life or theirs. At your death they will be slaughtered and eaten in your honor."

"Again, you honor me generously. To serve you is more than enough."

The Royal Mother laughed. "You are a lovely, cunning creature, Overseer Strong. I like that. Now what do I do with this human? He is an emaciated looking being. I do not see the use of him.

"If you will indulge me, my Royal Mother. May I have a personal request?"

"Such ambition. I will hear your request, my lovely servant."

"The human is with me. I call him Percy. I desire to keep him as my slave, bound to me like a crainn for life. Can that be done?"

The Royal Mother smiled and laughed. "So, it shall be. Hold out your right arm." Shadow did as told. The Royal Mother bent over and touched the Overseer's right arm. A trail of blue light formed a blue bracelet around her wrist. Instantly three lines of blue extended from the bracelet. Two lines went through the open pathway to the Fomorian world. The third leash lashed out to Percy and wrapped around his neck.

Percy grabbed at the leash trying to free himself. "Ms. Harrisford. What is this?"

"I am High Overseer Shadow Strong. You, Percy, are my slave. From now on you will address me as such. If you wish to live, Percy my friend, you must do so as a slave."

Percy dropped to his knees and bowed his head. All he could do for the time being was to accept it and wait for a better opportunity to come his way.

He sighed, "Yes, Overseer Shadow Strong."

Out of the rift two crainn crept. They climbed to the roof and leapt across to where their new master knelt. "Actually," the Overseer laughed. "I think they are quite adorable, my Royal Mother." She walked to the edge of the building and looked down.

"Please, Overseer Shadow Strong," Percy groveled from behind her. "This blue rope, or whatever it is, hurts. Remove it… Please."

The Royal Mother said to Overseer Strong, "If he resist in any way it will choke the life out of him."

"That would be a shame Percy," Shadow said. "We have worlds to explore together. You behave and everything will go well for you."

Chapter 45

Blessings

Bobby clenched his fists to relieve the tingling numbness in his hands. What had Cooper done to him? After Cooper laid his hand on Bobby's head, a strange feeling slowly crept through him. First his head started to throb, then his chest swelled and his heartbeat accelerated to an unnerving rate. Now he felt all pins and needles everywhere. But soon his headache subsided and the pins and needles faded away. He now felt more alive than he had ever been. Everything and everyone alerted his senses. Their thoughts came to him in fragments, which made their feelings, motives, and desires much clearer. Later, he began to see things that had previously been invisible to him. Faint but visible strings connected people together. Strings led from a person to family members and friends. Some strings were thick, while others were so thin he could barely see them. Bobby assumed the thickness of the strings probably indicated the strength of the connection between individuals. As he expected the line between him and Sam was thick and strong. Bobby saw a faint line forming between Jeff and Delia. A new bond had formed because of the shared loss of Amy. Of course, there were many other lines connecting everyone together. Cooper's lines connected to Sam, but also to the Shadow witches present. Thick lines connected them together. They were allies with a common goal. The thickest line among the Shadows connected the Priestess to Cooper. It rivaled Bobby's and Sam's connection. A lot must have happened in Cooper's world over the last two years.

Bobby wasn't the only one to feel these odd changes. Sam felt a euphoric new power coursing through her body. It burned inside her and made her heart pound. Nerves from head to toe pulsed, not with pain, but with a kind of pleasure. The adrenaline and every other pleasure producing glands in her body pumped chemicals through her system. It left her flushed, lightheaded, and a little amorous. Every time Bobby got near her, her body heat spiked.

"Are you alright," Bobby asked her? "Your face is flushed. It is quite red right now."

"Yes, I'm fine. But when you come near me, I get... excited. You know what I mean?" she said with a sheepish grin.

"Oh," he said, reading her mind. "I see. Is this what people mean when they use the word, *hot*? Cooper's gift is a little unexpected." These emotions emboldened her passions. She tried not to think about her feelings, but honestly, she couldn't help it. The constant flood of hormones were so... wow-ish.

"Good grief," she whispered to Bobby. "You're so freaking adorable, I want..." She didn't finish that thought. It was a new-found passion. Sam felt like she could do anything. The surge of confidence astounded her.

When Cooper removed his hand from Jeff's head, the boy suddenly saw the world for what it was. A world full of energy and life. He saw it in everything, even inanimate objects. Emotional energy flowed from the people and the Shadows as well. That energy vibrated continually from one person to another. To his surprise, energy had color, smell, taste, and sound. He felt the waves as the energy blew past him like the air on a windy day. There was a sense of magic about it. That too Jeff could both see and feel. While training back in Japan, he had felt a special quality in his instructors, especially Master Maeda and he had always felt something special in his grandpa. It felt like something more than just respect. Then a thought hit him smack to the face. What he had sensed was their magic. Without any doubt, magic existed and he knew how to use it. He remembered Master Maeda telling him that, when he finally understood the true nature of this world, he would be able to know and practice magic. This is what the Master meant.

Delia and Child were now at peace with each other in spite of the schizophrenic nature of two minds in one body. The male Shadow, the one Sam called Cooper, had done this for them and they were both grateful. Actually, the way the Shadow witches thought of his name was Ku Por. The two separate words had a greater meaning to them. Delia knew she would struggle with this Shadow existence for a long time. She was a strong-willed girl, but this was a staggering new reality. A fearful reality that caused her to cry herself to sleep at night. Child seem to understand, or at least tried to understand. Maybe together they both would get through this symbiotic nightmare.

Grandpa Maeda had been watching Delia all day and decided to meet her. "I suspect this situation is harder for you than for the rest of us. I know you have lost so much but please know you are not alone. Sam, Bobby and Jeff, they all love you. Because of that, I will love you too. Besides, I have always wanted a granddaughter. From now on you are part of my family." He hugged her. At first, she tensed her body, but grandpa didn't let go. Then she started to cry. "I know," Grandpa said, patting her back gently. "I know."

Chapter 46

The Mission Begins

Although it was only midday outside the dome, the magical shield blocked much of the sun's light. In addition, the shield had severed all above ground power lines, disabling the lights on the streets, in houses and local businesses. The sun looked like a dim spotlight hanging directly over their heads. A dim spotlight lighting their world.

Cooper and the Shadow witches took the lead. The cloaked humans followed silently behind. Even with the cloaking devices, the blue leashed crainns seemed to sense their presence. With each encounter the crainns ignored the Shadows, but they seemed to smell their unseen enemy. Two crainns didn't give up and followed the group a few yards behind them.

"Those things are following us." Bobby whispered. "Do you suppose they can see us?"

"I don't think so," his dad replied. "But they might be able to smell us."

Jeff whispered, "They are getting uncomfortably close. But you are right. I can smell us, so they probably can too.

"What do you mean you can smell us," Sam hissed."What is that supposed to mean?"

"Something Cooper did to me. I can smell things now that I couldn't before. Besides, I didn't say you stink," Jeff said. "But we do have a sorta musky smell. It's not that much different than how cats and dogs smell, just not as strong.

"So now I smell like a dog."

Ignoring Sam, he continued explaining. "Another thing I have noticed. These cloaking things on our wrist have an unusual odor. Are they magical?"

"Partly," Rich replied.

"I smell something similar coming from the Shadows... and from those things following us. Maybe that is it," Jeff said. "Maybe they can smell our magic."

"Come to think of it," Bobby said. "They do seem to be attracted by magical activity."

Bill said, "You may be onto something there. The Shadows are magical creatures after all."

Rich added, "I think the presence of our Shadow friends has them confused. Shadows are supposed to be their allies, yet they smell us among them."

"Let's stay close to Cooper," Bill concluded.

"But what happens when we split up," Sam asked. "The plan is to split up. Right?"

"This mission has three objectives," Bill reminded them. "The first is intelligence. The second objective was to find the grimoire and steal it. Objective number three is to save as many people as possible and hopefully facilitate an evacuation. If those creatures get too close, eliminate them." Of course, they all understood that the best way to save lives was to end the invasion. The enemies' rift needed to be closed. None of them knew if it was even possible to close the rift, but the grimoire might hold the answer they needed.

Cooper vocalized. "Two Shadows witches go with Sam. Others with me. Understand?" They all agreed. "Go. Be careful," Cooper said with a wave of his hand.

They were just about to separate when they heard the cries and shouts of people in obvious distress. Accompanying the distress sounds were the angry growls, bellows, and hisses of the enemy. Everyone receded back to a safe distance and watched as El Palmar residents were herded down the street. Bobby could see the strings of connection. The people huddled together in family groups, neighbors and friends. Men, women, and children clung to each other, afraid and crying for help. Many were wounded, bleeding. The herded humans did everything they could to keep away from the alien captors. The fear on everyone's face revealed the level of distress they felt. Fomorians and Shadow witches herded, prodded and pushed the prisoners. Any human who got behind faced an angry *crainn*. The beasts snarled and snapped, forcing the trailing individuals to run and catch up. The Fomorians had captured or killed almost everyone still hiding inside the dome. They intended to either keep or sell the stronger humans as slaves. Unfortunately, the infirmed and weak were an unnecessary drain on resources. The Fomorians had other plans for them. The crainns following Cooper's group left and joined the tormentors.

"These people are in serious trouble," Bobby said with a shudder. He closed his eyes and concentrated. "The thoughts coming from those demons are truly disturbing. I... I can't put it into words what I am sensing."

"There is some real dark, evil mojo going on here," Jeff added. "The colors are so disturbingly inhuman. Should we follow this caravan and see where they are taking them?"

"Do you think we can save them," Sam asked?

"We need to do something," Bobby said. "No kidding guys, this is bad. If you could see what is going on inside their minds... well... maybe it is better you can't."

Cooper closed his eyes. "Yes. Bad things will happen."

"Well I'm in. Let's do it," Delia replied.

Bobby turned to the group. "Dad, we will see you at the rift."

"Be careful, son," Bill said.

"Yes. You too Sam... all of you," Rich added.

"We will dad," Sam replied. "I love you."

The four friends ran off, before her dad could reply. Two Shadow witches followed after.

******

"All the enemy Shadow demons have left," Grampa Maeda told his daughter. "You are safe as long as you remain inside. These Shadows are our allies. They have placed a protection shield around the building. Nothing can get through."

"Shadow demons," Mrs. Sasaki said, still shaking from this horrifying event. "I still can't believe all that is happening. That you and Jeffrey knew all about things like this and never said anything to us."

"Sorry. It's the Maeda code of secrecy. Jeffrey was brought into my world by accident two years ago."

"Are you talking about the terrorist attack," Alan Sasaki asked?

Grandpa shook his head. "I still can't believe that people accepted that story without question. It wasn't terrorists. It was the Shadow demons, and a lot of people died that night. Monsters like these killed my father and my grandfather."

Alan Sasaki didn't know much about the Maeda Clan. "I thought your father died in the war."

"They did die in a war. It was a war with *yokai*. Jeffrey, his two friends, and Cooper are the real heroes from two years ago."

"Why are these Shadow demons helping us?"

"Because of Cooper. He is a great warrior and a loyal friend. It was his selfless act that stopped the demons and ended that first Shadow invasion. He saved a lot of lives. We thought we wouldn't see him again, but he came back as an even greater warrior than when he left."

"Okay," Mr. Sasaki said. "How do you want to proceed?"

Grandpa smiled and slapped his hand on his son-in-law's shoulder. "Follow me."

******

The four teenagers followed the captured humans at a safe distance. It was clear that many of the prisoners were wounded. The age of the prisoners ranged from babies to the elderly. A Shadow pushed an elderly woman and she fell down. Two Shadow witches prodded and threatened her with their staffs. The lady just looked up at the alien figures in horror, too frightened to move. A witch grabbed the woman by the arm and pulled her to her feet. The woman stumbled and fell again.

"Please," she pleaded. "I can't…"

"Grandma," a young woman in her early twenties called out. The granddaughter hurried to the old woman's aid, but a Fomorian warrior backhanded her to the ground. The warrior's leashed creature snarled savagely just inches from the elderly woman. The granddaughter screamed and covered her face. The Fomorian laughed over the accompanying human screams. At least it sounded like a laugh. The alien said something in his own language, and laughed again. Then he slowly let the blue leash slip through his hands. The *crainn* creature bit down on the old woman's arm and dragged her away. It shook its head, severing the arm. The Fomorian warriors present roared with delight. As the *crainn* took another bite, the granddaughter gagged on bile and dry heaved what was left on her stomach. Several other prisoners did the same. A small girl, holding her father's arms screamed in terror. She just kept screaming. The attack happened so fast that the father hadn't had time to turn the girl away.

"What the freaking hell," Jeff said, stunned. "And I thought the Shadows were bad." Jeff looked at Delia. "Uh... sorry. No offense."

"No argument from me," she said. "I don't know how we fight these monsters, but right now I would love to rip their heads off."

The Fomorian warrior took hold of the granddaughter by the neck and raised her off the ground. He held the terrified woman to his face and uttered in his own language, "*Shut up and keep moving. I do not wish to kill you. You are too valuable.*" The warrior let the woman fall to the ground. A couple of men tried to protest but were both hit with an unseen force that knocked them back. The next thing they knew, a Shadow witch stood over them. They struggled to their feet and backed away. The granddaughter scrambled to her feet and ran to the crowd of prisoners. No one gave further resistance.

This harsh treatment continued until they reached the destination, El Palmar High School football stadium. Terraced bleachers sloped down a hill side on one side of the stadium. On the other side of the field, the bleachers were part of a concrete structure. Tall fences surrounded the goal ends of the stadium, making it ideal for an internment camp. Several more groups of prisoners were arriving from different parts of the city. The Shadows forced hundreds of people through the stadium's main gate. Several more Shadows guarded the fenced perimeter.

"How many people do you think there are down there," Jeff asked from a vantage point on top of a nearby building.

"Maybe eight or nine hundred," Delia suggested.

"To be exact, it is nine hundred and thirty-nine," Child said inside Delia's head. "Seven hundred and seventy-two adults and one hundred and sixty-seven children."

Delia thought back, "That's pretty specific."

"I can sense each of them," Child replied. "When you get more used to your abilities, you too will sense things in such detail."

"Delia," Jeff said.

"What?"

"You went blank for a minute."

"Oh... Child says there are nine hundred and thirty-nine people down there," Delia said.

"Okay. Thanks for the update."

"Child says you are welcome."

Jeff smirked looking sideways at Delia. "Your split personality thing is crazy."

"More like a dual personality."

"Everything is too far away," Sam said. "I wish we had some binoculars?"

"No problem, I've got Child," Delia said. "She says some people look okay, at least for now. A few are pacing the perimeter of the field. Probably looking for a way out. Some are aiding the injured. The majority of the people look pretty desperate. The injured look like they won't make it without proper medical care."

"This level of cruelty... is frightening," Bobby said. "These monsters don't have any regard for life."

"They are monsters, after all," Delia said. "So, they act like monsters. Besides, from what I remember of world history, this sort of thing is not all that alien to us humans... you humans." Delia smirked.

Jeff smiled. "That was your first non-human sarcasm," he said. "Good job. Unfortunately, what you said is true."

Silence fell over them. Then Bobby said, "So, what do you guys want to do about this messed up situation?"

******

Grandpa Maeda and Alan Sasaki walked the first tunnel. It headed west on a downward slope. Eventually, they found the end. To their surprise, the tunnel ended in a pool of water. Grandpa tasted the water.

"Sea water," Grandpa said. "How clever of them."

"Why," his son-in-law asked.

"We are now under the ocean. The entrance is completely hidden. Very stealthy."

Alan nodded in understanding. "We should tell someone about this."

"We will. Let's head back and check out the other tunnel. See where it goes."

The two men returned to the main room and followed the second tunnel. Soon they came to a fork. The main tunnel turned and headed due east on an upward slope. The second led north.

"Which way," Alan asked?

"Let's go north,"

"Due east will no doubt lead into the foothills," Grandpa replied. "The northbound tunnel probably runs parallel to the coastline. Maybe this way leads out of the tunnel. So, let's go north."

Alan nodded and followed his father-in-law obediently. The tunnel curved gradually back toward the coast. Eventually, they saw natural light. The orange glow of the setting sun turned the tunnel walls to gold. That meant they were now outside of the enemy's defensive dome. The tunnel took a hard left toward the sun, leaving the opening just out of sight. Grandpa reached out and stopped Alan from turning the corner. It wasn't shadows being cast per say, but fuzzy moving shades of filtered light. Holding his son-in-law back, grandpa inched closer for a clear view of the entrance. His old eye hadn't deceived him. Two Shadow witches guarded the entrance. He quietly slipped back out of sight.

Grandpa raised two fingers, then pointed toward the entrance. "Shadows," he mouthed.

Alan's eyes widened in fear. The whole idea of a demon invasion left him stupefied. He had no idea what to expect if the guards found out they were there, or how to fight them. Hoping his father-in-law would retreat to get help, Alan started to back away. But, the old man had turned to sneak back toward the entrance instead. Not only was his father-in-law not making a wise retreat, he had drawn his katana. Aghast, Alan hissed at his father-in-law. Grandpa turned with a glare and put his finger to his mouth.

Alan rushed toward grandpa. He would insist that they withdraw immediately. He was too late. Grandpa Maeda slipped around the corner and ran toward the two unsuspecting guards. The stunned son-in-law threw his back against the wall trying to think, which wasn't easy with all the sweating and shaking he was experiencing. He gradually moved close, hugging the wall. Through salt burned eyes from sweat that dripped off his forehead, he saw the old man standing over two dead demons.

Grandpa Maeda turned to see his shaking relative. Grandpa sheathed his katana and put his hands on his hips. "Have a little faith in me," he exclaimed. Alan signed in relief. "Come on," grandpa said. Something tells me we better head back now. This is outside the demons' dome. That means there is a way to penetrate their defenses." He turned and headed back.

The Shadow witch appeared out of nowhere and hit the old man with ferocity. Grandpa flew several feet back into the tunnel before he tumbled into the hard wall. The demon was focused on the grandpa and hadn't yet noticed the other human clinging to the opposite wall. Alan froze in a state of pure panic. This had to be the moment he would die. Then the Shadow witch's head exploded.

******

Sam and Bobby crouched down behind a raised planter at the opposite end of the field. Planters such as this one surrounded the stadium. Every other planter had either flowers or trees planted. The two Shadow witches flew overhead. At the far goal, they could see Delia, as Child, walked toward the main gate with Jeff posing as a prisoner. Jeff's sword now hung around Delia's waist. At the gate she pushed Jeff forward hard enough to make him stumble and fall.

"*I have a prisoner,*" she thought to the other Shadows present.

"*Bring him here,*" thought a Shadow witch that acted as though she were in charge. Child grabbed Jeff by the arm before he could get to his feet and dragged him over to the Shadow leader, who in turn dragged him down into the football field. Child followed. She felt the magical barrier as they walked through it.

"Is this all the humans," Child asked. "Surely there are more than this."

"This is only one compound," the leader thought. "Five more prisons exist inside the dome. The Fomorians say that, as the dome grows, they will create even more."

Child grunted "We are noble warrior witches. Why are we guarding prisoners? Where is the glory in this?"

"Careful of your thoughts, witch," the Shadow chidded. "The High Overseer has made a solemn pact with the Fomorians. They give the orders now."

"I do not like this," Child sneered. "And I do not like them."

The leader Shadow grabbed Child by the arm and pulled her close. "Silence you fool. the Fomorians can hear our thoughts. The Overseer has already executed three of our sisters for such thoughts."

"Executed," Child said stunned. "This is far worse than what it was like on Tiarnas. From gladiators to mere servants of new masters. At least as gladiators we had status."

"*Enough,*" demanded the leader. "*Not another thought or I will kill you where you stand.*" Other witches gazed nervously at the two engaged witches.

Child sensed that the leader's outburst had more to do with fear than loyalty to duty. *"You will get us all killed. All we can do is wait until this is over and hope the High Overseer can protect us from the Fomorians."*

Child decided to end her thoughts. Inside Delia shuddered. From the moment Child used the soul eater spell on her, she had lived in fear. But this new revelation made her afraid on a level she never thought possible. She thought of her mother whom she hoped was still hiding at home. She needed to go home and check on her mom as soon as she could.

"There are still a lot of humans hiding," the leader said, calming down. "The Fomorians are only interested in the healthiest prisoners. They are allowing us to feed on the weak, sick, or old. For now, we are safe. At least we have food."

This revelation shocked Delia. Child walked away, transforming back into Delia. The other Shadows needed to see both her forms. It gave her deception credibility. Delia studied the people as she walked. Jeff had already blended into the crowd. They met on the far side of the field where Bobby and Sam hid. Jeff and Delia leaned against the fence with their backs to their two comrades.

"What are the chances of anyone surviving a jailbreak," Bobby whispered?

Jeff shook his head. "Honestly, not good at all. I ran into a couple of the cops that had arrested me. Believe it or not, they were actually relieved I had gotten out of jail. They might be able to help people get moving. The healthiest folks might stand a chance. The rest... I don't know."

Child had felt the new power surge when Shadow Cooper had blessed them. It gave her extra confidence. Child thought to Delia, *"These humans are better off staying here. Even if they escape, where will they go. They will get captured again, or killed."*

Delia said, "Child thinks these people will be safer staying here for now. At least here, they are off the battlefield."

"They might be safer now, but what will happen later, when those Shadows get hungry," Sam asked?

Delia looked frustrated. "I hate to say it, but maybe we should wait until we get some backup before we try something this big?"

"So, we come back later," Bobby said?

Delia nodded. Then Jeff, Sam, and Bobby nodded.

"I'll talk to those cops and let them know what's up," Jeff said. "So, they can get ready."

I'll meet you at the gate," Delia said. She transformed back into Child as she walked away. The people gave her a wide path as she approached. At the same time, Jeff headed back through the crowd to find someone willing to lead these people to safety.

Bobby and Sam were about to leave for the planned rendezvous site when a voice called out, "Bobby Williams? What are you doing?"

He and Sam turned to see his first hour teacher. "Mrs. Hanson," Bobby replied?

Mrs. Hansen stared at Bobby. "Are you Bobby? How do I know you aren't one of them?"

"Them," Sam asked?

"Those things," Mrs. Hanson said, backing away. Three girls from the high school hurried up to the teacher. They huddled behind her. "They can look like people we know, but they aren't."

"Mrs. Hansen," Bobby said. "All we can tell you is that we are who we say we are. We're on your side."

"You need to get out of sight before the creatures find you," Mrs. Hanson said.

"We are trying to get everyone out of here," Sam said.

"We need to go get help first," Bobby said. "I'm sorry, but you will have to stay here until we come back."

"I don't want to stay here," one of the girls spoke up. "I want to go home."

"You haven't been home? Have you talked to your parents yet?"

"No. None of us have. We were at school with Mrs. Hanson when we were captured and brought here."

"It is really bad out here," Sam said. "I am afraid there is no way to know what has happened to your parents. Just stay put for now. We will come back."

"We promise." Bobby said in agreement.

A stream of fire came from above them and hit the fence where Bobby and Sam stood. They jumped back just in time and avoided the strike. Bobby lifted his staff and shifted into a defensive position. To Mrs. Hanson and the girls, he appeared to point the glowing end of the staff at them. Bobby raised his weapon letting a bolt of light exit the end. The weapon blasted a brilliant white light past the attacking Shadow. Sam followed with her own attack, hitting the Shadow and dusting her into oblivion.

Mrs. Hanson and the three girls screamed. "How... how... how did... you do that," the shaking Mrs. Hanson asked?

"No time to explain," Sam said. "We have to go."

"Your staff thing," one of the girls said. "Was that like a laser or something?"

"Something like that," Bobby said, not wanting to explain.

"Do you even know how to use that thing, young man," Mrs. Hansen asked? "Why do you own such a dangerous weapon? Something like that should be illegal. Someone could get seriously hurt, or worse."

"My dad made it for him," Sam told her. "An early birthday presents."

"What kind of parent would create such a thing and give it to a child?" Mrs. Hansen huffed in disgust. "When this is over I shall have to talk with both your parents."

Sam and Bobby looked at each other in disbelief. "You're kidding right," Bobby said.

"Mrs. Hansen, these dangerous weapons will save your life. I am a lethal weapon all by myself. In fact, I'm a witch." Sam held out her hand and a ball of fire appeared.

The girls gasped. One asked, "A witch? Really?"

"That is so cool," said another.

"This is a war," Mrs. Hanson. "Dangerous weapons are a given."

"Look we have got to get out of sight," Sam insisted. "Be ready."

At that moment there was an explosive flash at the front gate and the magical shield disappeared.

"Go tell everybody to get ready for the prison break."

The teacher and three girls stood and stared back, not moving.

"These creatures are man eaters," Bobby told them. "If you don't want to be eaten, be ready to run at the first opportunity."

The shock of that revelation jolted them into action. "Alright," said Mrs. Hanson. "We will tell everyone to be ready."

******

Delia passed through the magical shield without trouble, but as the cloaked Jeff stepped through, there was an explosion that knocked out the barrier. This was the result of contrasting light and dark magic coming together. Unfortunately, it also knocked out Jeff's cloak. He stood there in shock, completely exposed.

Child turned back to Delia. "Jeff," the wide-eyed Delia whispered. "I can see you."

"Huh... what?" Jeff looked at the device on his wrist. The screen was black. He tapped it, but nothing happened. Panicked, he tapped it several times. Jeff looked up to see several Shadow witches looking at him in shock. If it hadn't been for the sheer surprise of the situation, he would be dead. He looked back to Delia.

Both of them said, "Demon dung."

Delia tossed Jeff's katana to him. He had just enough time to draw the sword from its sheath and slice it through the first attacking Shadow. Delia let Child transform and take over. Although Delia knew and understood everything that Child knew, at a moment like this, it was better to trust in the experts. Her experience as a warrior trumped Delia's desire for control. Child's actions were quick and decisive, as she fought her way through the gate. Jeff followed close behind. Keeping his back to Child, he fended off the blows from the raptor staff and sliced through any attacking Shadow witches who got too close. Fortunately for Jeff, the close combat conditions kept the witches from releasing their full power.

As soon as they made it out into the open, Child leveled her Raptor staff at the attacking Shadows. A burst of energy killed three more attacking witches. Their Shadow allies circled above, joining the battle.

The initial attack on Sam and Bobby had resulted in a big hole in the fence. Sam stepped through the hole and yelled, "Everybody, over here. This is a good time to run. So, come on... run heaven sake."

"Get to a safe place to hide," Bobby yelled as he turned and ran across the field to the front gate.

"Where is there a safe place," Mrs. Hanson bellowed. "Those things are everywhere." She put her hands on her hips. "Honestly," she blustered. "What is wrong with those two?"

Running through the crowd of prisoners, they quickly encountered the enemy Shadows. By the time they reached the others, only a handful of Shadow guards remained alive.

With a firm grip on Jeff's arm, So, come on... run for heaven's sake." Their Shadow witch allies above blasted a couple more holes in the fence. The humans ran for the exits. They then swooped down and picked up Bobby and Sam, taking off after Child and Jeff.

Jeff hung from Child's raptor staff for dear life with his eyes closed tight. Opening his eyes for a quick look, he closed them tight again. "As long as I keep my eyes closed, I'll be fine," he said. "Don't worry about me."

"That was freaking amazing," Delia thought to Child, ignoring Jeff.

Child thought, "That was exciting. Wasn't it."

"I know, right?"

"And fun."

"Fun in a very dangerous sort of way," Delia countered. "You were really amazing back there. I thought you said you hated being a warrior."

"Maybe I just hated who I fought for."

"Thank you, Child. You saved us all."

******

It took a minute for Alan Sasaki to regain his composure. He ran to his father-in-law, his wife's beloved father, his son's grandpa. He carefully lifted the old man's head. "Father," he whispered. "Father."

The old man opened his eyes. "I didn't see that one coming."

"That sounds like you, *Ichiro san*," said someone with a thick Japanese accent.

Grandpa tried to adjust himself up against the wall. The pain hit him when he moved. He tried to focus on the man who had just spoken to him. "Cousin, is that you?"

Master Maeda, followed by several heavily armed Maeda Clan soldiers, strolled over to Grandpa and Alan. Master Maeda wore traditional Japanese clothes, very old school *samurai* looking. The rest of the group wore either civilian clothes or black special ops soldier gear and armor. They carried a variety of weapons from swords to the latest military battle weapons.

"You are in some serious trouble here, Ichi," the Master said.

Grandpa winced, not just from the pain this time, but from hearing that childhood nickname again. He didn't care for it, but this was Master Maeda, the head of the Maeda Clan. Grandpa decided to refrain from calling the Master by his old childhood nickname for the sake of goodwill.

"Yes... at least one or two broken ribs." Grandpa coughed. "And maybe a punctured lung."

"Do not worry yourself, Ichi," the Master encouraged. "We will take care of you now."

"Forgive me Master," Grandpa said. "I would normally bow at a moment like this, but I do not feel so good."

Master Maeda laughed. "You are one tough old man, Ichi."

"What are you doing here," Grandpa asked.

"It appears that you have another demon infestation in California. We came to help."

"Yes... yes. That is true." Grandpa coughed again. "Sorry to worry you, Master. Although you should have phoned ahead. I would have gotten things ready for your arrival. Maybe even baked a cake in your honor. Forgive my lack of hospitality."

Master Maeda shook his head and waved his hand. "No worries, cousin," he laughed. "So, where does this tunnel lead?"

"Back inside the dome," Grandpa said. "It seems the domed shield does not penetrate into the ground. There is a fortress at the far end built by the enemy *kage oni*. They hid their presence from us in a shielded building... damn demons. The Shadow we call Cooper, the one that saved us two years ago, came back to mop up any Shadows left behind after he closed the rift. He has control of the fortress now."

"I see," the Master said. "A strange world we live in." He waved to his people. "Two of you help Ichiro san. Everyone else, follow me."

"By the way, this is my son-in-law, Alan Sasaki," Grandpa said, reaching out to Alan.

"Master Maeda, sir," Alan said with a bow. "It is an honor."

"Alan, go with the Master. Make sure our allies do not start killing each other."

Alan looked confused at first, then he understood. "Oh... Yes, father."

The Master and his soldiers followed Alan Sasaki back to the Shadow fortress.

******

Bill, Rich, and Cooper arrived outside the side wall of the DoD research compound. Cooper's witches landed next to him as he waited for Rich to enter the key code at the compound's rear entrance. The door opened and all disappeared inside. This entrance led directly to a stairway leading below ground one floor. The hallways at the bottom wandered from building to building. Bill led the way to the Center for Interdimensional Physics laboratory wing that housed his and Rich's offices and laboratories. They encountered no one, human or demon, along the way. Only a few employees had access to the underground halls, so the enemy probably didn't know it existed. Rich keyed in his code at another door. When the door unlocked, it sent a signal to the Security Center alerting them that someone had entered the building. Another alert appeared on an unmonitored computer screen in the Control Room.

A fatal flaw usually comes to light at some point when a mega-maniac sets his or her malicious plan into action. Pride, arrogance, or whatever, causes even the best bad guy to overlook small details. In this particular case Overseer Shadow Strong had ordered her witches into battle. She had abandoned the Control Room. The security guards were all dead, so no one saw the alert that told them that Rich Thomas, at least, had entered the building. No one noticed the cameras had picked up the team of humans and Shadows moving through the building unchallenged.

Once inside the Center, which was at the center of the compound, Cooper and his Shadow witches split off from the team and exited to the outside through an emergency exit. An alarm went off. Rich frantically disarmed the alarm and the area went silent. Closing the door behind them, the Shadows spread out to observe the enemy forces. Even if seen, they would easily blend in with any enemy Shadows still in the area.

Bill and Rich's offices were next to each other in the laboratory wing. The two men entered Rich's office and accessed video and data of the Center's Control Room and the rift chamber.

"Now," Rich said. "Let's find that book and get out of here."

"No way it is going to be as easy as walking in there and finding the grimoire just lying around," Bill said. "Then leaving without being seen."

"I am sure you are right, but they have left the place unguarded thus far."

Rich had had a good look at the grimoire when the disguised Shadow showed up with it. But after looking at the control room from every view the cameras could provide, it became clear that the book was not in the room anymore. He switched to the cameras in the rift chamber. These cameras were offline. That meant going in blind.

"We need to get in there," Rich said.

"We don't know what or who is inside that chamber."

"This will not be the first time we have taken this kind of risk."

"We were a lot younger then."

"If caught, the odds of survival are not good."

"If something happens to us, who will protect our families?"

"Damn," Rich sighed. They both sat there thinking about their mission. How were they going to steal a book that could be anywhere at the moment?

******

Master Maeda and his small army of special ops slayers remained cautious as the large chamber opened up in front of them. Grandpa Maeda had told them what to expect. Sure enough, there they were, six *kage oni*. The Shadow witches had sensed the intruders coming and had spread out, two front, two right and two left, ready to attack the intruders as they exited the tunnel.

"It's okay," Alan Sasaki said. He looked back. "Father. We need you up here."

"Hold on, everyone," Grandpa hollered. He and the two men helping him had just managed to catch up with Master Maeda's group. "Quick, get me up front." The two soldiers carried the old man out in front of the group. Grandpa put his hands up. "It is okay. These people are friends."

The Shadows seemed to understand and relaxed their stance. The Priestess moved forward to face Grandpa. *"Who are these humans,"* she asked in thought? She stood silent waiting for an answer.

"What does the *kage oni* want," Master Maeda asked?

"I'm not sure," Grandpa replied. "They speak by telepathy."

"Kathleen-chan," Master Maeda said. "See what you can do."

Kathleen, a dark haired and green-eyed woman in her late twenties dressed in black battle gear, moved past the Master to face the Shadow. She looked into the Shadow's eyes and projected her thoughts. "We are here to help. We," she indicated with the sweep of her arm that she meant all present, "wish to be your allies."

The Priestess took a minute to reply. *"You are a warrior witch. Are you not?"*

"That would best describe me, yes. How did you know?"

"I smell the magic on you."

"I use magic, but this is my weapon of choice." Kath held up her assault rifle.

"I see," thought the Shadow.

Master Maeda said, "Tell her we need to get to the rift as soon as possible. Can she lead us there?"

Kathleen did as the Master asked. "She says she can't leave the fortress."

"I can get you there," Alan Sasaki said.

Mrs. Sasaki protested. "Honey, no. Leave this to the soldiers. They can take care of it."

"Well, maybe this situation requires me to step up and be a soldier. We can't leave this place and our friends in it unprotected. Your father is unable to do this. So, that leaves me. I know this town as well as anyone." He turned back to Master Maeda. "Master, I will guide you."

"Very well," the Master said.

The Priestess sensed another concern. She turned to Kathleen and thought, *"I sense enemy witches coming. I sense their hostile intentions."*

"Master," Kathleen said urgently. "The Priestess says enemy Shadows are somewhere close. She says they are hostile and possibly on the way here."

"The Master said. "How many?"

Kathleen communicated with the Priestess. "She says maybe ten."

"Is that all? It is about time we get into this fight."

The members of his team smiled and grunted in agreement.

Kathleen turned to the Shadow. "We are ready," she thought with a smile. The Priestess smiled a big toothy grin.

******

They entered the deserted control room with considerable caution. Bill did a quick search of the room for the grimoire while Rich sat down at the Director's terminal. The system was still active but there was no data stream. The hypergravity chamber wasn't functioning.

"The Shadow must have destroyed the rift chamber after opening the new rift, Rich informed Bill. "But the rift still functions," he added. He tried to turn on the cameras in the HG chamber. The large monitor at the front of the room flickered with static and distorted images. By checking the cameras one at a time, he discovered that, although the rift interfered with the signal, one camera at the far end of the chamber still worked on its night vision setting.

Bill stepped up to his side. "The book is not in this room," he whispered. "What now?" Rich pointed at the main screen. Bill stood there wide eyed. "Will you look at that," he said.

They could make out the arched ribs of the HG chamber that circled the swirling vortex which rose up out of the floor. The scene was surreal. The contrasting light and shadows of the greenish chiaroscuro vision held the two men's attention.

"Wait," Rich said. "How many of the columns do you see?"

"One, two, three, four…" he counted to himself. "Is there one missing?"

"Humm," Rich wondered. "I need a closer look."

Rich stood and walked down to the front left corner of the control room and through the door that led to the HG chamber.

Bill said, "Are you sure you want to do this?"

"I do not know," Rich replied. "This is the last place to look for the grimoire."

They couldn't see anyone guarding the long hallway that ended in a set of doors with windows in the upper half. Rich, followed by Bill, hurried down the hallway. Through the windows they could see the HG chamber. The open rift glowed bright with ominous blue and black swirls. Sure enough, one of the chambers' columns was missing.

"Look," Rich said. "I didn't think she could do it but the Shadow removed the one column. The stump left shows the cut made a clean slice through the rib."

"Magic, no doubt," Bill said.

No one was inside the chamber room, so Rich opened the door and stepped inside.

"Can you see the grimoire anywhere?"

"No," Rich said. "It is too dark on the far side to tell if something is there. Stay here and I will take a quick look."

"Make it fast, my friend."

Rich hurried around the HGC and disappeared into the dark. Bill stepped inside the room. Curious, he slowly approached the rift. He tried to get a look down the open vortex but it was too far away. Looking up through the missing ceiling he could see nothing but the dark dome overhead. The invaders had created a ramp leading up to ground level. Pushing his fear aside, he scurried up the ramp and dropped to a crouch at the top. The emergency power remained on, some walkway lights and building entrance lights still worked. The scene above astounded him. There were several of the new enemy patrolling the area. He saw the tall being on the roof of the zeno-biology facility. She appeared to be female. She was a giant, tall, thin, and strikingly beautiful. If this was the leader of this new race of creatures, she sure did not look like them. Standing next to her was a Shadow. Bill saw that the Shadow had a firm hold on the grimoire

Bill quickly scurried back down the ramp and back to the hallway entrance. "Rich," Bill called out in a half whisper.

"I am coming," he replied.

Out of the rift appeared two more the crainn creatures, followed by their masters. Rich dove back into the darker part of the room. Bill quickly hid back in the hallway behind the doors and cloaked himself as well. Several more of the creatures and their masters enter up through the rift. Each of the masters looked around as they appeared, then immediately headed up the ramp to the outside.

Rich feared that even breathing would give him away. He had ended up on his stomach, flat on the floor, and facing away from the rift. He couldn't see anything. The growls, hisses, and unintelligible language of the masters were all he had to tell what was happening. His mind kept repeating the phrase, "Crap, what was I thinking..." He had never given much thought to the possibility that a god or a supreme being existed. He had studied the cultures of other worlds. All had some variation on the concept of god or gods. Even though he felt like praying the moment, which god should he pray to? He went with the Judeo-Christian one.

"Dear God, get us out of here," Rich whispered.

At that moment there was a pause in activity. Rich raised his head and looked back at the rift. No creatures remained in the room. Then he heard a voice in his head.

It said, "Run."

The voice sounded familiar. "What," Rich asked?

"Run. Now."

The voice implied that there wasn't much time. He scrambled up on his feet and ran around the rift toward the open door where Bill waited for him. But something stopped him in his tracks.

"Got you," Overseer Strong thought.

Rich felt the blue leash tighten around his neck. He turned to see a glowing blue leash lead back to the Shadow who had caused all of this trouble.

The Overseer transformed to her human persona. "I thought I smelled something human," she said while grinning maliciously.

Back in the hallway, Bill feared for his friend. "Why didn't he cloak himself," Bill said in a daze? Then realizing he had snuck up that ramp uncloaked. "Did I cause this," he asked himself.

******

Bobby grabbed his throbbing head. Fortunately, the Shadow witches had just landed. He fell to his knees. What had he just witnessed? The vision had come on so fast. If it was real, then Sam's dad was in serious trouble. He had yelled out to Mr. Thomas to run, but he must not have heard Bobby's warning. Then it was too late.

******

Shadow Strong pulled on the leash and it began to retracked, dragging Rich along with it.

"You are mine, Mr. Thomas," She said. Now I have a scientist and an engineer."

Rich looked around until he saw Percy standing nearby. He gave an angry glare at his former colleague. Rich then realized that Percy too had a blue collar around his neck. Percy had the look of a doomed man.

"Well," Rich said. "Maybe there is some justice in this universe." The Overseer laughed generously. "Well said, Mr. Thomas."

She turned her head, sensing something else that didn't belong. She hadn't seen Cooper, but she felt him. Holding the grimoire tightly she walked to the edge of the wooded area behind the buildings. Looking around slowly, she saw nothing unusual. Sniffing the air, she could sense the witches and, of course, the Fomorians, but something else was out there. She sniffed the air again. For some reason she could smell a male Shadow.

Cooper saw the grimoire in the witches' arms. No way he could get to her and retrieve the book without being seen. He and his Shadow witches needed to regroup. Retrieving the grimoire would require blood. Another being moved into his view. She stood on top of one of the nearby buildings. The female giant stood much taller than the Overseer. A crown of golden horns rested on her head.

Cooper thought, "So, there is the leader of the enemy. If we kill her, we end the war. Cooper disappeared through the trees.

******

The Shadow Priestess had just lifted the protection spell around the fortress when the Shadow witches attacked. One group of witches blasted through the building's second floor windows and began to work their way down to the main chamber. A second group blew away the gated parking garage entrance. Maeda's team had already entered the garage area and stood waiting for the shield to be lifted. The attack caught them off guard. Fortunately, Master Maeda's people stood battle ready when the gate flew off its track and landed in a pile of smoldering metal. The Shadows entered with individual shields up. Master Maeda and two others stepped forward to create a protection shield of their own. All hell broke loose as the two sides met. Guns flared and swords clashed against raptor staff Beams of blue hot fire and other attack spells glanced off the humans' shields. Their bullets stopped in midair as they struck the Shadow witches shields. The battle didn't last long, only ten minutes in fact. The start of the assault involved ten of the Overseer's witches. Five went up and into the building. Five attacked the garage entrance. Master Maeda's had a special ops team of twenty-four. No matter how powerful their magic, in a close space like the parking garage the five witches were outnumbered and out classed. Maeda's team surrounded and destroyed them all. Three humans were injured in the firefight.

Inside the fortress the Shadow Priestess raised the protection shield around the building to prevent more enemy Shadows from entering. This action trapped the enemy witches inside the fortress, but very little stood between them and these highly motivated witches. The allied Shadows sealed all entrances into the chamber. If the enemy got through both Shadow and humans' lives would be in grave danger. The Priestess sensed five to six of the enemy inside the structure. With the magical battle going on in the parking garage, she was unable to sense what was happening.

For the Maeda team, the battle was over, but they were now trapped in the parking garage. The priestesses actions had blocked the way out of the building, as well as the way back into the main chamber. A way back inside had to be found in order to secure the fortress for the humans and their allies. Losing this base at this critical moment in the battle meant disaster.

"Kathleen san," The master ordered. "Try to contact the Priestess." Kathleen closed her eyes and concentrated. *"Priestess,"* she thought out. *"What is your situation?"* A long pause that seemed like forever made Kathleen anxious. "I'm not getting through, Master."

"Human, Kathleen..."

"Wait, sir... *Priestess?*" Another long pause ensued.

"Human Kathleen, we are safe for now. Enemy witches are in the fortress above us. If they break through, we will not survive."

"Master. The Priestess says the enemy is in the building. They are trying to get into the main chamber. They are in danger of losing control."

"Can she drop the seal on the door and let us in," the Master asked?

Kathleen went silent. "She says the shields inside are all connected. If one is down, they all are down."

One of the older, more experienced soldiers, stepped forward. "Sir," Sergeant Doyle interrupted. "If we could get into the building through a window on the floor above us. We could engage the enemy from behind."

The Master turned back to Kathleen. "Can she drop the outside shield?"

"She says yes, but she doesn't want to leave it down for long."

"How many people do you need, Sergeant Doyle," the Master asked?

"Doyle said, "Me and four others.

"Choose your team.

"Sir, I need Kathleen to be one of the four."

"I agree, sergeant. Carry on."

The five-member team moved out as soon as the shield dropped. They shot two grappling hooks into the broken windows and scrambled up and through the window.

Kathleen thought, *"We are here."* The outside shield was restored without incident.

" We are on the battle arena floor," Kathleen reported to the Priestess. "No Shadows are in sight."

"Where to, Kathleen," Doyle whispered? She indicated across the floor to an open shaft.

Doyle took point with Kathleen right behind him. Hugging the wall, they moved to the opening and flanked it on both sides. The leader took a quick look up and down the shaft. It was too dark to see anything. Doyle pulled the night vision goggles down over his eyes and looked again. He saw four figures at the bottom of the shaft, about twenty to twenty-five feet down. They were attempting to force the entrance open. Doyle put up four fingers, then pointed down the shaft. Looking over his shoulder to Kathleen and pointed at her. Then he tapped his head.

Kathleen understood. She concentrated, opening her mind. She sensed the Priestess and the two Shadows in the main chamber with her. They were ready for an aggressive defense of themselves and the humans with them. She sensed the four Shadows at the bottom of the shaft. They seemed unaware of the human soldiers above them. Kathleen sensed something else. *"A fifth Shadow,"* she thought? She informed Doyle that a fifth Shadow hid somewhere close. Doyle indicated to everyone to be on guard. They all nodded.

Doyle pulled a grenade from his vest. This was going to be like killing fish in a fishbowl. At times like this the procedure was to hit demons with a one-two punch. First a flash grenade to confuse and blind the demons and, second, a standard grenade to blow them into bits.

The soldier on the opposite side of the shaft smiled and grabbed a flash grenade. The two men held the two grenades over the shaft. The flash grenade dropped. A second later Doyle dropped his grenade. They waited.

Kathleen heard the hiss of the Shadow demon behind her. She quickly turned and raised her weapon but the fifth Shadow batted it out of her hand. "Doyle," she screamed. The witch grabbed her by the neck. The four other soldiers pulled away from the opening as the grenades exploded. The flash and dust temporarily blinded them. When they realized what had happened to Kathleen, they raised their weapons, but the closeness of the enemy to the team member to the Shadow stopped them from firing. Doyle got a clear shot and fired a short burst. Anticipating the counter attack, the witch flew backward with blurring speed. The rounds missed. She threw the now unconscious Kathleen across the concrete floor.

The soldiers opened fire but, again, the Shadow was too fast. She launched an offensive spell at them. They spread out to compensate, but not fast enough. The spell obliterated one of the dodging soldiers, leaving a black hole in the wall behind him. The remaining soldiers kept firing, but the Shadow's defensive shield stopped the rounds in midair. These were magically enhanced bullets. Yet, they could not pierce the Shadows protection shield. She cast a stream of almost white-hot fire and another soldier died.

"This is going all to hell," Doyle thought as he dove trying to dodge another attack. He felt the pain of the hit immediately. The fiery spell burned his right leg below the knee. Ignoring the pain, he rolled on his back and fired another burst at the Shadow. The other soldier, the only one of them still standing on his feet, kept up his assault as he tried to get to Doyle. The Shadow dashed forward. She hit the man so hard he flew through the air and slid into the open shaft. He fell without a sound. Considering his condition, Doyle struggled to his feet and moved as fast as he could. He ended up backing into the wall a few feet to the left of the shaft. The Shadow witch turned and faced him with a malicious grin. Struggling against the pain, Doyle opened fire again until the magazine ran out. He attempted to replace it but the Shadow was already on him. The witch grabbed his neck with one hand, while pulling back the other fisted hand.

"I will crush your head, human," the Shadow seethed in anger.

"Oh no you won't," Kathleen screamed. She aimed at the side of the unshielded Shadow's head and pulled the trigger. The blast hit the witch's head, blowing it into dust. The Shadow fell to the floor dead. Just for good measure, Doyle obliterated the rest of the monster with his weapon.

Doyle slid down the wall and let out a burst of air from his lungs. "Thanks, sis," he said.

"You are welcome," she replied. "I thought I was about to be an only child."

"Well, are we sure that was all of them," he asked?

Kathleen Doyle nodded, "Affirmative, Sergeant." She closed her eyes. *"All is clear, Priestess."*

******

Child let go of Jeff as she landed on the open beach at the edge of the old University of California campus and transformed into Delia. The two Shadows helping Sam and Bobby also landed.

"It looks like we got away," Jeff said, breathing easy again. "I'd rather not do that again."

Delia shook her head. "Sorry, no such luck. Child says there are at least two witches in pursuit."

"Damn. So much for catching a break."

They all looked back from where they had come. The sky was too dark to see anything.

"Let the Republic Shadows deal with this," Bobby said. "We need to move on."

"Yeah. If we stay here, we will be sitting ducks," Jeff said. Child thought to the Shadows and they took off immediately.

The foursome ran for the cover of the nearby buildings. Before they could reach cover, a flash of fire exploded right next to Delia. She transformed back into Child and returned fire. Another blast hit the ground next to Jeff. Child could not locate the source. The illusive witches landed behind them. Child sensed it and called to the Republic Shadows to return.

"Crap," Jeff shouted. "Where did they come from?"

Child mumbled a spell that set her hand on fire. She flew at the enemy witches with all her might. She shoved her fiery hand into one opponent's chest, destroying the enemy's upper body in a blaze of fire. The second enemy Shadow reacted quickly. She was already on top of Child when an explosion of magical power came from above, killing the witch.

"Ding dong the witch is... DEAD," Jeff sang hopping around. "Yes." He turned to Child, who had become Delia, and smiled with pure admiration. "I am so impressed," he said as he walked toward Delia.

Another screech came from above. Child was half transformed when she was hit by a new blast of magic. She fell, immediately transforming back to Delia. The third enemy Shadow dropped to the ground next to Delia's unconscious body. The Shadow was so focused on Delia that she didn't see Jeff. He took her head off. Delia awakened.

"Are you alright," Jeff said as he dropped to Delia's side? Sam and Bobby joined them.

"Yes. I think so," Delia said weakly. *"Child, are you alright,"* she thought? No reply came. "Child. I said, "Are you...?" Something felt different... wrong. Delia panicked. *"Child, are you okay?"* Delia put her hands to the side of her head. "Child," she said out loud.

Jeff asked, "What's wrong?"

"It's Child. She isn't answering me."

"She's must have gotten knocked cold like you did."

"It's just that I can't feel her either. Where is she? We need to keep fighting." Delia fell into a full-blown panic attack. "Child, wake up. I can't do this on my own." She stretched her arm around herself and squeezed tight. "Child, where are you?"

"Look, why don't you rest here for a while," Jeff said. "Give her a chance to recover."

"Yeah, maybe... Sorry."

Another Shadow appeared in the air.

Heads up," Jeff yelled.

"Wait," Bobby said. "She is one of ours."

******

Delia watched as her friends flew away. What was she going to do? She had relied on Child to take care of the dangerous stuff while she remained safely tucked away inside Child's body. The soul eater spell had backfired on Child. Instead of the Shadow taking the body and mind of the human, the human had taken over the body and mind of the Shadow. Delia showed a brave front, but she had not really come to terms with the situation. According to Child, Delia should have died, but she didn't. Now she feared that Child was hurt or worse. If so, then Delia was on her own. Most of what Child knew, Delia knew as well. But there is a big difference between knowing and understanding. Experience is a big factor when it comes to developing one's skills. Delia tried to transform. Nothing happened. She let her mind go back to remember what it was like to transform. How did it feel? What was Child thinking when she initiated a transformation? Delia relaxed and did what Child had done. This time it worked. She bent down and picked up her raptor staff. She wanted to find her friends and help win this battle, but things had just changed dramatically.

Delia bolted into the sky. As she flew over the rooftops, she saw many of the giants with their strange attack dogs. These creatures scared her to death. Without Child to explain things to her she was at the mercy of her new and dangerous reality.

Delia landed in her own backyard and transformed to human form. The house was dark, but she could sense that her mother was still there. Child still hadn't responded to her constant call for help. Afraid and worried, she felt more alone than she had ever felt. Even worse than the day her father had left without a word. Delia held back the tears. She had to keep it together for her mom's survival. She didn't want to die, so she would do what needed to be done to stay alive.

A loud crash came from the front of her house and then a scream. "Mom," Delia shouted. She ran to the back door. Finding it locked, she pushed on the door. To her shock, the strength her Shadow body hadn't gone away. The door tore off its hinges. "Mama. It's Delia. Where are you?" She ran through the house checking rooms. Loud noises of cracking wood, plaster and breaking glass came from the front of the house. Delia hurried upstairs to check the rest of the house. She found her terrified mother hiding in the master bedroom closet. "Mama."

"Delia," her mother asked in disbelief? "Is it really you?"

"Yes mama." They embraced.

"When I didn't hear from you for so long I was so afraid. I thought you must be..."

"I'm sorry mama. I am sorry I made you worry."

"Where have you been all this time?"

"I can't tell you right now. I need to get you out of here."

There was another loud crash. Her mom screamed again. "What are those things?"

"They are demons or aliens or something. I'm not sure." Her mom's eyes looked even more terrified. "If we don't leave now, mama, we will both be killed."

"Okay, but how?"

A series of loud crunches and bangs made her mom scream again. The growling and sniffing sounds got closer. One of those creatures was coming up the stairs. Delia picked up the wing back chair her mom always used to relax and read before bed. She threw it through the back window. "Come with me mama," Delia urged.

"But I can't jump out a second-floor window, Delia."

"I'll carry you. Just come with me."

"How can you possibly carry me?"

Delia wrapped one arm around her mom and lifted her. "Put me down," her mom protested.

"Sorry, but we have to get out of the house."

The crainn creature crashed through the bedroom wall and landed in front of them. Holding her screaming mother tight, Delia jumped through the window. Delia noted that her mom was as light as a feather. The crainn followed them out of the window. They backed away, but her mom tripped falling on her back. Delia transformed into the Shadow demon form. Her desire to protect her mom caused the instinctual defensive reaction. She charged the crainn.

Delia swung her staff at the crainn's head. The creature batted the staff away. Then jumping on the creature's back, Delia slammed her right fist as hard as she could into the top of its head. It twisted and stood on its hind legs trying to get her off its back. It spun around to fling her off, but Delia wrapped her arm around its neck in a choke hold. The move wasn't that effective but it did keep her on its back.

The creature turned its head unnaturally backward and sunk its teeth into her shoulder. Delia screamed in pain and let go and bolted away. The wound began to heel almost immediately. Ignoring the lingering pain, she stood and charged again. Delia was pissed off and the Shadow part of her took full control. With her long fingers she grasped the front of the still standing creature's throat. Her claw like nails dug in deep. It took a swing at her, which she blocked just before kicking the beast in the abdomen. She repeated that action five or six times before the beast reacted. It fell to the ground, landing on top of her. The hold on its neck helped her to keep its snapping jaws away from her face. She pushed with all her might, right hand on its neck and left hand on its chest. She screeched an unearthly sound and let go the full fury of the witch. From her hands extended glowing blades of fire, causing lethal wounds to the creature's neck and chest. The creature flopped to one side. Delia stood triumphant, withdrawing the fiery blades which morphed back into her hands. Delia looked at her mother who was transfixed on her. This was what Delia wanted to avoid. In deep sadness she morphed back into her human form.

"The demons captured me," said Delia sorrowfully. "They did something that was supposed to kill me, but instead it made me like them." She looked at her mom. "Are you hurt or anything?"

Delia fell to her knees. Blood soaked her clothes. For some reason the shoulder wound had healed. Most of the blood, the creature's blood, was green.

She began to sob. "I'm sorry mama... I didn't want you to know... to find out what they did to me." She now sobbed uncontrollably. "Please... don't hate me... or be afraid of me. I have become a monster Mama... but inside it's still me. I'm so sorry this has happened to you. I feel so alone. Now you will be alone too."

Mrs. Bowen got to her feet and slowly went to her devastated daughter. She knelt down next to Delia and embraced her. "You are not a monster," she whispered. "You are my loving daughter who nearly died saving her mother. No monster would do that. You are still alive somehow, that is what matters. As long as we both live, we will never be alone."

"I love you mama."

"I love you too, sweetheart," her mother said. They continued to hold each other tight until another loud noise came from the house.

Delia nodded. "Okay," she said through the tears. "There is one more thing you need to know, mama, but I am also some kind of a witch." She waited silently for her mom's reaction.

"A witch? Well now, doesn't that sound useful." They both laughed and hugged again.

"We need to leave now," Delia said. "I need to get you to a safe place." Delia grabbed her mom and they were gone in an instant.

******

The Fomorian Royal Mother sensed the enemy Shadows and their human allies. The enemy had clear intentions. This was a war after all. She expected them to fight back and admired their bravery, but with such a small number of warriors, what did they hope to achieve other than certain death? Still, these individuals had magic. That made them dangerous enough. She would not underestimate them. Instead she would trick them in a way that would put fear into their hearts and minds. That would stop their advance.

"High Overseer Strong," the Royal Mother said. "It seems that there are Shadow witches that are not loyal to you."

"I sensed them as well, my Royal Mother," Shadow replied.

"Is there a reason for concern?"

"Witches can be powerful, but none are stronger than me... or you my Royal Mother. Besides, what could a few individuals possibly accomplish against the most powerful race in a thousand universes?"

"Ah, so true," the Royal Mother uttered. "They are courageous. I will give them that."

The Royal Mother looked around. Her warriors had routed out the humans everywhere they hid. Soon the dome would expand, capturing more territory.

"If they want a fight, I will let them die as brave, but foolish, warriors."

Shadow Strong, however, had sensed something that made her livid with hate. One of the Shadow witches approaching the compound was one of hers. This traitor had dared to turn against her. That required the worst punishment possible.

******

Jeff, Sam and Bobby stopped in front of the entrance gate to the DoD research facility. The tall wall that surrounded the facility loomed to the right and the left. Under the dark dome the wall disappeared in both directions. All three of them stood still, entranced by fearful visions.

Jeff gazed mystified by the huge black Torii arch that now loomed menacingly in front of him. The two tall posts were about twenty feet tall and two feet in diameter. The ends of the massive horizontal beam that spanned across the top extended beyond each post by about four feet. The two ends turned up slightly. A second beam crossed between the two upright posts about three feet below the larger top beam.

"What the heck," Jeff asked? Jeff remembered the Torii arches that had appeared at the gym on the night Amy died. He shuddered in a moment of renewed grief. He backed back a few steps. "What is going on," he said to the others. They didn't answer.

A thick mist flowed through the arch. A small wooden boat drifted toward him, floating out of the mist. Standing at the bow was a vague figure. As it got closer the face became clearer.

"Amy." Jeff exhaled her name. His grief was renewed as pain stabbed his heart.

"Why did you let them kill me," the wispy figure asked?

"Amy... I..."

"I am left here in darkness... all alone. Killed by demons of the underworld, I now walk in darkness." Amy's face became distorted with anger. "Because you let them kill me," she screamed. Jeff fell to his knees. The tears of agony flowed.

Bobby ran beside Jeff as they approached the DoD compound, when Jeff skidded to a stop. Then Jeff was no longer beside Bobby but a few feet in front of him. Jeff had a terrible and fierce look on his face. His face was red with anger.

"What's wrong," Bobby asked? Bobby hurried up to his friend. He put his hand on Jeff's shoulder and said, "What is it, Jeff?"

"Don't touch me," Jeff barked. Jeff raised his arm and knocked Bobby's hand away. He began to pace back and forth and then began to circle Bobby in confused frustration. He unsheathed his katana as he continued to circle.

"What is going on, Jeff," Bobby said, more than a little unnerved by his friend's demeanor. To draw his katana like that was a shocking provocation. "Jeff, what are you doing?"

"It is all your fault," Jeff growled.

"What? What are you talking about?"

"Amy and I would have been so happy together, but now she is gone."

"I know, buddy. I feel the pain of her loss as well."

"Shut up," Jeff threatened, brandishing his katana. "You have no... It's your fault she is dead. If you hadn't dragged me into your weird, alien life, I wouldn't have become the target of the Shadows. Amy wouldn't have become a target. She would be alive right now."

"Come on, Jeff. That's not fair," Bobby objected. "I didn't want any of this either, but it happened. I can't do anything about that."

"You arrogant ass," Jeff growled.

Jeff came at Bobby in full force. Bobby barely had time to block the blade with his staff. Jeff pulled back and swung again and again. He pushed Bobby back with every blow. All Bobby could do was block the blows. He didn't want to fight back. He didn't want to hurt his friend. Jeff struck again and caused Bobby to trip and fall. Jeff was over him instantly with the katana raise, ready to kill.

Sam Stood still. She was in shock. Her father stood weak and shaking in front of her, covered in blood. He fell to his knees. "Daddy," she shrieked. She dropped to her knees next to him.

"There is my little girl," Rich Thomas said. He coughed and blood came out of his mouth. "Honey, where have you been? I was counting on you to save me, but it seems you are too late. Where were you?"

Oh, Daddy, I am so sorry. We got here as quickly as we could."

Her dad fell on his side and rolled onto his back. "Did you? Humph. You never seem to take responsibility for your mistakes."

"What," she said in shock? Sam pulled his head over onto her lap. "Daddy... Daddy. I don't know what to do to help you."

"Help me," he said with a laugh, coughing up more blood. "You cannot help me. You are too late - always too little too late."

"I am so sorry I didn't get here sooner."

"If you had not taken the time to help a bunch of strangers escape from that prison compound, you would have been here in time to stop that Shadow from attacking me."

Sam's heart felt like it was about to break. "I am so sorry. We will get you back to the fortress. The priestess is a healer." Rich closed his eyes. "Daddy, no... please stay with me."

"No, don't worry about it. What is done is done. You will just have to live with the guilt. Of course, that kind of guilt can ruin a person's life."

No, Daddy." Sam sobbed. "I love you. Please... don't go."

"Love? What a laugh." Rich coughed and then closed his eyes as life drained from him.

Then just as the tormenting visions had started, they were suddenly gone. Sam, Bobby, and Jeff were standing next to each other. They each took a look around bewildered.

"Jeffrey-chan. Are you alright?" Standing in front of Jeff was Master Maeda.

"Master," Jeff gasped. "How did you get here?"

"What just happened," Bobby said, still trembling.

"You were under a powerful spell. A spell designed to invoke your deepest fears," Master Maeda said. "It started to happen to us as well, but I cast a counter spell before it overcame me. Then we found you, I had to do the counter spell again. You should have no further problems. Now come, we need to bring this to an end."

"Wait. Who are you," Bobby asked.

"This is my grand uncle," Jeff replied. "Master Maeda."

"Master Maeda," Sam said? She was still reeling from the vision of her father's death. She Wiped her face with her sleeve. "The one from Japan?"

"We will do introductions later," the Master said. "Clear your heads and get back in the fight. The worst is yet to come." Maeda's team moved on. After a moment of hesitation Bobby and Sam followed. Unfortunately, what they had seen and experienced in their visions would stay with them. But Jeff lingered behind. The black Torii was still there.

"Jeff, aren't you coming," Bobby asked.

"I'll be there in a little while. I think I have something else to do first."

Delia landed next to Jeff. "What is with this arch thing? It wasn't here before," she said.

"I feel like I am supposed to go through the Torii arch. Do you want to come with me?"

"Okay, sure. Lead the way."

They both faced the arch and walked between the two massive posts. They vanished from sight.

****

Bill turned to Cooper. "Well, you are the warrior here. What do we do now," Bill asked Cooper? "As long as they hold Rich a prisoner, anything we do could get him killed."

"Maybe," confirmed Cooper. "But we must cut the raptor's head off." He made a cutthroat sign with his hand. This was the Tiarnas way of saying, *cut the head of the snake*. We need a magic book... or we die."

"Getting close to the giants' leader is an impossible task."

"The Shadow witches call her the Royal Mother," Cooper said.

"Must be like a dowager queen," Bill said.

"Sorry, I not know that word."

"Don't worry. It doesn't matter," Bill said. "So, how do we get close to her?"

"Cooper smiled mischievously, pointing to the device on his finger. He wore the old cloaking device Rich had given him two years before. It was too small for his wrist, so he wore it as a ring. "Have invisible magic. You do too. We sneak up unseen. We fight other demons only if we have to. You get the book. I attack the Royal Mother."

"Sounds like a suicide mission,"

Cooper grimaced. "Maybe."

Bill worried. Rich was like a brother to him. "We do need to get the grimoire," Bill said, shaking his head in disbelief. Cooper was considering attacking the well-guarded Fomorian leader. "We should wait until everyone gets here."

"Agree," Cooper said.

Bill nodded that he understood. "I wish they were already here."

"Me too," Cooper said.

"We all are going to die. Aren't we?"

Cooper's eyes went large. "Have faith. I not die yet."

The sounds of a nearby battle got their immediate attention. "Sounds like our friends are here.

"There are others I do not know," Cooper told Bill. He turned to the Republic Shadows. *"Bring Sam and Bobby here,"* he thought.

The Shadow witches flew away.

******

As soon as Jeff and Delia walked through the gate, it disappeared. The creepy black Tori arch was finally gone, but the illusion continued. They were in a dark no-man's-land. They walked in silence for a while, but Jeff always felt the need to talk when he was in a stressful situation.

"Where are all the demons," he asked. "We should have run into some by now." Delia said nothing. "You know, this is a little funny." She glanced at him as if to say: *What the hell are you talking about?* He went on. "I mean this whole fatalistic place is kind of calming. I feel at ease when I should be shaking in my shoes. We could totally die tonight and I seem to be alright with that. Is that weird? Why am I not afraid?"

Delia shrugged. "An hour ago, I would have agreed with you," she said, breaking her silence. "But now, I don't want to die. My Mama is safe. She is not afraid of me."

"That's good. You have been given a reason to live, but I on the other hand…" His voice faded. His mood darkened. "Amy is gone. I can never get her back. She was one in a million. There will be no replacing her."

"I know. I'm sorry."

"Not your fault."

A glowing ball of light appeared in front of them. It grew larger and brighter until it encompassed Jeff and Delia. They stood there in amazement.

The light was beautiful and warm.

Jeff squinted his eyes and said, "I see something."

"Me too, it's a person"

The silhouette moved closer until she stood directly in front of them.

"Hello, my dear friends," she said. "How are you doing?"

She wore an elegant, floor length white dress. Her long dark hair draped over her shoulders accenting her feminine features. She was so beautiful, angelic, and so happy.

"Amy," Jeff whispered as tears filled his eyes.

Delia gasped, putting her hands to her mouth. "Oh, my dear friend."

"I have missed you both so much," Amy said softly. "They let me come to you."

"How," Delia said. "Is this really you?"

Amy stepped closer and took Delia's hand. "I needed to give each of you a message." She turned to Jeff, who was stunned and speechless. "Jeffrey, my dear boy," she said. "I want you to know how much I love you and I will always love you."

Jeff choked on a sob. "I miss you so much, Amy. You were the only person who saw me as I wanted to be. I love you and my heart is broken. How do I live without you?"

"But live you must, my love," Amy said, tears running down her soft cheeks. "I am here to tell you that you are known by us. We want you to understand how important you are to the future of the human race. You are needed and you are valued. Live on my love, and fulfill the purpose for which you were born. If you could see the future, you would know, as I know, who you are going to become."

Jeff shook his head. "But without you..."

Amy stopped him by putting her hand over his mouth. "Jeffrey, believe me when I tell you," Amy said. "You will never be without me, I will be with you every step of the way. I will be your special angel." She held Jeff tight. Their tears blended and there was magic of a celestial magnitude. It filled Jeff with a new-found joy. His eyes were opened and he saw what Amy saw.

Jeff gasped at the vision. Eyes wide, he looked at Amy's angelic face and said, "Thank you. I will always Love you."

Amy turned back to Delia. "Delia my dear friend. What happened to you was a hard thing, but know this. You will soon understand why you need Child in your life. Your future of both your worlds depends on the two of you working together. You will be the saviors of millions."

"But Child is gone," Delia said, mourning the loss for the first time.

"Child has been with me for a short while. She is a beautiful soul. We will give her back to you. Embrace her as your friend the way you embraced me. Child needs you." Amy held Delia tight as she did Jeff. Their tears joined and, again, magic happened.

Delia gasped as she felt someone enter her body. She joyfully said, Thank you, Amy. " I will never forget you."

Then a familiar voice spoke. *"Thank you, Amy, my new special angel,"* Child whispered.

Amy stepped away from the two people who meant more to her than anyone else. "Jeffrey, take care of Delia. Delia and Child, take care of Jeffrey. I am counting on you."

Then Amy faded away. The real world returned.
******

As they ran to catch up with Master Maeda's team, Bobby reached out to get Jeff's attention. Jeff was in deep thought, so when Bobby took hold of his arm, it nearly scared the wits out of him.

"Jeez, dude. You just took years off my life."

"Our visions came from the leader of the Fomorians," Bobby said. "She is like a queen."

"What," Jeff replied.

"The leader of the invaders. She messed with our minds. Somehow she made us see things."

"I am going to kill that witch for what she put me through," Sam swore, spitting anger.

Delia landed next to them. She said, "The other Shadows are calling her the Royal Mother."

Bobby said, "You're back. Now that we are all here, let's do this."

"Evidently, she knows we are coming," Jeff said.

"I guess we just move on," Delia said.

"What does this demon Queen... Royal Mother... look like anyway," Jeff asked.

"Something tells me we will know when we see her," Bobby replied.

"Well, I guess what will happen, will happen," Jeff said resigned to whatever fate had in mind.

"Why don't I feel comforted by that," Sam moaned.

"Guys, Child is back," Delia said. "We are here for you. Like Jeff just said. What will happen, will happen."

"Did you actually quote me," Jeff said as he drew his katana.

"Don't worry. I won't make a habit of it." Delia used her new found ability and two fiery blades morphed from her hands. "I'm ready."

"That was so cool, and... super hot," Jeff said with a smile.

"Shut up, Jeffery," Delia quipped. Jeff laughed

By the time they reached the Maeda team, the next conflict had already started. Giant Fomorian warriors with their leashed crainn creatures had charged in from multiple directions. There weren't as many Fomorians as there were humans and Republic Shadow, but the sheer size of the enemy made them fearsome. They overcame their fear by joining the fray. Guns blazed and grenades exploded as the magical rounds and explosives hit the enemy. Those who fought with traditional blade weapons began hand to hand combat. This took out the first line of enemy warriors. Human and Shadow voices roared as they returned blows just as fearsome as the enemy.

Some Republic Shadows attacked the enemy from the air. The Maeda soldiers, surprised by this new development, raised their weapons to fire on the incoming Shadows.

Sam yelled over the noise, "Don't shoot. They are with us."

Bobby yelled to Sam, "Cooper needs us."

"I know," she replied.

Two of the Shadows flew around the fight, scooped up Bobby and Sam.

******

"Excuse me, my Royal Mother," implored Overseer Shadow Strong with a bow of her head. "It seems I have been betrayed. May I leave your presence to discipline the traitor."

The Royal Mother nodded and waved her away dispassionately. "Do as you must," the Royal Mother said. "Leave your slaves. They will not escape." Shadow Strong put the grimoire down next to the Royal Mother and entered the battle to find Shadow Child.

Jeff pulled back to catch a breath. He had cuts, abrasions, and blood on his face and arms. "I feel so strangely calm for some reason," Jeff shouted to Delia.

Delia was in her Shadow form, so all she could do in response was to glance at him as if to say: *What are you talking about?* She glanced at another giant fist with the raptor staff, then lowered it to the assailant's chest and blasted a hole through it.

"I mean this whole thing is so fatalistic," Jeff said, swiping his blade through the front legs of another criann. It fell forward, gouging its face into the pavement. "Why am I not afraid?"

Delia just shrugged. She leaped away and transformed to human form. "That's because you are an idiot," she mocked.

"Must be," Jeff said, "I have a reason to live." Although Amy is gone, I feel her with me now. I will live to fight for her."

"Yes," Delia agreed. "The same for me."

The High Overseer landed behind Delia. "How dare you betray me, Shadow Child," the Overseer thought in dark anger. "The sentence for treason is death, you impish witch."

Delia pivoted quickly. She sneered, a little surprised that she understood the Overseer while in her human form. Delia looked into the Overseer's eyes and thought, *"I'm sorry. This is Delia Bowen. Shadow Child is unavailable at the moment, but if you leave a message, she will get back to you as soon as possible."*

The Overseer looked confused, then she transformed to human form as well. Then she said, "You insolent little bitch, how dare you mock me."

"Whoa, sexy babe," Jeff joked.

"This is High Overseer Strong," Delia said glaring at her opponent. "The one who ordered Child to do this to me. Even Asura and Asuri were her victims. She caused all of this to happen. She did this. If it hadn't been for this witch, Amy would still be alive. I will kill her." Delia morphed her hands into the two fiery blades.

"And I will help," Jeff said, his mood changing to hate. Rage filled him. Delia took a deep breath.

Overseer Strong laughed heartily. "Well then, Shadow Child, I am happy to let you try." The Overseer's hands also morphed into fiery blades.

"Shadow Child is not alone," Delia shouted. "I am Delia, one of the girls you order Asura to kill. Now you must deal with me as well. Child and I stand together."

"What are we talking about?"

"The Soul Eater spell didn't work on us and we are not afraid."

Shadow laughed again. "It does not matter. Shadow Child, you are a pathetic warrior and a useless witch."

"Shut up," Delia screamed. They struck more aggressive blows back and forth. "Child is far greater than you ever will be."

"I doubt that."

"We have a righteous cause. Good will defeat evil."

The Overseer laughed again. "Not in a million worlds is that true. Besides, it depends on who is defining what is good and what is evil. In my experience, evil is the position of strength. Let me show you."

Delia attacked with her fire bladed hands. Jeff was about to attack with all his anger and hate driving him. The force of the Overseer's spell hit Jeff in the chest. It knocked him back. He hit the ground rolling. By the time he got to his feet, his senses had returned. It was time to use what he had learned. Master Maeda always said, "Anger only clouds the mind."

Delia attacked with her fire bladed hands. Shadow successfully blocked every one of Delia's blows.

"Delia drop back. Let's do this together. We can't defeat her with just weapons alone," Jeff whispered as they continued to back away from the powerful witch. The overconfident Shadow stepped toward them with a menacing glare.

Child responded as Jeff joined her side. *"Then together."*

"Together." Delia nodded. They halted their retreat and concentrated on whatever violent action came into their minds.

 "Ready for some more," the Overseer mocked?

Jeff looked at Delia. She nodded back. Jeff extended his katana. Delia extended her arm and hand toward the Overseer. They both closed their eyes and said together, "As I will, so…it…will…be," Delia finished spitting out the words.

Jeff's blade lit up. It extended at the speed of light and shot through the surprised Shadow's chest. At the same moment an energy wave emitted from Delia's bladed hand hit her opponent in the stomach with the force of a missile.

Shadow was thrown back twenty-five to thirty feet. The wound inflicted by Jeff tore open, allowing demon blood to flow. The Overseer moved to her right, but Jeff was there to stop her. She ran left, but Delia threw up a force field that stopped her again. The battle still raged behind them. There was one way out. She took to the air. To the Overseer's surprise, another force field appeared above her, pushing her back down.

Enraged, she attacked Delia head on. "I will rip you to pieces," the Overseer screamed.

Before Delia could counter the attack, the Overseer was on top of her with one hand around her neck and the other hand forming a fiery blade

Jeff had to get closer fearing his blade might hurt Delia by accident. Just as the Overseer raised a bladed hand and preparing to stab Delia in the throat, Jeff kicked the Overseer's magically enhanced hand, knocking the blade away.

Angry, the Overseer pointed her blade at Jeff and thought, *"Extend."* The blade extended in a blink of the eye. Jeff parried the strike with his blade. He marveled at the odds that he had survived that strike and fell backward because of the force of the contact.

In this moment of distraction, Delia made her move to escape the enemy Shadow's grip. She jammed her arm between her body and the Overseer's hand and flipped herself over with all her strength. The cartwheel movement disconnected the grip. Once away, Delia thrust her hand forward. Her power pushed the Overseer onto her back.

The Overseer's chest wound opened up further, causing more blood loss. She tried to sit up but Jeff swung his blade at the side of the Overseer's head. She raised her hand and formed a blade, stopping a possible fatal blow. Even so, Jeff's blade sliced down into her arm. The Overseer screamed in pain. Delia kicked the injured Shadow in the face, knocking her back on the ground. Two fiery blades extended from Delia's hands. She slammed them into the Overseer's shoulders, pinning the enemy to the ground. The hated witch stopped struggling as she lost consciousness.

"Blades become solid and bind this witch," Delia spit out. "As I will, so it will be." The blades turned black and detached from Delia's Shadow hands. She transformed into her human form. "That is for Amy," Delia spat.

"For Amy," Jeff parroted.

"For Amy," Child declared.

Both of them rejoined the advancing Maeda team. They felt strong, because a special angel was with them.

******

The Royal Mother felt the change in the battle. Until now she felt unconcerned. This was merely the final burst of resistance from a conquered enemy. But suddenly she felt alone... too alone. The ancient book that her Shadow ally had brought to her possessed significant, valuable information, but the Overseer had not returned to guard it. Not that she could not defend it herself. None of these lowly creatures dared to approach her. Still, something felt wrong. The Royal Mother could not sense Shadow Strong. She must have lost the fight with the traitor Shadow. Even more unsettling, she sensed that a new dangerous power now closed in on her. For the first time, a twinge of doubt entered her mind.

"Lord General," she roared. The sound of her voice filled the dome. "Return and stand by me."

The giant Lord General, who was at that moment fighting at the far side of the dome, turned and ran at his Royal Mother's command. His feet hit the ground with a deep thud as he took leaps and bounds to avoid obstacles. It only took the giant six minutes to cross the diameter of the now six-mile-wide dome. His final leap landed him on the rooftop where the Royal Mother stood. Fortunately for him and the Royal Mother the structure had been designed to handle the stress of such an impact. Nonetheless, the building shuddered as he landed. The Lord General kneeled. "What is your wish, my Royal Mother?"

"Something is wrong," the Royal Mother said. "Stay with me... and recall all warriors to this place. There is a... danger."

"As you wish, my Royal Mother," he replied. This request surprised him. From this vantage point he could see nothing that concerned him. "The first stage of the invasion is nearly over, my Royal Mother. We are ready to expand the dome."

"That is good," the Royal Mother said. "We must end this."

"My Royal Mother. Look." The Lord General pointed at the two humans running around the battle toward the Royal Mother. In amused surprise, he let out a boisterous laugh. The two humans stopped and pointed at the Royal Mother. "Look at them, as bold as they please. Do they really think they can challenge us?"

At that moment, Cooper appeared behind the Lord General. He leaped onto the giant's back, stabbing his sword into the back of the enemy's skull. Cooper disappeared as quickly as he had appeared. Blood gushed from the Lord General's head. The giant stumbled and fell, rolling off the building's roof. In the confusion, the Grimoire disappeared.

Sam watched the big being fall. That was when she also saw her dad. "Daddy." She wanted to run to him, but only took a few steps toward him.

"Stay back Sam," her dad shouted. He strained against the blue collar. It flared, causing him to cry out in pain.

"Daddy," Sam screamed again. Bobby held her back as she tried to get to her dad.

"No, Sam. Stick to the plan," Bobby reminded her.

"Stay strong, honey." her dad said. "I am alright for now."

"I am so going to kill you," Sam shouted at the Royal Mother.

The Royal Mother blinked, dumbfounded. Then she laughed. Standing at the edge of the roof, she leaned over. "You can try... if you wish to die." She laughed again.

"Fine, but I won't be the one dying," Sam yelled back.

Bill appeared on the ground with the grimoire in his hand. "Bobby, use the anti-magic light." Bobby flipped his staff around and fired a blast of light. It spread outward with considerable force. The powerful light hit the Royal Mother. Her robes blew wildly from the concussion, but she didn't move an inch. The anti-magic did, in fact, cause her some pain. Just not enough to stop her from retaliating immediately. She screamed fiercely. Blue-white flames escaped her hands as she waved about in uncontrolled rage. Everything around her ignited. The fire burned all the way through the roof and set the building below on fire. At that moment all the nearby leashes disappeared, setting the criann,.. Rich, and the traitor, Percy free.

Bill ran to get behind Sam and Bobby. The Lord General had landed face down on the ground below, but he wasn't dead. Magic had begun to heal his wound. In a rage he jumped to his feet. Cooper now stood between him and his three friends, or rather five friends, as Jeff and Delia had just joined them. The giant roared. His eyes flared and his blue tattoos pulsed from blue to red. The Lord General took a deep breath and blew out blue fire.

Cooper thought out, *"Protect."*

A circle of magic appeared in front of the six of them as a searing hot flame left the giant's mouth. The shield deflected the blue fire straight back at the Lord General, inflicting pain and injury on the giant. He coughed and spit up blood. His lighted tattoos turned black. Dazed and even angrier than before the Lord General charged Cooper, but his opponent was ready, already jumping upward. Cooper slammed his extra hardened fist into the giant's face. The giant staggered back, bleeding again.

Delia took to the air, landing on the Lord General's shoulders. She swung her fiery blade at the giant's back, but his hardened armor kept it from piercing. Jeff and Bobby followed Delia's lead, rounding the giant to the right and left. They both struck the back of the giant's knees. The blows didn't penetrate, but the force buckled the weakened Lord General's legs, and he fell to his knees.

Sam's move came next. She ran forward slamming her hands on the giant's armored chest. Her energy electrified the armor. The Lord General convulsed and fell forward again.

Bill ran to Rich and Percy, who were hugging the side of the burning building.

"Let's get out of here," Bill said. "You too Percy. You have got some explaining to do."

Percy looked conflicted. This deal he had made with the High Overseer Shadow Strong had gone to hell. If he went with these guys, he would be arrested and thrown in jail. But if he stayed here, he would be dead for sure. If the High Overseer wasn't dead, she would protect him. Of course, he would live the rest of his life as her slave. None of these options appealed to Percy, so he turned and ran, preferring to take his chances on his own.

"Percy," Bill shouted.

"Let the fool go," Rich said.

The Lord General's helmet dislodged His helmet dislodged from his head. He tried to get back up, but fell flat again.

"This beast won't die," Jeff yelled in frustration.

Delia jumped up onto the Lord General's back. Extending both hands into searing blades, she scissored the blades on either side of the giant's neck and drew the blades together, cutting through the flesh and bone. The Lord General's head rolled to the side. Finally, he was dead. "I guess there is always a weak spot somewhere," Delia said, relieved.

The Fomorians came running in force at the call of their distressed Royal Mother. There would be little time to finish the objective before being overrun by the enemy. Only two of Cooper's witches had survived the ordeal. They joined their comrades as the Maeda Clan's team approached the defiant Royal Mother. She floated above the burning building.

Maeda's team formed a semicircle in front of the Royal Mother. She reacted by creating a protective shield. No matter what the small army of warriors tried, they would not penetrate such a powerful shield.

Cooper turned around to see a couple hundred of the enemy warriors and their leashed beasts flowing into the compound. They only had a minute to decide what to do. Stay and fight (and probably die), or run like hell. "We must go," Cooper said. "Too late."

Bill and Rich made a run for it with Bill in the lead and Rich close behind.

"We go now," Cooper barked.

"Just where do you think you are going slave," High Overseer Shadow Strong screeched.

"Look out, dad," Bobby shouted.

The High Overseer already had a squirming Percy in tow. A second blue leash extended at the speed of light from the Overseer's hand to Rich Thomas' neck. The Shadow then darted toward the rift, lifting the two men off the ground. The three figures disappeared down into the rift.

"Daddy," screamed Sam. "Daddy..." Sam gasped for breath. She screamed, "NO." The scream was so loud and powerful that the ground seemed to shake. She fell to her knees and sobbed with an agony she had never before experienced.

Bobby knelt behind Sam and embraced her. He held her tight. "Dear God," he whispered. "Please help us." At that moment, Bobby's mind expanded. He saw everything inside the dome. "Sam. I can see them all, Sam," he said.

Hundreds of white glowing lines left the huddled coupling. The lines shot out in every direction. Each line found an enemy Fomorian or an enemy Shadow. The forward advance stopped. The warriors jumped back from the lines of light. It was too late. The lines had already been attached to each of the warriors, including the Royal Mother.

"I see every one of these hateful beings... every one of them," Bobby said to Sam. "See what I see. Do you see them?" Sam nodded her head. "Then follow the lines and kill them. Kill every one of these devils," Bobby shouted.

Sam looked up. Her eyes red with grief and... rage. She screamed so loud that the ground actually shook this time. But, it wasn't the scream that caused the quake, it was her power. She felt a power as immense as the ocean. The power drowned her grief and fueled her rage all at once. The power left her body in an explosion of light. Balls of light followed each line that Bobby had laid out. The humans around the young coupling fell to the shaking ground in fear. Each ball of light hit its dark target. The Royal Mother and the other Fomorians close by were the first to die. The light entered the Royal Mothers body. Rising up into her chest, it expanded.

The Royal Mother screamed, "Stop this. Stop this now." For the first time in thousands of years, a Fomorian royal feared for her life. "What is this?" She exploded.

"This is the power of a magical coupling," Bobby boldly spoke with bitterness in his voice. "Fear awakened us, love unified us, self-confidence empowered us, but took grief to finish the course of our fate. Grief enraged us. You all are a witness to our transformation."

The enemy exploded as the balls of light reached their hearts. Cracks of fire flashed across the overhead dome. Sam's power decimated the Fomorians, along with their Royal Mother. The dome vanished as did all the other domes that had appeared around the world. The rift to the Fomorian world closed.

Master Maeda and his soldiers got to their feet. They stared at Bobby and Sam, uncertain about what they had just witnessed and uncertain about what to do about it. The Master stepped forward with his katana raised. pointed at the young couple. As if they had read their Master's mind, his people also stepped forward. They raised their weapons at the two grieving teens. They spread out to form a circle around them.

"Whoa... whoa, whoa, whoa," Jeff shouted. "Master, what is going on?"

"Their power is too dangerous," the Master proclaimed. "Far too dangerous to be left unchecked."

Suddenly, the Shadow Priestess and the remaining Shadow witches dropped from the sky. They landed in between the couple and Maeda's soldiers. Delia joined the Priestess to lend her support. The Priestess turned to Delia. *"Please translate my thoughts."*

"This witch and the decerner are under our protection," Delia said, translating what she heard in her mind…

"This is too much power given to one person," the Master warned. "It is too dangerous. It could threaten the very existence of human life on this planet. I cannot allow such power to exist… to wander free."

Delia told the Priestess what Master Maeda had said. The Priestess continued, "We will take over the training of the young witch. She will learn how to control her power. The enemy is gone for now, but they will return to avenge their Royal Mother. This world and all worlds like it need these two to defend them. Otherwise you will lose your lives. This enemy will kill us all, or worse, enslave us for thousands of years. Shadows have finally found their freedom. We will not give it up easily."

Master Maeda thought for a moment. Then he sheathed his katana. "Stand down," he said. Everyone relaxed and breathed a sigh of relief.

Epilogue

When the time is up, the play ends. At least that is what is supposed to happen. When a half-a-dozen warriors stopped the war against the Shadow Empire and the war against the undefeated Kingdom of Formoria, time seemed to stop across multiple universes. These victories would become stories of which legends are made.

Such epic events were bound to attract the attention of other demon races in the universes. Like the gunslingers of the legendary American west, there will always be someone who wants to prove they can draw their gun faster. These events that saved humanity had the frightening potential to bring on the wrath of a thousand universes.

How will the Earth survive such man-made disasters? One thing I know for sure, the Earth you know and love will never be the same again.

From the Journal of Robert James Williams (2070)

Damaged Still

By Samantha Thomas

My wounds,
Although healed,
My scars are
Ugly and painful.

Authors Notes

In Celtic mythology, Lugh (or Lug) is primarily considered a god of the sun and light, renowned for his exceptional skills in various arts and crafts, a striking appearance, and his role as a patron of heroes; notably, he is often featured in Irish and Welsh legends, with his unique lineage stemming from Balor, the fearsome king of the Fomorians, a race of dark, supernatural beings.

<u>Shadow Invasion: Demons or Gods</u>:
Coming soon - Projected for Summer 2025

www.ingramcontent.com/pod-product-compliance
Lightning Source LLC
LaVergne TN
LVHW051036070526
838201LV00009B/216